The Mermaid
from Jeju

The Mermaid from Jeju

❨ *A Novel* ❩

Sumi Hahn

alcove
press

Published in the United States by Alcove Press, an imprint of The Quick Brown Fox & Company LLC.

Alcove Press and its logo are trademarks of The Quick Brown Fox & Company LLC.

Library of Congress Catalog-in-Publication data available upon request.

ISBN (paperback): 978-1-64385-954-5
ISBN (hardcover): 978-1-64385-440-3
ISBN (ebook): 978-1-64385-441-0

Cover design by Melanie Sun

Printed in the United States.

www.alcovepress.com

Alcove Press
34 West 27th St., 10th Floor
New York, NY 10001

Trade Paperback Edition: November 2021
First Edition: December 2020

10 9 8 7 6 5 4 3 2 1

For my dear Mike
and Griffin, Raven, & Kira

HISTORICAL TIMELINE
1910–1945
KOREA OCCUPIED BY JAPAN

AUGUST 1945

United States drops atomic bombs on Hiroshima and Nagasaki, forcing Japan's surrender. 60,000 Jeju residents return home. Korea is divided along the 38th Parallel, with the USSR occupying the North and the US occupying the South.

NOVEMBER–DECEMBER 1945

US Army Military Government established on South Korea. Despite Korea's pleas for independence, the Allies divide Korea between two occupying foreign powers in a trusteeship between the Soviet Union, the United States, China, and Britain.

MARCH 1947

Jeju's April 3 Incident begins with police firing shots into a reunification demonstration. Six people are killed, including a child.

Workers and officials strike in mass protest. Thousands of people arrested and jailed; some are tortured to death

APRIL–AUGUST 1948

To protest the elections of May 10, the Jeju Chapter of the South Korean Labor party attacks police stations and other areas under jurisdiction of the US Military Government. Thirty military police officers are killed, many of them former Japanese collaborators. The US Military Government deploys more troops to Jeju while also purging the Jeju constabulary of any officers sympathetic to the South Korean Labor party. Rhee Syng Man is declared president of the Republic of Korea ("South Korea") in July. In response, the Democratic People's Republic of Korea ("North Korea") declares Kim Il Sung the Premier of North Korea on August 25, 1948.

OCTOBER 1948–FEBRUARY 1949

President Rhee Syng Man declares martial law on Jeju as the US Military commences a scorched earth strategy against Communists. Most of the 14th Regiment mutinies before deployment to Jeju, not wanting to commit atrocities against their own people.

JUNE 1950

The Korean People's Army crosses the 38th Parallel and invades Seoul, officially starting the Korean War.

PHILADELPHIA, 2001

That summer, the embolus lay snug in its hollow behind Mrs. Junja Moon's right knee. The little clot gave no twinge nor any other hint of its existence. Trembling in the brisk current of Mrs. Moon's bloodstream, it was unaffected by the hours she spent pickling kimchi and unmoved by her attempts to improve her golf swing. The red blob was even impervious to her rare fits of homesickness, when she turned on the shower to muffle her sobs for Jeju Island, which she fled in the winter of 1948.

At 6:47 PM on August 29, 2001, a sharp pain shot up Mrs. Moon's right leg. Did she forget to stretch after her golf lesson? She summoned her husband, Dr. Moon, from the living room, where he was watching an instructional video and practicing his putting.

"Time to eat dinner, yobo." She bent down to rub her calf, which ached a bit. Dr. Moon grunted in acknowledgment as the golf ball rolled into the cup.

The family of four sat down and gave their proper Christian thanks for the food. As napkins were adjusted and chopsticks readied, Mrs. Moon gathered her thoughts to address her visiting daughters: Hana, whose name, the delivery room nurse had promised, sounded American, and Okja, who was named after her grandmother.

It was a matter of urgency that her daughters find husbands and that she be given grandchildren, preferably grandsons. As a pillar of the Korean American community in Philadelphia, Mrs. Moon wanted to plan weddings and hundredth-day birthdays instead of church dinners and golf games. Most of all, she longed to stop the polite inquiries about her daughters, who, though smart and attractive, were still spinsters at the overripe ages of forty and thirty-seven.

Mrs. Moon cleared her throat to speak. The little clot popped free and fell into the red rapids of her bloodstream, where it took a short thrilling ride to the spongy swamp of her upper left lung. Mrs. Moon mistook her sudden heart palpitations for anxiety. She pounded herself on the chest as she gasped, recognizing the clamor in her body: she was drowning, even though she was on dry land. Her fingers scrambled at her throat, trying to seize oxygen from the air.

Her daughters and husband froze, chopsticks midway to their mouths, as Mrs. Moon rose from her seat, grabbed the edge of the table, and coughed out a spray of red that landed on an empty plate.

☽

When his colleagues described the deadly embolism, Dr. Moon swayed on his feet as the floor betrayed him. All the scientific words receded from his head, which filled with a roaring mist. He had taken Junja away from her ocean home, and now she had journeyed elsewhere, without him.

A soft keening brushed his ear. Dr. Moon blinked at his daughters, whose tears splashed his face, filling his mouth with the warmth of salt. Their hands were holding his, their fists an anchor. He closed his eyes again.

He remembered a bright day on the Jersey shore, when the girls were small and quick like rabbits. They had been gathering stones to put into red plastic buckets. Junja squatted down to watch. Her hands had stroked the sand as she talked.

"What are you doing, Hana?"

"Working."

"You're so busy, Okja. Why?"

"We're gonna catch fishies, Umma."

Junja's voice had grown soft. "You have no fishing stick. No net. How are you going to catch fish?"

Hana shrugged. "With our hands."

Junja smiled. "You are smart, like haenyeo."

"What's haenyeo?" Okja squinted at her mother as her big sister left to get another bucket of water.

"Haenyeo is like a Korean mermaid. From Jeju Island, the most beautiful place in Korea. I lived there when I was small like you."

"Are they real mermaids, Umma? Or pretend ones?"

"Real ones. They brought food for my family every day."

"I wanna see them!"

Junja had stroked her daughter's hair. "When you are bigger, I will take you." She leaned in to whisper. "Here is a secret: A long, long time ago, when I was a girl, I was a mermaid too."

Part One

_____

The oar breaks, but never the true timber from Hallasan
The rope snaps, but never the strong coils from Seonheul Cape
Warship on the ocean, please go away
Any direction at all but here

—from "The Songs of the Jeju Haenyeo," recorded by the
Haenyeo Museum

One

"Junja!"

Hands shook her so hard her teeth clattered like pebbles. "Wake up, Junja!"

She'll be forced to scrub abalone shells and carry buckets of water to the cistern if she doesn't obey. But she's so tired, she'd like to sleep now.

"Junja!" A slap landed hard on her face.

Her eyes opened—too bright!—she shut them.

Out of her mouth spilled the tides.

Junja's eyes blinked open as she gasped.

Mother was standing over her, the sea streaming down her skin like silver. Junja started sneezing. Mother fell to her knees and cradled her head on her lap, stroking her hair.

"You are alive, Junja." Mother's hands were so warm. "You dove too deep, but the sea king returned you, and you are safe on land again . . .

Grandmother's voice: "We must ask her what she saw while she was there."

"Hush—not now," said Mother. "Don't worry her."

Grandmother's whisper was hot against her ear: "Remember your sea dream, Junja. When you wake up, dry and warm, remember the true dreams you dreamt under water . . ."

Wrapped in Junja's fist was something hard and jagged that hurt. She opened her hand. Lying in her bleeding palm was a shell. She held it up to her mother, who shrieked while lifting it up high.

"She never let go!"

Shouts of joy and admiring murmurs. Junja looked around. She was lying in a circle of women all draped in wet ribbons of ocean, like Mother and Grandmother.

"You are a true haenyeo now," whispered Mother. "You belong to the sea, like I do, and like your grandmother. You have visited the sea king like Sim Cheong, the beggar maiden, and returned alive, bearing his gift."

Mother smashed the shell with a rock and clawed out the meat. "Eat this," she commanded.

Junja turned her head. She couldn't stomach any more of the sea.

Mother pushed the briny blob past her lips and made her swallow. The little piece of sea mass plummeted down Junja's body, making her cough as it settled deep inside her.

She spat out a stone.

☽

Ever since her near-drowning, Junja was allowed to follow her mother and grandmother to the seashore, instead of staying home to watch her little brother. That task now belonged to second sister Gongja, who was only eight but already knew how to make a fine millet porridge.

"I could probably cook a chicken too," boasted Gongja.

"But you don't know how to kill the chicken," yelled Jin. "Or pluck out its feathers and clean the innards!

"Pretty soon you'll have to take care of yourself, useless boy," said Gongja. "Because I'll be old enough to do water work with Ummung and Halmung and Junja."

"Hush," Mother said, crouching down to look her son in the eye. "Heed your noonah well. Don't forget that Gongja is your mother while we are gone. Behave like a man. Both of you must weed the garden and feed the chickens. When you finish, write the alphabet three times. Over there, on the dirt near the garden fence, so the chickens can't walk over it. Then, you may play."

Mother rose to gather the supplies they needed for their day of work, dividing everything between her eldest daughter, her mother, and herself: picks, knives, scythes, hemp nets and rope, twig baskets, dried gourds, lengths of cloth, kindling, and fresh water.

The three of them walked down the rocky path toward the beach, large bundles balanced on their heads. The dawn sky was inky, but their eyes were accustomed to the darker pitch of the ocean. They navigated the shadows, their bare feet steering.

"Aigoo," said Grandmother, "My feet are too old for these bad black rocks."

"Aigoo," said Junja, giggling, "My feet are too young for these bad black rocks."

"Such noise!" scolded Mother. "You will wake the clams in their beds."

"Tell me, what do you remember of your sea dream?" Grandmother asked, when Mother walked a few steps ahead of them to kick the large stones away from the path. Grandmother had asked this question every morning and every night for weeks, hoping that something would dart out of the crevices of her granddaughter's memory and be caught.

"I cannot remember much, Halmung," apologized Junja. "I remember falling and falling. Everything was dark and cold and wet. I couldn't breathe, and I couldn't move. I remember thinking, 'I am dead now. Instead of helping Mother, I am only bringing her sorrow.' Suddenly, I could move again. The sea king and his maidens watched as I swam back up. I kicked and pushed toward the light. When I woke, I was holding something in my hand, something I knew I couldn't let go."

"You kept the pearl," said Grandmother, "but you lost the treasure."

Junja stayed silent.

"Your sea dream was the true treasure, but the sea king tricked you with a pearl so you'd return to this world holding onto a stone instead of the truth." Grandmother sighed.

Mother had traded that pearl for a large sack of white rice and a new garden hoe. Junja didn't understand how a dream could have been more helpful, despite Grandmother's stories about her great-great-grandmother, who had captured a sea dream and shared its riches with everyone in her village.

"She dreamed her entire life in that sea dream. After she coughed the ocean out of her body, her mind cleared, leaving behind a detailed picture of everything that was going to happen in her life. She knew when typhoons would blow, which winters would freeze solid, and which summers would shrivel up in drought. She knew which parts of the ocean were teeming with delicious living things and where there were only barren rocks and sand. When she met the man she would marry, she told him, 'I dreamed about you, and you will be my husband.'

"It wasn't always easy to bear, knowing what would happen. Usually she would bite her tongue. On the day her mother drowned, she tried to stop her, begging her not to go out. The mother, wiser than her gifted daughter, continued on her way, because knowing never stopped the sun from rising or the tides from coming in."

"Did your great-great-grandmother know how she'd die as well?" Junja wondered if knowing about your own death could somehow delay it.

Grandmother clucked. "She probably did, but she never told another person that secret. She grew so sad, knowing when everyone else would die, that all sorts of troublesome spirits were able to enter and cloud her mind.

"One night, she slipped and hit her head on some bad black rocks. When she woke up, she was as simple as a child of two. The villagers had to tether her to a tree so that she wouldn't wander off a cliff. While no one was watching, she loosened the knots and slipped away. They found her body washed up on the beach, head cracked like an egg. It was the sea king's way of reminding us that whatever comes from the sea will always return to it."

☽

On the beach, bonfires were blazing. Women scurried about, stoking flames, coiling lengths of rope, and inspecting gourds for breaks and nets for tears. Some of the divers were singing a song that keened like the wind. Others were rubbing their hands together as they chanted prayers to the sea god. Seabirds hovered as the sky began to brighten. Junja added her family's kindling to the community pile.

"Gather your dolchu," an elder barked. Junja hurried to the water's edge, where speckled black-and-white stones had been washed clean by the night tides. She found a smooth one, the size of a summer squash, and showed it to her grandmother, who hefted it with an approving grunt. The first group of divers were standing before the fire in their water clothes, eyes shut, faces glowing with heat.

"Water time! Water time! Go into the sea!"

The divers secured their seaweed scythes and shellfish picks. They spat into their masks and rubbed the bubbles over the glass. Junja's mother, hands in thick wool mittens, stirred the embers with a stick and pulled out stones to cool on the sand.

With the warm anchor stones nestled in their hemp slings, the first group stood ready, led by an elder who would guide them to the first dive site.

The barefoot women waded into the water, arms wrapped around their gourd floats. The anchor stones warmed their bellies. Their linen swimsuits darkened before puckering to cling to their skin. As the women kicked their way through the surf, the sound of singing grew fainter, giving way to the slapping waves and the pounding of their pulse.

The ocean sucked each diver down greedily. But the women were prepared for battle. They swiped their knives at the fingers of sea grass that clutched at them. They used picks to pry away shells clinging to underwater rocks. They worked the waters, humming the chants of their forbearing mothers, who had explored the deep before them.

☽

You must leave the ocean before your fingers and lips grow numb. Grab your fistful of treasure and fly back up toward the light. When your head breaks the surface, release the air you held captive in your chest, letting it fly away in a whistling scream.

Rest your cheek on the gourd, which bobs on the water, dreaming of the steady ground that once moored it. Place your shell inside the net bag and thank the sea king for his gift. Close your eyes and imagine the sun's fire sinking deep into your belly.

Swallow another gulp of shining air.

Dive into the depths one more time.

Two

1948

Mother packed a large clump of dripping seaweed into the bottom of the big wooden basket as Junja watched, envious. The abalone, snug in their shells, were packed in next and covered with more seaweed. Mother threw a ladle of sea water on top before tying the basket shut. Junja held the carrying rack steady while Mother secured the basket to its wooden frame.

For her annual trip to Hallasan, Mother was wearing braided straw shoes and socks that had never been mended. Her crisp shirt was closed by five wooden buttons instead of the usual ties, and its bright persimmon had not yet faded to mud. A silver hairpin, borrowed from Grandmother, glinted in the coil of hair at the nape of her neck. Under the soft light of the setting moon, she could have been her daughter's reflection.

Junja took a breath before trying again. "Please, Ummung. You promised I could go this year." Ever since Mother had announced her intention to fetch a piglet from Hallasan, Junja had been begging to make the trip in her stead. The girl's voice was a murmur because everyone in the house was asleep, but the chickens opened their eyes to glare. "Let me go, please! I swear I'll be fine." Junja had never ventured more than a two-hour walk from the village by herself, and she had not yet visited the sacred mountain, seeing it only from a distance.

Mother hefted the pack, feeling the security of each knot with her fingertips. The weight of the basket reminded her that someday she would not be able to make this trek. When that time came, she would have to see her friend, the pig farmer's wife, during market trips in town. Junja's mother recognized in her daughter's eyes the same restlessness she had felt at that age.

Junja watched Mother press her lips together. The girl had reached her eighteenth year without paying her respects to the mountain god. The lapse was understandable with so many strangers on the island. It was impossible to walk into town these days without passing at least half a dozen carts. Motorized vehicles rumbled by with such frequency that the old man living near the big road talked about starting a roadside stall. Yesterday alone he had counted two buses, four motorcycles, and a military truck, full of soldiers.

Despite its novelty, the traffic added to an overall sense of unease. Mother was probably fretting about the diver who had agreed to take her place while she was gone. The woman had witnessed an eel entangled with an octopus, illuminated by a beam of light. The purple tentacles had clung to the dark eel, whose jagged teeth were sunk into the octopus's head. A glowing halo had outlined the creatures' deadly embrace, so mesmerizing the woman that she almost failed to surface in time. The spooked diver had stayed out of the water all week but insisted she was up to the task. Mother's worries were obvious: Was that woman fit to lead her dives during her absence?

Sensing her mother's hesitation, Junja thrust her arms through the carrying straps. She stood, gasping when the full weight of the pack settled on her. She pretended to clear her throat. "See how easily I can lift everything? If I go, you'll be able to get so much done. Please, let me help you, Mother!"

Mother shook her head. "Manipulative little wench!" She always scolded her children before relenting to any of their requests.

Junja muffled her excited yelp and threw her arms around her mother's neck. "Thank you!"

Mother shook the girl off. Her voice was brisk. "I'm not letting you go because you want to, but because it'll help me." She was already thinking ahead to everything she could do with the extra hours. "And you're long overdue for a visit to the mountain god." She squinted at her daughter, who had copied her mother by putting on her best shirt, just in case. Junja's hair was hanging in a braid down her back, and her face had been scrubbed. She looked presentable enough, but her feet were bare. "Put on your shoes."

The girl made a face. "They're too small. Besides, it's more comfortable walking without them."

"Shoes aren't for your comfort. You need to look respectable when you reach the pig farmer's house." Mother sat on a black stone to remove her shoes and socks. "You can borrow mine."

Mother's socks felt warm against Junja's skin. Though the girl managed to pull them on, the straw shoes were tight.

"How are they?" Mother peered down at Junja's feet.

Junja tried to wiggle her toes. Mother's shoes were too small, but she didn't want to give her an excuse to change her mind. Anything would be better than another dull day harvesting seaweed, which was what Junja would be teaching the junior divers in her charge today. The shoes, as well as the truth, would have to stretch a bit.

"They feel fine."

"Well, I guess that settles it. You'll go to Hallasan in my place." Mother closed her eyes to think. "You'll pass two shrines along the trail, but you won't have time to stop on the way up. Pay your respects after you deliver the abalone."

When Mother placed a heavy gourd in a sling around her neck, the girl had to refrain from grunting at the added weight. "Don't drink from the gourd. It's seawater to keep the kelp wet. You can drink from streams along the way, once you're on the pass. The first stream is at the foothills of the mountain, after you pass the last sweet potato field. A couple hours later, you'll see a large rock that resembles a dol hareubang. Take the pack off there and pour the seawater onto the seaweed. By this time, you'll be very close, only three thousand paces away. The sun will be high, so you will need to walk quickly, or else the abalone will die, and the trip will be wasted."

The weight of the pack made Junja stagger as she took her first step.

"You're eighteen years old now and very strong," Mother said to steady her. "Even stronger than I was when I first climbed the mountain."

"What if I stumble?" Junja considered whether this wasn't such a good idea after all. Gathering seaweed was boring, but it wasn't hard work.

"Then you will get up and keep walking."

"What if I take too long, and the abalone go bad?"

"Then you will disappoint the pig farmer's wife, and we will eat no pork this winter. And I will think you are a stupid girl instead of a clever one. Do not speak about bad fortune, or your breath may give it life. Put those kinds of thoughts out of your mind," Mother hissed, willing the bad luck away from her daughter toward herself.

She draped a small purse around Junja's neck, tucking it out of sight in her shirt. "One coin for the cart, two for the constable at the pass. Tell him why you are going, using these words exactly: 'I am delivering goods from the haenyeo of Lonely Rock Village to the pig farmer of Cloud House Farm.' If he asks you to show him what's in the basket, then do so quickly."

Junja nodded. Her sudden misgivings faded, giving way to excitement about her first trip away from the village by herself.

"Make sure you give the wife of the eldest son my greetings as well as my apology." Mother bit her lip. "Keep your wits about you. If you see anything suspicious, leave the road and try to avoid being seen."

"What do you mean by 'suspicious,' Ummung?" Junja tried to reach down to tug at her sock, but the bulky pack limited her movement.

Mother pretended to adjust the bindings on the pack. Just the other day, Nationalist soldiers had done the unthinkable, entering a bulteok while divers were warming themselves by the bonfire. The men had stood there, leering, until a stooped granny chased them out with a stick, muttering. If the men had understood her, they would not have laughed, as she had cursed them in the old tongue, which no mainlanders understood.

Junja's mother undid and retied a knot. She never thought she would miss those Japanese vermin. They, at least, would not have sullied themselves by entering a lowly female space.

"Just make sure you pay attention to everything around you. Don't get distracted. You don't want to be surprised by a snake or a boar on the mountain." Mother shooed Junja toward the direction of the big road. Her parting words served as both reminder and talisman, to ward off forgetfulness and misfortune.

"Your load will feel light, and you will move with sure feet. You will climb the mountain path, passing two bangsatap. When you reach the dol hareubang, you will water the contents of the basket, knowing that you are almost there. Walk quickly. Someone from the pig farmer's family will meet you. You will stay one night and come home tomorrow with a healthy piglet."

☽

The night stars were still winking in the western sky as Junja closed the wooden gate at the main entrance of the village. She balanced against the wall to remove a pebble embedded in the sole of the shoe. Her feet felt stifled. The pack pulled at her, hard, and she had to remind herself that she was a haenyeo, a woman stronger than most men.

The footpath from the village widened gradually as it merged with the paved main road. Junja slowed her steps, hoping for an agreeable farmer with a cart to pass by soon. On the dirt, the straw shoes had been tolerable, but on this hard surface she could feel every ridge and bump in the braiding.

The discomfort reminded Junja to stamp her feet and spit on the pavement, just like Grandmother always did on the roads that the Japanese built. Grandmother told her that when she was a girl, everyone walked or rode their horses all over Jeju by using the dirt-trailed olle. "It took days to travel from one end of the island to the other, but it was a beautiful journey that we made on special occasions. We would take food and visit friends and relatives in villages along the way. Each olle had a guardian spirit, a special tree, rock, or stream that we would pray to, or leave small gifts for, like flowers or nuts. When the Japs invaded, they bulldozed and paved most of the ancient footpaths, which our ancestors formed a thousand years ago. Modern roads were better, they said. Travel would be easier for everyone. Ha! Faster roads and the contraptions that used them only made it easier for those bloodsuckers to steal from us."

By the time the first horse-drawn cart made an appearance, only the morning star and humpbacked moon still hung on the glowing horizon. The eastern sky was a pale violet, streaked with orange, while Hallasan was a looming silhouette of a woman, luxuriant in repose. At this early hour, Junja could almost see the goddess of the mountain breathing, her bosom rising and falling as she stretched out, long hair cascading down to the sea.

Junja waved her arms to attract the cart driver's attention. "Are you heading toward the mountain pass, sir?" Junja hoped that her bow was convincing enough, restricted as she was by the pack.

The man shook his head and urged the horse to go faster.

Junja spluttered as the cart wheeled away. Not a word of greeting or even apology! She had never encountered such rudeness before. All sorts of stories were being whispered about the strangers on the island; now she had one of her own.

Another cart appeared around the bend moments later. Junja's relief, however, turned into disappointment when she saw that a passenger was already sitting beside the driver. Her feet dragged as the pack grew even heavier.

The cart slowed down when it pulled up alongside her. The passenger addressed Junja in a voice that was noticeably deep and sonorous. "Excuse me, miss, but where are you going with that large pack?"

A young man with a kind face smiled down at her. He was wearing the same baggy hemp trousers and rusty shirt that all Jeju men wore, except that his head was clean-shaven.

Junja lowered her head in respect before speaking. "Good morning, sunnim. I'm going up to Cloud House Farm to deliver abalone from Lonely Rock Village."

The monk beamed. "What a fine coincidence! I'm headed up that way too." He turned to the driver, who cut the monk off before he could ask his question.

"Nope, my horse can't pull all three of us that far. Not with that load she's carrying."

The young man's smile didn't flicker. "I see. Then one of us must get off the cart to assist this young maid with her heavy burden."

The driver snorted. "Won't be me. My cart, my horse."

"Then it is I who must go." The monk gathered his walking stick and bag and thanked the driver, handing him a small coin. "May you travel safely, sir." He climbed out of the cart and offered his place to Junja with a smiling nod.

The girl was gratified by the young man's generosity. If she took this cart, she would be sure to reach the mountain in time. A delay would cost her the abalone as well as the piglet, so she had no choice but to accept his offer. Still, it would be rude to agree too quickly.

"You're too kind, sir. I can't possibly take your place. I'm sure another cart will come this way soon."

The monk held up his hand as his face crinkled into a wide grin. "Unlike you, miss, I don't have a heavy burden that needs to reach its destination before the sun climbs too high. As you said, another cart is sure to come this way soon."

Junja hesitated again, out of decorum. She tried to bow, forgetting that she was prevented from doing so by the pack. She bent her head as deeply as she could. "Thank you very much, sir. Thank you!"

The monk helped Junja climb into the cart. Once she had settled in place, the driver clucked to his horse, who flicked his tail before he began walking. Junja waved to the monk, who raised his walking stick and grinned as the cart pulled away.

The girl turned to the driver. "That's the kindest monk I've ever met."

The man scratched his ear. "He wasn't uppity like a lot of 'em are. And he didn't speak in riddles either. He sure talked a lot, though. You're not going to talk my ears off too, are you?"

"No, sir."

"Good. I need to pay attention to the road. You can't be too careful these days, with strangers popping out from every tree and rock."

Junja remembered her mother's warning. "Are the roads dangerous?"

The man considered. "I don't know about dangerous. More like strange. Lots of strange things happening."

"Like the cart that passed me just before you arrived!" Junja jumped at the chance to share her outrage. "The driver didn't even slow down when I waved. When he saw me, he drove even faster, as if he didn't want to be seen."

The farmer spat. "Bastard almost ran me off the road. Could've made my horse go lame. No manners at all! Definitely wasn't a local. Makes you curious about what schemes he's up to, scurrying around like a rat."

After grumbling for a few moments, the farmer roused himself for one final outburst. "Damn foreigners even charge us to use our own roads. As bad as the Jap bloodsuckers." He spat again. "That reminds me: Do you have coins for the pass?"

Junja pointed to the bag around her neck. "Yes, sir. And for you too."

With that satisfactory reply, the man didn't say another word to Junja for the remainder of the trip.

Three

On the approach to the foothills of Hallasan, the patchwork fields of the lowlands turned into forests of tender green maple and blooming cherry. The cart came to an abrupt halt, pulling up to a break in the trees where a dirt pass met the main road. The farmer jumped off the cart, surprising Junja, who thought that he was going to help her down. Instead, he wandered into the woods, where he took a long, loud piss.

At the entrance to the pass, a constable in a green uniform was hunched under a blooming cherry tree, asleep. A breeze from the mountain stirred a flurry of loose blossoms, which showered upon the sleeping man. Pale pink petals capped his bushy head and blanketed the pistol cradled in his crossed arms. His green hat was lying on the ground, full of pink. The sound of his snoring grated through the humming and twittering of insects and birds. The air was thick with tiny wings that Junja waved away from her eyes as she approached the sleeping figure.

"Sir?" Her whisper disappeared into the crunching gravel of the cart driving away.

The man's nose twitched as a blossom landed on his nose, but his snoring did not change in volume.

Junja swallowed and raised her voice. "Sir? I have toll money for the pass." She didn't dare touch a strange man.

When he still didn't respond, Junja decided to tiptoe past. Just as her foot took a step back from the huddled figure, a hand darted out and grabbed her sock.

"Where do you think you're going without paying?" The constable reached for his hat and put it on, showering more petals on his head. His mainland accent was strong. A city man from Seoul, Junja guessed.

"I didn't want to wake you, sir. I have the money right here." Junja pointed to the bag around her neck.

The man grunted as he rose. The girl could not help staring. She had never seen such a bulging stomach before.

The constable placed the gun back in its holster and hiked up his pants as circled her. Petals fell out of his hair and beard. "You were going to sneak past me, eh?" His menacing tone was foiled by a belch.

"No, sir. I thought I could pay you upon my return. This is the only way back, after all."

"What's in that basket? Weapons for Communist rebels hiding in the mountains?" The man's eyes narrowed under his unruly head of hair.

Junja took a deep gulp of air before reciting what her mother told her to say. "I am delivering goods from the haenyeo of Lonely Rock Village to the pig farmer of Cloud House Farm."

The constable swallowed as he rubbed the bulging mound of his stomach. "How can I be sure?"

"You may inspect the basket, sir."

"What's inside?" The man growled.

"Seaweed, sir. And abalone."

His lips twitched under the bushy beard. "Abalone are one of the redeeming features of this forsaken island. Is that all you've got? Just seaweed and abalone?"

"Shall I take off the pack, sir, for you to inspect?"

"Of course."

Junja suppressed a sigh as she began unwinding the first layer of bindings that secured the wooden frame against her body.

The constable held up his hand. "I don't want to spend all day watching you take off your pack and then help you put it all back on again. Damn country bumpkins think you have all the time in the world. Just gimme the toll."

Junja opened the drawstring purse and pulled out two coins, which the man snatched from her fingers.

"When do you plan to return?" The constable peered suspiciously at the coins before hiding them away.

"Tomorrow morning, sir. I'll have a piglet then."

"That's another thing you Jeju folk do well: pork." The man's expression softened. "But I still can't find trotters as good as my mother's." His stomach rumbled as he waved her to pass. "Move along, then. Move along."

Junja gave in to a sudden impulse. "Would you like some bing-ddeok, sir? I have enough to share." She pulled a cloth packet from her waist bag and unrolled it, revealing two fat logs of millet pancakes filled with seasoned carrot, turnip, greens, and egg.

"That's mighty kind of you. A man gets awfully hungry working outside, guarding the road." The constable grabbed the fatter of the two rolls. He took a large bite and chewed noisily as Junja wrapped up her remaining roll and tucked it away. Bits of food flew out of his mouth, sticking to his beard and mustache.

The constable grabbed Junja's arm, speaking through a full mouth. "This is good. Really good. Did you make it?"

"No, my mother did."

"Does she live nearby?"

"In Lonely Rock Village, sir."

"Do you think she'd be willing to sell food to a hungry officer like myself?"

"I will ask her, sir, when I get back home."

"You do that. Tell her to ask for Constable Lee at the military office in Seogwipo."

Junja bowed again. "I really must go, sir. If I don't hurry, these abalone will die."

"Go along, then! What do you think this is, a social call?" The constable gave her a shove.

The girl started trotting to make up for lost time. She halted when the man shouted at her.

"Wait! What's your mother's name? I'll look for her if you forget!"

"Goh Sookja."

The constable waved the girl away.

☽

Junja squinted up at the sun. The air was warming quickly, and she had lost track of how long she had been walking since lunch. Blackbirds were winging their way overhead, squawking. As soon as she heard the gurgling stream, Junja pushed through the trees. She took off the pack so that she could scoop handfuls of water into her mouth. She rinsed her face and neck before putting the pack back on.

The wide footpath, which had sloped gently at first, grew steeper and narrower as it threaded through evergreens, losing its smooth stamped surface and looking more like a faint trail scratched out by animals. The pack pulled at Junja like an anchor. Sweat trickled down her back, stinging where the straps had rubbed her skin raw. Grit and pebbles had needled into the straw shoes.

With a grunt, Junja kept walking, ignoring the pain in her feet and the lightheadedness that made her want to lie down and sleep. So intent was her concentration on keeping her foothold that when the blur of fur and snout jumped up into her face, the girl was too startled to be afraid.

A boar? She staggered backward, bracing herself for an agony of hooves and tusks.

The heavy pack thudded against a tree, breaking her fall. Junja kept her eyes closed, arms crossed over her face. This was all her fault, for not following Mother's directions to pay attention.

"Are you all right?"

At first, the girl thought that the beast had spoken to her in a human voice, like beasts often did in the stories Grandmother told. Junja peeked through her arms. Below her was a large yellow-white dog. He was looking up at her, pink tongue lolling out.

"What did you say?" The girl looked down at the dog, which closed its mouth and cocked its head at her question.

"My dog didn't say anything at all." A tall boy with a walking stick stepped out of the green shadows. One bushy eyebrow was raised in amusement, and his shaggy cropped hair was pulled back from his forehead by a scholar's manggeon. Except for that black headband, he was dressed like any other man on Jeju, in baggy pants and a shirt the color of dried mud.

"Who are you?" Junja grew alert. This ungainly boy looked strange enough to be a mountain troll, a dotchebbi who would steal her basket and torment her. If only she hadn't thought those horrible thoughts! Mother was right; she had breathed bad luck into her venture by saying those stupid things.

"My name is Yang Suwol. Pleased to make your acquaintance." The boy's speech was polished, like a scholar's, and his bow stiff.

His prominent nose was crooked, as if it had changed directions midcourse, and his jaw was shaped like a spade. His eyes seemed to disappear into his cheeks when he grinned.

Was he smiling or smirking? Junja scowled when she realized she could not move. "Your dumb mutt shouldn't be running about scaring people." She tried to take a step away, but the pack didn't budge.

The boy crossed his arms as the crook of his grin deepened. "My dog did not scare you; you scared yourself. And he's not dumb; he's the cleverest dog on Hallasan."

Junja grunted. The pack was wedged tightly between two saplings.

"Actually, he's more intelligent than some people."

The girl's eyes blazed. "Don't just stand there. I've got to bring this basket to the pig farmer's wife of Cloud House while the abalone are still alive."

The boy yelped, leaping forward to tug at the basket. "My mother's been waiting all morning!" He braced his legs as he tried to pull the basket free of the trees.

"Careful! If you break it, everything will spill."

The basket creaked ominously but held together as it slipped free. The weight resettled on Junja's shoulders, making her gasp.

The tall boy did not speak as he began loosening the ties at Junja's waist.

"What are you doing?" Junja was shocked by the boy's casual license. Who did he think he was to stand so close that she could smell his musk? She flushed.

The boy cleared his throat. "I'm going to take the pack from you. Your feet are bleeding." He was taking care not to touch her as he began to unwind the bindings.

Junja looked down. One of mother's straw shoes had fallen off. The white dog was sniffing a bloom of red oozing through the socks.

"It doesn't bother me too much."

"It bothers me, though." The boy motioned to Junja to remove the gourd around her neck. The sweeping motion of his hand was so elegant that Junja could not help noticing how long his fingers were, with clean nails trimmed close to the tips.

She hesitated before deciding that there wasn't enough time to argue. She gave the gourd to the boy, who set it down on the ground before lifting the pack off her shoulders.

The sudden absence of her burden made Junja's body feel curiously light, as if she might float off the ground. She grabbed a tree as the ground seemed to tilt beneath her.

"This is really heavy! I can't believe you carried it this far." The boy looked at Junja with respect. "Who are you?" He hoisted the pack with a grunt onto his back.

"Goh Junja."

"I guess it's true what they say about you haenyeo being tougher than most men." The tall boy settled the pack on his shoulders and began winding the ties around his waist. "Could you help secure this thing, please?"

Junja bound the pack to the boy, handing him the loose ends of the ties, which he joined in a complicated knot low on his waist. After planting his stick, the boy took several brisk steps up the mountain path. The white dog followed, but then stopped, whining in concern.

Junja was holding onto a tree as the world seemed to whirl around her.

The boy crossed his arms as he studied her. "Dizzy?"

Junja nodded.

"You need water." The boy handed her the gourd, motioning for her to take a drink.

Junja pushed it away. "That's saltwater, for the pack. I was supposed to pour it over everything when I reached the grandfather rock. The sun will be high in the sky soon, and the abalone will die." She turned her head so that the boy couldn't see her tears of frustration.

"Don't worry, miss. I'll take care of everything."

Junja tried to stand. "I have to go with you . . ."

"You'll slow me down if you follow. I won't forget to water the basket. Please stay here, and I'll send someone to get you. Do you understand?"

A sudden wave of dizziness made Junja slide to the ground. She managed to nod as she closed her eyes.

The tall boy and his white dog loped away.

☽

"Wake up, big sister!" A high voice pierced Junja's ears; small hands shook her shoulders.

Junja opened her eyes.

A little face was staring at her, so close that the eyes seemed to have merged in the center, above the nose. Junja took the small gourd that the child was offering.

"Mama says you must drink this while you are sitting down. Little sips, or else you will throw up." The child opened her eyes dramatically, revealing a flutter of long, thin eyelashes and eyes as bright as a bird's.

Junja took a sip. "Who are you?"

"Everyone calls me Peanut. I'm seven, but people say I look younger. I don't think that's true at all." She cupped her chubby cheeks with her grimy fists and thrust out her lower lip. A fringe of black hair fell straight above her eyes while the rest of the little girl's hair fit like a cap that reached below her earlobes.

The girl was indeed unusually small for her age, but Junja didn't say so. "You look exactly as you should look, I think."

"Big Brother said that you carried that huge pack up here all by yourself! He said you were a mermaid too. Is that true?" She wasn't a pretty child, but her eyes were bright with curiosity. Her resemblance to her brother was unmistakable.

Junja sat up when the girl mentioned the pack. "Were the abalone still alive?"

Peanut made a face. "Mama poured water on them, and they moved. She was gonna make me hang the seaweed to dry, but I said I wanted to find you instead. No one is faster than I am because I know all the secret trails the rabbits use."

The little girl peered down at Junja's legs. "You didn't answer my question. Are you really a mermaid like Suwol said? Does that mean you can swim like a fish? And are you really stronger than he is?"

Junja smiled before taking another sip of tea.

Peanut hung her head and sighed. "Mama said I was s'posed to be quiet until you finished drinking the tea. And then we're s'posed to start walking home."

Junja rose, holding onto a tree for support. Her legs were trembling and her feet ached, but the dizziness had subsided enough for her to start moving again.

Peanut took her by the hand to lead her up the path. The sky was bright, and the small spring leaves shook in a slight breeze. The mountain stood massive and still, unlike the shifting sea.

The two girls walked in silence until Peanut tugged wordlessly at Junja's arm. The little girl's hand was clamped over her mouth, cheeks ballooned out on either side.

"Why are you covering your mouth like that?"

Peanut let out her breath in a loud gasp. "Mama said I'm only s'posed to answer questions."

"Do you still want to know if I can swim like a fish?"

"Oh, yes, yes, yes!" Peanut hopped from one foot to the next.

"Well, when I'm in the water—"

The child interrupted. "When you're in the water, your legs turn into a fish tail, right? That's how come you can swim as deep as a fish, right? Can you breathe water like fish too? Have you seen the sea king?"

Junja laughed. "You're just like a rabbit, hopping from one thought to another. When I'm in the water, I use my legs like a fish uses its tail. And, no, I don't breathe water like a fish. I hold my breath. For a long time. And, yes, I've seen the sea king. His ladies in waiting too."

Peanut's expression flickered from disappointment to awe. "What did he look like?"

"Big and fat like a manatee, with a long bristly mustache. He wore robes of green and purple seaweed, held together by a belt of shiny pearls."

The little girl's mouth dropped open. "He must be very rich!"

"He is. The sea king owns everything under the sea, even the treasure from sunken pirate ships."

Peanut balled her fists, quivering with excitement. "I wanna be a haenyeo like you! I'll find the sea king's treasure and become rich enough to eat rice candy and drink honey water whenever I want. And my piglets will sleep on new straw every night."

"If you keep shouting like that, you won't have enough breath to walk home!" The little girl's brother was standing at the bend of the path above them.

The white dog scampered down to the two girls, panting.

Peanut ran toward her older brother. "Carry me, Ohrabang! Please!"

When Suwol pretended to refuse, Peanut began to pummel her brother with her small fists. "Carry me! Carry me!"

The boy handed his walking stick to Junja. The little girl climbed onto his back. Suwol clasped his hands under his sister's bottom, holding her up. Peanut grinned, and the dog leapt ahead.

Four

Junja had expected the pig farm to resemble her own home, a stone hut with a thatched roof, kitchen garden, and muddy pigsty, surrounded by black doldam walls. She blinked, confused, at the forbidding stone walls guarding the entrance, rearing up high as if they enclosed a military fortress. Once she passed through the front gate, she understood. Cloud House Farm was a nobleman's compound. The curved tile roof of the main building jutted out proudly, shading the smaller structures next to it.

The expansive courtyard bustled with people. A slight man staggered by with an earthenware urn roped to his back, followed by a stout woman barking directions. Two men balanced astride wobbly stick ladders while replacing the thatch on a tidy hut near the main house. A clutch of young children chased chickens while two older boys pulled squealing piglets on ropes. A group of squatting women were pulling out handfuls of freshly decanted dwenjang, placing the dripping soybean ferment into straw baskets to drain. Under the shade of a red maple, a tiny boy played with a pile of pebbles and sticks.

"So many people live here!" Junja looked around in fascination as Peanut slipped off Suwol's back.

Suwol shooed away several small children who had toddled over to stare at Junja. They were naked from the waist down, too young for a chamber pot or outhouse.

"I have seven little uncles and dozens of cousins. What about you?"

Junja considered for a moment. "There's only five of us: Grandmother, Mother, little brother, little sister, and me."

Peanut interrupted. "What about your father? Wouldn't he make six?"

"My father . . . isn't with us anymore." Junja didn't want to admit the shameful truth, that he had moved away to the mainland, abandoning his family.

"That's so sad. I would miss my daddy so much if he died." The little girl's face turned tragic for a moment, before brightening as a cat streaked across the courtyard. "What about animals? Do you keep chickens? A dog or cat?"

"We have chickens, but no dogs. There's a village cat, though."

Suwol threw a stick. When the white dog bounded away, Peanut followed. Both dog and child scampered away in response to a woman's call.

Junja laughed. "Your dog seems to think he's human."

"Boshi is the smartest dog on Hallasan. Which means he's the smartest dog in all of Jeju. Maybe even all of Korea."

"Boshi?" Junja stifled a giggle. "Like boshintang, the soup?"

The boy grinned. "That's what Mother threatened to turn him into if he didn't behave."

Peanut ran back with a small wooden box and several strips of cloth. "Mama says I'm s'posed to take you to the spring, so you can wash your feet. You're s'posed to cover the hurts with this medicine and cloth, so they don't swell up red. And then mama says you're s'posed to go to the shrine, like your mama always does. I can take you there!"

The little girl turned sideways, tugging her earlobe. "Big brother, you're supposed to do something with the pigs. I forget what, but Little Uncle said so."

Suwol laughed. "Peanut, whenever you lie, you always pull your ear. Everyone knows you're not allowed to go to the spring. Give the bandages and salve to Junja."

Peanut thrust the box and cloth strips into Junja's hands before turning to glare at her brother. "You think you're so smart just because you're studying to be a baksa! Wearing a scholar's head-band doesn't make you one!"

Suwol motioned to Junja to follow him. The two of them walked away while Peanut stamped the ground, howling.

"How long will she scream like that?" Junja looked back as Peanut's wails grew louder. Mother would take a switch to her children's legs if they behaved that way.

The boy kept walking. "She'll only get louder if you pay attention. Just ignore her."

☽

The spring was a dozen paces away from the main house, past a small ridge. Suwol clambered up and then reached over to offer Junja his hand. "We're taking the shortcut."

As the girl stepped up, the wind whipped her hair into her face. Junja pulled the strands away from her eyes, gasping. Below her lay the coastline: pale sand, dark rocks, shimmering ocean. The sky above was a bright expanse of blue.

"It feels like the top of the world here, doesn't it?" Suwol's cropped hair was ruffled by the wind.

Just like blackbird feathers, Junja thought.

The boy turned around to grab a bucket wedged into a rock cleft beside a small stone well. He hefted the wooden lid off the well and tossed the bucket, which was tied to the lid by a length of rope, into the darkness below.

"Everyone else uses the new pulley well over there," Suwol motioned with his head as he pulled the rope, hand over fist. "I prefer the old well. The view's better here." He placed the brimming bucket on the ground next to Junja, who had already taken off her straw shoes and socks.

The girl dipped her cupped hands into the bucket to drink. "Oh! That's sweet!" She soaked one of the cloth strips to wipe her wounds.

Suwol kept his head turned to give the girl some privacy as she tended to her feet. He squatted nearby, picking at a blade of grass as he talked. "The shrine's a few steps from here. If you think you can go further, I could take you all the way to the temple. It's just an hour's walk."

Junja studied her feet with regret. "I don't think I should walk too much more today. And I should be helping out with dinner soon." She wished she could say yes. "Maybe you could take me another time."

"Does that mean you'll be visiting again?" The boy asked his question so quickly that Junja became flustered.

"I don't know. That would depend on my mother. She was supposed to come, but I convinced her to let me take the trip instead. I've never been to Hallasan before."

"You've never seen the Five Hundred Generals up close?" Suwol pointed toward the distant ridge of craggy boulders that seemed to be gazing out to sea.

This was the first time Junja had come close enough to see the rock pillars guarding Jeju's southern coastline. Grandmother often told stories about them, claiming that the boulders housed the spirits of the warrior sons of Jeju's creator, a giantess who formed the entire island in just seven bursts of effort. The giantess had died while cooking her sons one final meal. When the sons learned of her sacrifice, their grief had hardened them into stone. Junja bent her head toward them in respect.

"The monks say that the Five Hundred Generals aren't warriors at all, but sages who reached full enlightenment." Suwol knew that Junja was thinking of the story that every child on Jeju grew up hearing. "That's why they built the temple up there, because they consider the area sacred."

"My grandmother says that every family has their own story about the stones, but that they're all similar enough to be the same." Junja, who had finished wrapping her feet, stood up. She walked next to the boy for a better view of the rock pillars.

Suwol looked at the girl beside him. Her eyes were shining, and the brightness of her smile made him grin. "Whatever the truth is, there's definitely something unusual about them. I've climbed up to see them many times and met people with strange and wondrous stories."

"What kind of stories?"

"Some people have heard the pillars talk. Others have seen faces appear, or felt warm tears on the surface."

Stones, Grandmother had taught Junja, housed all sorts of spirits, usually benevolent. "Do people really travel all the way up there?" After the distance she had walked, Junja found it hard to believe that some people went even further.

Suwol nodded. "Lots of people—not just the monks. There's a meditation hut near the peak that the monks allow everyone to use. The view up there is even better, but it's another half day's walk from here."

A buzzing whine interrupted their conversation. Both Junja and the boy shielded their eyes and squinted.

A gray airplane hung low in the sky, trailing a line of dirty smoke.

Suwol suppressed a curse. "That's the second one this week." He frowned as he watched the plane's passage toward the water.

"Is it Chinese?" Until a few years ago, all the war machines had been Japanese.

The boy shook his head. "American."

The plane cast its shadow on the sea, a black twin that rippled on the water.

"What's it doing?" Junja felt chilled by the sight.

"Searching."

"For what?"

"For something that isn't there."

Suwol glared at the airplane until it dipped under the horizon. He stayed silent for so long that Junja decided to make her way back to the house, to ask about helping with dinner. Just as she took a step away, Suwol remembered himself.

"Come, let's go to the shrine."

☽

The mountain shrine was a smooth ledge protruding from a mossy seam of rock that looked like it had been cleft in two by a giant's ax. Junja could hear water running below the surface, under jagged boulders piled atop each other as though they had tumbled from a great height. Tendrils of vine and fern fell from both sides of the gully, like green waterfalls spilling from rocks. Sunlight beamed through the trees, illuminating every tiny insect and mote in the air.

"This is the same spring that feeds our wells," Suwol said, confirming Junja's guess. "The water comes close to the surface here before diving back deep underground." Suwol bowed toward the ledge in respect. "When it rains, or if the goddess is moody, the shrine is hidden behind a waterfall."

"I'm fortunate the mountain is making it easy for me today." Junja bowed to the shrine before reaching into her waist bag. She pulled out the small handful of rice and dried jujubes Mother had given her for an offering. She placed the delicacies on the ledge, next to a small indentation filled with sand.

"Did you bring incense or candles?" asked the boy.

Junja shook her head as her cheeks flushed. "I was carrying too much." Though she knew that the gods didn't insist upon such niceties, Junja wondered if her gifts were too meager for this impressive shrine.

"Every drop of sweat spent to climb the mountain is worth a stick of incense." The boy spoke formally, as if making a pronouncement.

"Who told you that?"

"I read it somewhere." Suwol reached into his pocket and pulled out a candle. "Unlike you, I haven't already proven myself by climbing up this far, so I brought this along." The boy settled the candle into the small mound of sand. "May I join you in paying my respects?"

"Of course."

Suwol lit the candle and knelt next to Junja in front of the altar. They pressed their palms together in front of their chests and closed their eyes, to offer their private prayers to the god of the mountain.

With her eyes closed, Junja sensed the shrine's peaceful massiveness. Fluttering leaves stirred the air, mixing the richness of damp earth with the sparkling scent of water. As she repeated the mantra of gratitude under her breath, she imagined the old man of the mountain holding a wooden staff, companion tiger by his side, their eyes bright as flames. Mother, who had seen the god in all her forms, had told Junja that the mountain spirit might also make her presence known as a white-haired woman with a white stag.

The boy and the girl ended their prayers by prostrating themselves on the ground three times. They bowed in all four cardinal directions before thanking the sky and the earth.

As they turned from the altar, Junja waited for Suwol to break the silence. She cleared her throat, but when the boy still didn't speak, she blurted out a question, unable to contain her curiosity. "What did you use to light the candle? Was it a lighter?" Suwol had not used a match, but a small object resembling a lighter that belonged to one of the men in her village. The man was so protective of his American-made Zippo that he never let anyone touch it.

Suwol pulled a slim cylinder out of his pocket and held it out. "You want to try it?"

Junja gingerly lifted the brass lighter, which surprised her by being cool to the touch. "I thought it would be hot. How do you make a flame with it?"

"You have to pull the flint wheel back to make a spark." Suwol demonstrated.

Junja ignited the lighter on her second try and gasped in delight. "How clever! Where did you get it?"

"It was made by Austrian soldiers, from an empty bullet cartridge. The lighter used to belong to a Japanese general before it became my father's. He gave it to me when I turned eighteen."

The small object suddenly seemed to burn Junja's hand. She hastily returned it to Suwol. Her words were careful. "Was the general someone your father knew?"

Suwol raised an eyebrow. "Are you asking if my father was friendly enough with the Japs to be given a gift by one of their generals? The answer would be no. The lighter was left behind when the dog Hirohito pulled his troops." He spat.

Junja breathed out in relief. Everyone in her family loathed the Japanese, refusing to touch anything that once belonged to the bloodsuckers. The traitors who had collaborated with them were lower than thieves. "I'm glad they're gone."

Suwol nodded. "I am too." His face darkened. "But their replacements may be just as bad."

Junja, who had been warned not to talk about the political situation, changed the subject. "Could you show me the way back to the house, please? I don't want your mother to think I'm avoiding my duties in the kitchen."

Five

Dinner that night resembled a village feast, with as many dishes of banchan as there were people. Suwol's mother, as the wife of the eldest son, wore her authority lightly, issuing soft-spoken orders to all the women in the kitchen with a gracious smile. A diminutive, plump beauty with dimples and the fairest skin Junja had ever seen, she was obviously not from Jeju, a difference that was underscored by her soft, undulating accent.

"Little Auntie, could you bring out more of your bean sprout soup? It's so good that I don't think one pot will be enough."

"Won-Bin's Mother, that batch of chive kimchi may be a tad past its prime. Could you taste it, please, before setting it out?"

Because the spring weather was so mild, the menfolk, including Suwol, were eating outside in the main courtyard, while the women and children ate in the kitchen courtyard.

Suwol's mother offered Junja a bowl of gosari. "We pick these ferns from a special spot on the mountain, where they taste the best. It's your mother's favorite food to eat whenever she visits. Try!"

Junja hesitated, feeling guilty. She understood now why Mother made the yearly trip up the mountain to visit her friend. The two of them had met when the small woman first came to Jeju as a young bride; they had been close ever since. Though Suwol's mother had welcomed Junja warmly, her disappointment had been obvious. "At least you resemble your mother enough for me to pretend you're her." As Junja helped prepare dinner, the small woman had peppered Junja with questions about her mother's health, disposition, and work.

Suwol's mother held out the bowl of gosari and urged Junja again. "Go ahead! Eat!"

Junja took a small taste to be polite. The meaty brown tendrils were tender and earthy. "Delicious!"

"Then you must have more." Suwol's mother dropped a fat clump of fern into Junja's rice bowl with her chopsticks.

"This is far too much!" Junja gasped at the amount, which could have been shared by her entire family at dinnertime.

"Your mother could eat twice this amount!" The small woman's dimples winked as she smiled. "For folks on the mountain, gosari is as commonplace as seaweed is to folks on the shore." She gestured to Junja's bandaged feet. "Do your feet feel better now? That honey salve is very effective."

"They don't hurt at all, thank you for asking. I think the water helped too. Your mountain spring is the most beautiful place I've ever seen."

Suwol's mother laughed. "Suwol's father always says that too. I, however, want to stand in my kitchen courtyard and pump water straight into a pot. That would be far more beautiful than lugging around heavy jugs of water, don't you think?"

"Oh, that would be so nice." Junja sighed. It was her duty to keep the earthenware pots filled with water from the village well. She made that trip twice a day, staggering under the urn strapped to her back.

"The world is changing very quickly." Suwol's mother patted her hand. "Someday every house in the village will be connected to the well by a pipe. When that happens, I promise, your mother will be first in line!"

A ruckus in the kitchen courtyard distracted the women. Suwol was being swarmed by a group of little children led by Peanut, who were all clamoring to be picked up and tossed in the air.

"What is that boy doing here?" Suwol's mother rose from the floor, brushing her skirts smooth. Junja stood as well.

Suwol limped toward the two women while dragging a tiny boy who was clinging to his right leg. Suwol nodded to Junja, before addressing his mother. "Did you eat well, Mother?"

"As well as you did."

"Then you must have eaten very well indeed." Suwol rubbed his belly and belched.

The small woman laughed, hitting her son's arm. "You should be with the men, not here playing with the children."

Suwol bent over to peel the child off his leg. He placed the child on the ground and thumped his bottom. "I'll play with you later, Little Pup. After Big Auntie and I finish talking."

As Suwol stood, Junja noticed a long lock of hair fall into his eyes. He brushed it away while talking to his mother. "A monk stopped by with news from Seogwipo. He asked if the girl carrying the large pack got here safely. I wanted to make sure he was talking about the same person." Suwol turned to Junja. "Did you meet a monk on the way here?"

Junja nodded. "He gave me his seat on the farmer's cart. His kindness allowed me to arrive here on time." She wished she could thank the man again. "Is he still here?"

"No, he isn't."

Suwol's mother interrupted with a frown. "What kind of news from Seogwipo would compel a monk to stop by at this time of day?"

The tall boy shrugged. "Nothing very interesting. I think he just wanted to make sure that Junja got here safely."

Suwol's mother looked at her son sharply. Suwol was shushing the tiny boy, shaking his head and holding his finger to his mouth. The explanation was entirely plausible, so she relaxed. "Well, that was very kind of him. Next time, make sure you invite him in to eat something. Men! When will they ever learn some manners!"

Suwol ignored his mother's admonishment. Instead, he allowed himself to be dragged out of the courtyard by the little children. Suwol had overheard his father urging the monk to join the family for the evening meal, but the man had declined with regret. He explained to Suwol's worried father that he needed to return to the temple as swiftly as possible, because the news he was bearing could not wait: hundreds of Jeju citizens were being rounded up and jailed, on orders of the US military. People needed to be warned. They needed to be ready.

☽

Junja sighed with pleasure as she stroked the soft quilt, recollecting the day that had led her here, to a bedroom with silk blankets in a nobleman's compound. All the food at dinnertime had been served on wooden dishes, instead of sea shells. At the end of the meal, Suwol's mother had passed out lacquered cups of omija berry juice, chilled with pieces of ice that Suwol and his uncles had brought back from the lake at the top of the mountain. It had been Junja's first time trying the mountain berry famous for tasting like all five flavors at once, and everyone had laughed at her mystified expression.

The patriarch of the Yang family, Suwol's grandfather, had insisted on bringing out a large wooden box to show the visitor. Inside lay a curved sword, made from steel that had been layered a thousand times. It was a relic from the court, a gift from the last true king of Joseon to the most trusted member of his royal guard. The old man shed a tear as he described how all the loyal guardsmen were banished before they could be murdered by the Japanese. Junja had knelt on the floor to bow to the old man, who was delighted by the pretty girl's show of respect.

After Junja helped the women clean up the kitchen, Peanut had led her to the pigsty, where they fed the scrapings from dinner to the grunting piglets. The little girl had pointed out her two plump favorites, promising one of them to Junja, who had begun yawning.

Peanut had been leading Junja back to the main house when they ran into Suwol outside in the main courtyard. He was taking a break from his studies for some fresh air. His fingers were smudged, and a streak of ink stained his shirt over his heart. The three of them had gazed at the glittering sky together, searching for constellations. While Suwol and Junja were confessing that they shared the same favorite, the seven stars of the Big Dipper, Peanut kept tugging at Junja's arm, eager to show her the guest room.

The little girl had refused to sleep with her parents, insisting on keeping Junja company. Her two playmates, Princess and Baby, had begged to be allowed to sleep with the guest as well. Junja found herself telling the three little girls the story of Sim Cheong the beggar maiden, who sacrificed herself to the sea king so that her blind father might see again.

The girls, who already knew the tale, had pressed Junja for details about the palace under the sea. The end of the story disappeared into descriptions of crabs hiding behind curtains of sea grass, dolphin teams pulling giant conch carriages, and octopuses trailing after their owners like dogs trotting after humans.

☽

The crickets grew louder as the night deepened. Junja, who was accustomed to the lull of the surf, found it difficult to fall asleep in that din. On her final trip to the outhouse, she noticed an illuminated window in the main house. Perhaps that was Suwol's room, where he was studying.

Junja slid the door to her room shut and crawled back onto the sleeping mat. She pulled the silk blanket back over herself, marveling once again at its lightness. She had expected such a thick quilt to be heavy, but it rested on her like a pile of feathers. Beside her, Peanut and her two little cousins were a tangle of snores.

The crickets seemed to rise in volume, growing more shrill. Junja pulled the quilt over her ears and shifted position. She wondered if Suwol had fallen asleep yet, then chided herself for being silly. Someone studying to be a baksa would be studying late into the night, surrounded by lanterns. He was probably consulting books and writing on rice paper with a long wooden brush. Most likely he was grimacing in concentration, the wings of his black hair kept out of his eyes by a band of cloth around his forehead.

☾

The next morning, one of the aunties roused Junja, who had finally fallen into a dreamless sleep after much tossing and turning.

"My apologies for oversleeping! I didn't even hear the roosters crow!" Junja was mortified about appearing so inattentive and lazy. She started rolling her bedding. The little girls were nowhere in sight.

"The mountain air makes people sleep deeply," said the auntie. "A good thing, because you'll be well rested for your walk back. I brought more salve and new bandages for your feet. When you get home, soak them in seawater and dry them in the sun. There's porridge in the kitchen, in one of the small pots. Help yourself. Peanut will bring your piglet to you."

"Thank you for your hospitality." Junja bowed to the woman, who smiled as she left with the bedding, which would be aired out in the sun and beaten before being returned to a camphor-scented wooden trunk.

The kitchen was empty, except for Boshi, who was curled in a small hollow near the stone hearth. The dog stretched, the ridge of his fur bristling as he arched, before scampering over to Junja. He wagged his tail and placed his paw on Junja's knee.

The dog's dark eyes followed every mouthful she took. When Junja finished, she ran her finger around the bowl and held it out for him to lick clean.

"Boshi is especially convincing when he wants food." Suwol was grinning in the doorway, walking stick in hand and pack on his back. "I'm going to escort you to your village because I have some errands to run. My parents are paying their respects at the family shrine, so Mother asked me to say goodbye to you."

Junja was surprised by her sudden rush of pleasure. "I'm sorry I didn't get to say goodbye to your mother in person. Please let her know how grateful I am for her hospitality." Her bow was heartfelt.

Peanut peeked into the kitchen. She was holding a rope that was tied around the neck of a furry black piglet. "I picked my second favorite for you, because he's a little fatter than my first favorite, who's really smart and loves me too much to leave." The little girl bent down to pick up the beast and held it up to Junja, who flinched. She knew too well that the bulk of a black pig's diet came from the outhouse.

Suwol winked. "Don't worry. That one was just weaned a few days ago. It's only eaten leftovers. No adult fare until later, if you know what I mean." He handed Junja her drinking gourd, now heavy with spring water, and the basket pack, lightened of its load. He took the piglet from his little sister and set it back down on the ground.

"Peanut, tell Mother and Father I'll send word with the straw farmer if there are any delays. Take good care of Boshi while I'm gone, all right?"

The little girl nodded and threw her arms around Junja's waist. "Come back and visit again soon."

Junja smoothed Peanut's hair. "If you visit me, we'll look for the sea king's palace together."

"Promise?"

"Promise."

Six

As she walked down the mountain path alongside Suwol, Junja marveled. So much had happened since yesterday morning, which seemed like it belonged to another life. Something about herself felt altered, as if she had grown an entire year in a day.

Suwol surprised the girl by echoing her thoughts. "Some days go by and nothing in my life seems to change. Wake up, study, work, eat, sleep. Then do it all over again. But yesterday wasn't like that. And today feels different too."

Junja couldn't help smiling. The piglet snuffled the humid scent of the ground, straining at the rope as it grunted.

Suwol stopped walking. "There's something I want to show you. It will delay your return home, but I think you'd like it very much. Would you like to see it?"

"What is it?"

"Is it all right if I don't answer that question? I want to surprise you. I promise you'll be pleased."

Junja laughed. "I'm so curious now that I have to say yes. As long as we don't take too long. I promised my mother I'd help her today."

The boy grinned. "You won't regret this." He studied their surroundings, poking his walking stick into the underbrush until he found what he was looking for, a gnarled evergreen with a twist in its lower trunk. "We leave the main path here." He lifted a branch, gesturing for Junja to duck under it.

The two walked alongside each other for several steps until Junja, conscious of the proximity forced upon them by the narrow path, slowed down to allow Suwol to lead.

The boy, glancing behind him, cleared his throat. "How are your feet? I hope they aren't bothering you."

Junja felt a swell of gratitude for his concern. "The wrappings are so thick I could probably walk on a field of stones and not feel a thing."

"Good . . . Because if your feet hurt, I'd carry you on my back." Suwol looked behind him again. "You sure they don't hurt?"

"Quite sure." Junja demonstrated by kicking a stone.

"You must be so relieved." Suwol's pace quickened abruptly, forcing Junja to run to keep up. Because the girl didn't say anything more, the boy held his tongue for as long as he could before blurting out the first question he could think of. "Are all haenyeo strong like you?"

A memory welled up, of a slim girl who used to play cat's cradle with her. Junja blinked, relieved that Suwol couldn't see her face.

"We can't afford to be weak."

"How long have you been doing water work ?"

"Five years." Junja stared at Suwol's back. What a strange boy to be so curious about women's business.

"What age do girls start diving?"

"We start swimming as soon as we can walk. But the diving doesn't start until we're thirteen or fourteen. As soon as our bodies have some fat on them. Otherwise, the water would be too cold. That's why women do the diving, because we last longer in the water than men."

Suwol turned around. "Is that true? Or is it one of those old wive's tales that's been repeated so many times everyone believes it?"

"Why do we do all the diving, then? It certainly isn't because men work harder than women."

Undaunted by the prickle of irritation in Junja's voice, the boy continued his interrogation. "How old are you?"

Junja answered, to be polite. "I was born in the year of the sheep."

"I'm a dragon." Suwol looked pleased by his advantage of years and adjusted his language accordingly. "The dive—what's that like?"

Suwol's relaxation into informal speech surprised Junja, who could not take such liberties as a woman. She wondered if he was being condescending, but the boy didn't seem to be talking down to her. She decided to accept that this young scholar was treating her like a friend, and her mood grew more buoyant.

"Diving is always cold and exhausting. But it's also fun, especially when the harvest is abundant."

"It's quite dangerous too, isn't it?"

Junja thought again of the slim girl, how her body floated up, cold and blue. The sea, Grandmother had explained, was ruthless in its culling.

"That depends on your fate and whether the sea god favors you." Junja took a deep breath. "Some girls die on their first dive. And there are old grannies who've gone out thousands of times, who can barely creep about on land but swim faster than anyone else in the sea." Just like her own grandmother.

When Suwol didn't respond immediately, Junja thought that perhaps he had satisfied his curiosity at last.

But the boy asked another question. "That whistling sound you haenyeo make when you surface—why do you do that?"

"Sumbisori?" It's just what we do, Junja thought, as she tried to remember what she had been taught. "We make that noise to make sure all the bad air comes out. And to let the other divers know that we've surfaced."

Suwol stopped walking. He was grinning, and that smile rearranged his motley features in a way that made it impossible for Junja not to smile back. "Could you please make your sumbisori right now?" He planted his walking stick and waited.

"Here?"

"Yes!" Suwol's eyes glinted.

Junja considered. This bright mountainside was nothing like the shadowy depths. Without the sea bearing down and the desperate need of her body, was it possible to make the same noise? Not if the boy kept looking at her like that. She flushed. "You'll have to turn around first."

Suwol swiveled immediately. "Take all the time you need. I'll stay put until you're done."

Junja closed her eyes, drawing air deep into her belly. She imagined herself plummeting. The water pulsated and swirled, as vital and vast as the mountain she was standing on. Her hands reached out, searching for the light above. The breath she was holding started fluttering against her chest. She let it escape.

Birds shot out of the trees as the piglet jumped, squealing. After a moment of surprised silence, the mountain resumed its usual din: insects buzzed, birds chirped, leaves rustled.

"You sound like a hawk." Suwol turned around. His smile was so wide that it swallowed his eyes.

Junja blushed.

☽

To the crow flying overhead, the boy and girl walking through the forested foothills of Hallasan were curious enough to merit a second pass. There were no interesting smells or shiny baubles worth stopping for, so it swooped up and flew away, loud in its disappointment.

Junja almost jumped when Suwol's hand touched her shoulder. His voice was so close to her ear that she could feel the heat of his breath. "Look over there."

He was pointing down, toward a small shoot unfurling from the ground.

"Gosari." He held out his arms. "This is my secret spot. It's warmer down here, so the ferns bud earlier. If we pick for an hour, we could gather enough for you to take home to your mother. You could eat them all summer."

The boy stepped into the patch of green curls and squatted down to unfold two large squares of cloth. "One for you and one for me." He gestured to a place beside him.

Junja crouched next to the boy, pulling one of the squares toward her. She could feel her heart pounding. Why did it sound so loud? Could Suwol hear it too?

"You can use this knife." Suwol laid the blade on the ground, making sure to turn the sharp tip away from her.

Did he plan all of this just for her? Deep inside Junja, an unfamiliar sensation bloomed, soft and warm.

The two of them worked wordlessly, side by side, close enough for the boy to sense the warmth of the girl's body mixing with the cooler mountain air. Junja could feel the whoosh of Suwol's breathing, more sensation than sound. Their knives cut the stems, while their hands twisted the ferns free.

Small clouds drifted across the sky. The sun climbed higher. The boy and girl laughed and murmured. Gosari, young and tender, began spilling over the squares of cloth.

Suwol's hands stopped.

Time to go, Junja thought. She closed her eyes and sighed, not wanting to leave. If she could, she would live forever in this quiet green moment.

Suwol shifted, moving so close that Junja could smell his musk. Her skin prickled, suddenly aware. She could hardly breathe, and she didn't dare move.

His finger touched her, lightly, on the cheek.

The boy's voice was so soft that the girl wasn't sure whether the words were being spoken aloud or whether she was imagining them.

"When I first saw you on the mountain, I thought you were a gumiho. So fierce and wild." He swallowed. "And, last night, after looking at the stars . . . I couldn't concentrate at all." His finger traced the curve of her lip.

Junja looked up.

Tiny images of her face were reflected in Suwol's eyes. How had she lived her entire life by the sea without knowing that he was here, on the mountain?

Her hands trembled as they rose toward his face and then stopped. Junja felt herself flush. She scooted away to fuss with her bundle of ferns, trying to hide her face.

Suwol pulled his hand back. "My apologies. That was presumptuous of me. I'm sorry. Please don't be mad."

The girl shook her head. This wasn't anger, but something else that felt just as hot and red. What would Mother think? Junja could almost see her mother's face, contorted by emotion.

"Don't you feel as happy as I do?" The boy looked anxious.

Joy and dread pierced Junja in equal measure. What kind of happiness was this, to be shadowed by such anxiety? She glanced at the forest undergrowth. If someone had been watching, what would they have witnessed? His fingers touching her face. Her hand rising and then stopping. Nothing terribly shameful. She shushed the boy. "Something might hear you." It was never a good idea to tempt fate by crowing about one's happiness or good luck.

Suwol laughed. "I'm not very superstitious."

Junja managed a smile. "I'm being silly, aren't I?" Still, she couldn't help shivering. Had a cloud passed over the sun?

As they tied their bundles of fern, a heaviness tugged at the girl. Even when Suwol took hold of Junja's hand, the girl couldn't let go of her dark premonition.

☽

"Have you ever thought about the kind of life you'd like to live?" Suwol released Junja's hand to poke at the undergrowth with his walking stick. The girl's anxiety spiked with this break in contact, so when he grabbed her hand again, she squeezed his hand and smiled.

"I'm not sure what you mean." Junja puzzled over Suwol's strange question. Life was about survival and duty, working to feed and care for one's family. She had always done what needed to be done. Water work, housework, fieldwork, schoolwork . . . For a woman on Jeju, life was nothing but work, as Mother always said.

"What I mean is, do you want to be a haenyeo, like your mother and grandmother? Or do you want to do something else and live a different kind of life entirely?"

The questions puzzled Junja with their assumptions. Did he think she had a choice in such matters? She didn't want to appear dull, so she chose her words carefully. "My mother always says that in her next life she doesn't want to be born a haenyeo. Maybe I wouldn't either."

"I'm asking you about this life, not the next one."

Junja shrugged. "In this life, I'm a haenyeo."

Suwol's stride lengthened as he spoke. "My father's family has always lived on the mountain. No one has ever left. I want to be the first. I want to go to America."

Might as well fly to the moon on the backs of magpies. "Why America?"

Suwol stopped walking. "Did you know that people in America don't have to draw or pump their water? All they do is twist a metal handle, and water flows right into their homes."

Junja tried to imagine such a device, but could not fathom how it would work without flooding the house.

"I swear it's true. And here's something more amazing: they use porcelain chamber pots connected to pipes. When they finish, they pull a handle, and everything washes away."

"Where does it go?"

"I thought that maybe it went to the pigsty," said Suwol, "but apparently it goes somewhere far away to be cleaned."

"Then what do their pigs eat?"

"Apparently, there's so much food in America that they feed their pigs corn."

"I don't believe you."

Suwol took a breath. "Actually, I didn't start this conversation to talk about what pigs eat, but to ask for your opinion. Do you think I'm crazy? Or would you want to go to a place like America too?"

Was he asking her to join him? Junja didn't dare presume. "What would you do there?"

"I'd want to learn English at one of their universities. That's what I'd do first."

"How do you know so much about America?"

"Remember the missionaries who visited Jeju?"

Who could forget? Though they had no right to complain, the Japanese officers had raised a ruckus about the foreigners. There had been rumors in the village about these strange people starting a school that children could attend for free.

Suwol continued, "The missionaries stayed with us for several days. Father let me listen to their stories. They talked a lot. Especially about their god."

Junja had heard about their god as well. An entire neighboring village had converted all at once, to ally themselves with the deity that had cast out the Japanese. Their minister visited Junja's village often, trying to convince everyone that the Christian god was more powerful than all the gods of Korea combined.

"My grandmother says that anyone with a lick of sense would know that the gods of Jeju would not allow a foreign god to meddle here."

Suwol rolled a stone away from the path with his stick. "Not everyone believes in gods and spirits, you know. Some people believe that only the physical world exists."

Junja's eyes opened wide. Birds flew in the air. Fish swam in the water. Men walked on land. And spirits lived in the shadow realm of dreams, darting in and out of the world of men and animals as they pleased.

"How do these people explain bad luck? Good fortune? Coincidences? What do they think happens when we die?" Junja could hardly believe such people existed.

Suwol shrugged. "They think that when we die, we're gone. That's it. The end."

Junja shuddered. Such people were missing an elemental sense, like the baby that had been born without eyes. The thing had been mercifully smothered, and the shaman had purified the home of its taint. People who denied the spirit world were monstrous like that baby, missing parts that made them fully human. Without a spirit sense to guide their actions, such people would be capable of unthinkable deeds.

Alarm prickled her as she considered the possibilities. Junja could hear Mother's voice chiding her, reminding her that careless thoughts invited bad fortune. She muttered a good luck phrase under her breath.

Seven

Down by the main road, the cherry blossom trees had shed all their blooms, which lay in brown tatters on the ground. The constable that Junja met the day before was no longer guarding the pass. In his place was a thin man missing his front teeth, who scratched himself as he lisped through the interrogation. Halfway into Junja's explanation about the abalone and the piglet, the man waved them forward.

"All right, all right. Go ahead already."

As they walked out of hearing distance, Suwol cursed, startling the piglet, which dove into the green undergrowth. "Dogs. Acting so tough because the Americans loaned them some guns. I should take a tanker to Seoul and interrogate every mainlander walking over the Han Gang Bridge."

Junja glanced around to see if anyone could have overheard Suwol's outburst. She was startled by a green military motorcycle approaching on the road. She peered up into the forest canopy. Were Nationalist soldiers hiding in the trees as well? She tugged Suwol's arm and shushed him.

The motorcycle slowed to a stop when it reached them. The soldier took off his goggles before speaking. He pointed to the vacant sidecar. "You two wanna ride?" His accent revealed him to be a local. "I'm headed to Seogwipo, if that's where you're goin'."

Suwol was glaring at the young motorcyclist, so Junja decided to answer. "I'm going to Lonely Rock Village, which is on the way. He's headed to Seogwipo, though."

Suwol interrupted. His voice was clipped, but his language was polite. "Why are you wearing that uniform, sir?"

The young soldier rubbed his recently shorn hair. His face, darkened from sun, looked pleasant, and his hands were callused. "You think I had a choice in this? Where were you when they were conscripting? Hiding on the mountain, right?" He winked at Junja and snorted as if he had made a funny joke. "Wanna ride or not?" When Junja nodded, he grinned.

Suwol waved him away. "We don't want to ride a Yankee motorcycle."

Junja was quick to contradict him. "Yes, we do." She turned to Suwol. "I've never ridden something like that before."

"You don't need to. And neither do I." The boy crossed his arms.

The girl frowned. "We might have to walk for hours before someone else comes along."

"Fine with me. I'd rather walk the whole way."

"Well, I wouldn't." Junja placed her pack on the floor of the sidecar and stooped to lift the squealing piglet.

Suwol watched, fuming, as Junja, her pack, and the piglet settled into the sidecar. The motorcycle driver handed her the extra pair of goggles and shrugged at Suwol. "If you wanna come, you'll have to sit behind me and close your eyes. Your choice."

When it became clear that Junja was going to ride the motorcycle without him, Suwol climbed on at the last possible moment. Rather than wrap his arms around the driver as instructed, however, he opted to hold onto the back of the seat.

The young cyclist shouted to Suwol over the racket of the engine. "Your little sister, right?" He gestured to the sidecar.

Suwol's answer was lost in the din, but the cyclist heard what he wanted to hear. "I could tell, the way you acted. All familiar like. She's cute. Think she'd go for a guy like me?"

"I doubt it."

"Typical big brother. Don't be too overprotective. You don't want her to become an old maid." He glanced at Junja, whose gleeful smile encouraged him to gun the engine and speed up. "She likes to go fast, doesn't she?"

Suwol, who had grabbed the cyclist when the motorcycle lurched forward, tightened his embrace.

"Easy there, ohrabang. I need to breathe to drive this thing. Whatcha doin' in Seogwipo anyways?"

"Errands."

"That could mean anything." The cyclist glanced at Junja. "Lemme give you a tip, on account of your sister there. Things are a little tense in the city right now. You might wanna steer clear. But you didn't hear that from me. In fact, you never saw me, and I never gave you a ride. Get what I'm sayin'?"

Suwol swallowed. "What's going on?" He had been hoping the monk was mistaken.

"Commies are being jailed and questioned."

"How do they know who the commies are?"

"Oh, we have our ways. Most of the time you can tell just by looking at their eyes."

"That seems to be a rather inexact method."

"That sounds like something a commie would say. You're not a commie are you? 'Cuz I'd need to report you if you were."

"I'm just another Jeju native like you. And like her." Suwol pointed his elbow at the sidecar.

The young soldier glanced at Junja and revved the motorcycle again. "Your sister's too pretty to be a communist, so I guess you aren't one either."

☽

Junja was still shaking her head in wonder as the motorcycle roared away. Suwol, who had declined the offer of a lift all the way to the city, had bowed to the young man, thanking him for his advice, but looked troubled as Junja chattered about the miraculous machine that had brought them so quickly to the village.

"I can't believe we're already here! It's like magic! Thank you, sir!"

Suwol had been too preoccupied to join the parting conversation. Junja attributed the boy's dark mood to the flirting cyclist, who asked for her name and promised, with a broad wink, to return and give her another ride. She had been about to answer when Suwol responded for her.

"I'm Kim Dok Mun, and she's E-Hwa. Actually, we don't live here. We live near the pass, where you picked us up. We're bringing some ferns to trade with the haenyeo here." He had loosened one of their bundles to reveal its green contents.

"Why did you lie to that guy?" Junja asked the question after the cyclist rode away.

"Because it's never a good idea to give your real name to a soldier, if you can help it. You never know what might be done with the information."

Grandmother and Mother would have agreed. "I wasn't thinking. Thank you. Did you tell him that we were brother and sister too?"

"He made that part up himself."

The two of them walked from the main road toward the village, stopping every now and then for Junja to yank the piglet, which insisted on sniffing every plant. Several passersby shot Junja odd looks that the girl attributed to the unknown boy walking besides her. When they reached the public reservoir at the heart of the village, Suwol suggested that they stop to refill his gourd.

Junja took a long swallow from the ladle before giving it to Suwol. The piglet tugged at her, so she glanced down to shush it. When she looked back up, a ladleful of water hit her in the face. Junja spluttered as she wiped her eyes.

Suwol was grinning, holding the dripping ladle. "You gonna take a ride with every soldier on a fast motorcycle, little sister?"

"Only with your permission, ohrabang!" On the last word, Junja threw the contents of the bucket at Suwol, who retaliated by throwing more ladles of water from the reservoir. The two of them were soaked through and laughing loudly when one of the village grandmothers scuttled toward them, wringing her hands and wailing.

"Junja—go home quickly! Your mother! Something terrible happened!"

The smile dropped from Junja's face. After a shocked pause, she ran through the dusty streets, dripping water and dragging the alarmed piglet behind her. Suwol chased her, his longer legs allowing him to catch up to the girl. She was panting, wild-eyed. He took the leash for the squealing piglet out of her hands.

Outside Junja's house, standing among the clucking chickens, a group of haenyeo stood sentry, damp in their water clothes.

"Her daughter's here at last!"

"Has she returned in time?"

"Hurry, hurry!"

Grandmother opened the door, silencing the women.

Junja rushed forward. "What happened? Where's Mother?" Water dripped from her hair onto the front stoop. Suwol helped Junja take off the pack.

The old woman looked at the boy and the piglet and then down at the dark puddle of water pooling below them. She said nothing as she pulled her granddaughter inside and shut the door.

Junja could not see in the sudden dimness. She closed her eyes as the old woman pushed her through the doorway to the room where they all slept.

A woman she didn't recognize was lying on her mother's mat. Junja's younger sister and brother were beside her, clutching each other and hiccupping with sobs. A white-haired woman was rubbing prayer beads between her hands. Beside her, a young girl shook a rattle over the prone body.

When the shaman sensed Junja's presence, she stopped her ministrations and motioned for her to come closer.

Junja fell to her knees, shaking her head. That swollen face did not belong to Mother. That was a stranger lying on Mother's pillow.

Grandmother's voice was too loud. "Your eldest, Junja, has returned."

This person could not be Mother. This was a shriveled thing, mottled with bruises. Mother would never lie down during the day. Mother was never sick. Junja began to shiver.

The swollen eyes tried to open. A word escaped the bleeding lips. "Junja."

Grandmother nudged the girl. "Answer, quickly."

Junja shook her head, trying to rise, away from the imposter on the floor. Grandmother pulled her back down. She wiped the girl's damp hand against her clothes before wrapping Junja's hand around the woman's.

The woman on the mat coughed. A pink froth bubbled out of her mouth. The stranger's eyes were staring at something beyond Junja's shoulder. The girl looked in that direction but saw nothing.

The woman's hand gripped Junja's, hard. "The piglet?"

Mother's voice. Unmistakable. Horror surged through Junja.

"I-I got a good fat one. He's outside." The girl was trying not to retch. She was rubbing her mother's hands, which felt like ice. Mother squeezed her hand. Surely everything would be all right. Mother's grip was still so strong.

"Good girl . . ." Mother's voice trailed away as her eyes closed.

Junja shook her mother's hand, which still held hers. "Mother?" The girl's voice rose high.

Mother's eyes opened again. She looked at Junja as if she wanted to say something more, but no sound came out of her mouth.

The hand that Junja held grew soft.

☽

When Suwol saw the white-haired woman and the girl leave the house, he stopped them.

"What's happening? Is Junja's mother all right?"

The shaman glanced down at the girl standing by her side. The girl stared through Suwol, her black eyes glittering. She cocked her head.

The white-haired shaman finally answered. "Her mother was badly hurt."

"During a dive?"

The white-haired woman studied the boy before answering. "The others brought the girl's mother home." She nodded toward the waiting women, who stood by, silent as stones.

"Shouldn't you go back inside? To help?"

The shaman gave her beads, knives, and rattles to the little girl, who put them into a basket. The woman turned her gaze up, staring at the sky above the thatched hut. The trees shivered in a sudden breeze. She turned her white head to listen.

Inside the house, someone started screaming.

The boy blinked, stunned, as the haenyeo surged past him, pouring inside. He started to follow before remembering the piglet. He stopped to tie the beast to a fence.

The white-haired shaman touched his arm. "Are you kin?"

He shook his head. "I helped bring the piglet."

The woman studied Suwol, intrigued. "Not related . . . yet the course of your blood runs the same."

"I don't understand." The boy thought of his mainlander mother, who had always feared the shamans of Jeju.

The white-haired woman grabbed his arm, urging him to listen. "Stay away from the mountain."

"I can't. Hallasan is my home."

The shaman dropped her hand. Not all truths were meant to be told. Instead, she gave him a blessing, as the little girl by her side watched.

☽

One by one, the villagers brought nourishment to the mourning household, leaving their sympathies tidily bundled on the front stoop. While the gut was still numb with shock, foods needed to slip down, for easy digestion: watery soups, porridges, custards. Later, the offerings grew more tempting to whet appetites dulled by sorrow: roasted mackerel, glistening with fat; wild garlic shoots pickled in soy sauce and honey; steaming abalone and mussel stew.

Junja dutifully served these meals to her grandmother and siblings. Her brother and sister were already smiling again, the fullness of their bellies distracting them from their pangs for Mother. Junja, however, could only choke down a few mouthfuls. She gave her scrapings to the piglet, which squealed with joy.

After three days of mourning, Junja and her grandmother returned to the sea. The other divers urged them to rest longer, worried that their sorrow was too heavy. They promised to share their catch.

Grandmother waved aside their concerns. Junja's cheeks were too pale, and the girl was visibly dwindling. The depths would numb any sorrows that were submerged. The old woman calculated and concluded: better for the sea king to take his tithe than for the girl to succumb to sorrow. Still, the old woman prayed for mercy.

Their dives were abundant, a god's way of compensating for what had been lost.

At night, after Junja fell asleep, her grandmother chanted by her side, trying to ease the girl's anguish.

Every morning, Grandmother asked the same question. Every time, Junja's answer was the same.

"Nothing, Halmung. I didn't dream anything at all."

Instead, little brother Jin and little sister Gongja shared their dreams, their voices shrill against Junja's monotone.

"I dreamt I was growing huge," said Gongja. "I grew as big as the house and was wearing it like a dress. My head crashed through the roof, and my arms stuck out of the windows. I grew as tall as a tree!"

Grandmother nodded, keeping an eye on Junja. "Twelve is the right age for the growing dream. It means that your body is readying itself to become a woman. You will dream this dream several times more. Once your body has gone through the change, the dream will stop visiting you."

Jin piped up. "I dreamt that I was flying like a bird. If I hopped up like this and raised my arms, I would float up in the air. That's how I found Ummung in the sky. She was flying too, so I followed her. We flew away toward the mountain together."

Grandmother smoothed the little boy's hair. "Do you remember where you flew with your mother?"

Jin thought for a moment. "We flew away from the village, over the mountain. I don't know where I went. But Ummung wasn't with me anymore when I got there."

"That's as it should be," said the old woman. "Your mother lives in the spirit world now, and you are too young to join her there. You have to finish this life first before you can be reunited with her."

"What does my dream mean, Halmung?

"You will be going on a trip soon."

"Really?" Jin jumped up.

Grandmother glanced at her eldest grandchild. Junja was taking the breakfast dishes to the kitchen, where she would scour them with sand before rinsing them.

Grandmother leaned toward her youngest grandchild. "Don't tell anyone about your flying dream. Such a good dream must be kept safe from jealous imps."

The little boy nodded. Dotchebbi were always stealing his favorite rocks and sticks, hiding them so that he couldn't play with them. He was a smart boy and knew how to keep a secret.

Eight

Junja woke with a start under the light of a half moon. As she listened to the sound of breathing around her, she began to remember where she was. At home, in the village, on her sleeping pallet on the floor. Grandmother was lying next to her, with Jin and Gongja on the other side.

The girl closed her eyes, trying not to awaken completely. She wanted to drift for a while longer, in that quiet place where everything she wanted to forget remained distant, on the edge of memory. Yet she could not stop the incoming waves of her restless mind.

The moon lighting a path through the night sky against a choir of crickets. The bracing sweetness of a mountain spring. Suwol's fingers, white against the green ferns. Blood staining Mother's socks, red rusting into brown.

Junja curled into a ball, trying to squeeze the sensations out of her chest.

That ache pushed Junja out of bed, away from the warmth of the other sleeping bodies. She felt her way along the uneven wooden floor on her hands and knees. Mother's chores were now hers. Time to start the fire for the morning porridge.

On that morning when she had taken Mother's place, Junja had lain drowsing in bed until she remembered that Mother was going to the mountain. The girl had bolted up, making Grandmother mutter, to join Mother in the kitchen. As Junja added kindling to the flames, Mother had ladled water into the black pot holding the leftover millet from the evening meal. Junja had stirred the porridge as she begged Mother to let her go to the mountain instead. Mother had shaken her head as she added eggs and minced green onion to the pot.

Junja dressed herself in the dark, feeling bereft as she put on her mother's house shift and hair wrap. She wanted to cocoon herself in Mother's fading scent. When Grandmother first saw Junja dressed in those clothes, the old woman had muttered darkly about gwishin. She was too practical, however, to waste anything and allowed her granddaughter to wear her dead daughter's belongings.

Junja had always known that her resemblance to her mother was uncanny. She had never imagined, though, that she would be forced to take her mother's place so soon. If a person's fate was written on their face, as Grandmother always said, what did that mean for Junja? And what about her little brother and little sister? With their round faces, wide eyes, and pouting mouths, those two looked just like their father.

When he abandoned his family, Junja had been twelve. Father had scarcely been mentioned since that time. Mother had erased him from their lives completely by giving the children her mother's family name. Grandmother had recently begun talking about him again, giving away secrets that the children never knew. Only yesterday she had revealed that Father had grown up on the mainland, near the big city of Seoul, where it was too cold for tangerine trees.

"City folk should never marry country folk, and mountain folk should never marry coastal folk," Grandmother had lectured. "Too many differences! See what happened to your parents."

Mother could have had her pick of any man. They were drawn to her, Grandmother boasted, though she was not considered a conventional beauty. Her face was too angular, her mouth too wide, and her stubbornness betrayed by her jawline. But she was striking: tall, with long, well-shaped limbs. And she was a top-rank haenyeo, a woman worth two men. Her best feature, Grand-mother said, were her light brown eyes. "The color of dark honey. Spirit eyes, though she didn't live long enough to come into her vision."

Mother had shrugged off so many suitors that by the time she was twenty-six, no man dared approach her. Villagers called her the stone maiden for dashing so many hopes. One summer day, on a trip to Seogwipo, Mother spied Father on the docks.

"A beautiful man," recalled Grandmother. "So pretty that every woman who saw him tried to lure him. Your mother decided that she would catch him for herself.

"He was surrounded by giggling women, all gazing at him with easy promises in their eyes. Your mother was too proud and too cunning to join that sorry group. Instead, she took off her outer layers and stood on the dock in her water clothes. Her hair was unbound, so it flew in the wind. Your father noticed her because she was the only woman not paying attention to him. She was pretending to study something under the water. When she sensed him watching, she jumped.

"She dove deep, her eyes blind from the sun, her fingers search-ing. She told herself, 'If I find an urchin, I will bring it to him. If he eats it, he will be mine.'

"There shouldn't have been any urchins near the docks. The water is too cloudy there and too shallow. But the sea king must have been in a mischievous mood, because her hand pierced itself on a spiny ball.

"When your mother surfaced, your father was leaning over the water, reaching out to offer assistance. Did she take his hand then? Of course not. Instead, she looked him in the eye, showed him the urchin, and said, 'Eat this, and tell me what it tastes like.'

"She stayed in the water, watching as he tried to open the spiny creature. She laughed when its quills made him bleed and curse. Still, he kept trying. Finally, one of the other women took pity on him and brought him a black rock. He hammered open the urchin and laid its insides bare. Your father took out the orange flesh, put it inside his mouth, and swallowed.

"'What does it taste like?' Your mother demanded.

"'It tastes like marriage!' he crowed.

"After a short courtship, they married. They were very happy, in the beginning. However, your soft, city-bred father did not take to life on the water. He was a terrible fisherman. Because your mother supported the family, his shame ate away at his love. He grew weak because men need pride to be strong. One day, he took the skiff, saying he was going to catch sollani. He left, whistling a tune, and never came home.

"At first, we thought the worst, that he had died at sea. But when his boat was found, the man who bought it swore that he had paid a fair price. Enough, he said, for your father to buy a one-way ticket to the mainland."

☽

When Junja opened the kitchen door to get more kindling, a round bundle was squatting on the stoop like an overgrown mushroom. Another belated condolence meal, she thought. She had to start the fire and boil some water first, before deciding whether to serve the gift for breakfast or set it aside for later.

The girl hesitated between the matchbox and tinder box, pushing the memory of Suwol's lighter out of her mind with an irritated mutter. She had managed to avoid the boy every time he visited the village by saying that she was still in mourning. Junja picked up the tinderbox. It was almost summer, so she had no excuse to waste a match. When the sparks caught, the dried grass curled into a flame under the black iron pot. She added a handful of small sticks before stretching. Yawning, the girl studied the contents of the pantry, wondering why she was feeling so hungry. With a yelp, she remembered the bundle on the stoop.

Junja hefted the bundle onto the stone slab next to the cooking fire. She unwound the layers, rolling the cloth strips carefully so that she could return everything to its owner. Her heart seemed to skip as a lidded clay pot emerged, with a covered wooden bowl set on top. She knew only one family who could afford such fine dishes. She held her breath as she opened the lid to the bowl. Inside was a generous cluster of gosari.

The girl restrained herself from rushing outside to see if anyone was there. How could she think about Suwol while she was still mourning Mother? She chided herself for her selfishness, which had made her shirk her duties. If Mother had gone to the mountain as she had planned, she would not have gone diving that day. Though Grandmother insisted that Mother's fate had been shaped before she was born, Junja could not escape her role in that disaster. She had wanted to take her Mother's place, and the gods, in their spiteful way, had allowed her.

Junja opened the lid to the pot. The scent of stewed chicken rose up, striking her like a physical blow. The girl could not stop herself from tearing off a wing and gorging on the tender flesh. She gulped down mouthfuls of food like someone gasping for air. With each swallow, she began to feel less vaporous and more solid, as if she had been on the verge of disappearing.

Junja cracked open the tiny bones and sucked them clean before looking back into the pot. Red dates, garlic, ginger, and a knotty plug of ginseng had enriched the soup. She filled a bowl with broth and removed some of the sticky rice stuffing. She pulled off another wing.

Junja took the food outside to the kitchen stoop. She ate slowly this time, savoring the broth and tender meat. When she finished, she set the bowl down and picked her teeth with a wooden splinter while watching shore birds float in the sky. Her attention drifted to her mother's vegetable patch, where small green shoots were poking up between the bristly young cucumbers and spiky garlic stems. Mother never allowed weeds in her garden. The girl fell to her knees to pull out the trespassing plants. Her fingernails turned black as she clawed the earth with her hands, pulling out everything that did not belong.

When her frenzy abated, the rows were tidy and clear, just like Mother always kept them. Junja felt ravenous again, so she returned to the kitchen. She pulled more sticky rice out of the chicken's cavity and topped the bowl with gosari before returning to the stoop.

"Is that chicken I smell? Or am I dreaming?" Grandmother was standing in the doorway, scratching her shoulder.

Junja untangled her legs. "It's an entire chicken, Halmung, with jujubes and ginseng. There are chestnuts in the rice stuffing too."

"What? Who could afford to be that generous?" The old woman guessed that the cook was not a Jeju native. Chicken stewed in such a costly fashion was a mainlander affectation.

"It came from the Yang family of Cloud House Farm." Junja had no doubt after tasting the ferns.

"Of course. That makes sense. Your mother was friendly with the wife of the eldest son." The old woman motioned to Junja to remain seated as she peered into the pot. Almost half the chicken had been eaten. So she hadn't imagined the brightness in Junja's eyes after all. When the appetite returned, so did the person.

"The eldest grandson was with me when I brought the piglet home. These gosari taste just like the ones I ate there."

Grandmother tried a bite. "This is quite good." Her praise was grudging.

Junja placed her empty bowl on the counter. "I think we should wash the bedding today. The sun will be hot enough to dry the quilts quickly."

The old woman looked sharply at her granddaughter, who had not noticed such details since the tragedy. "You started dreaming again, didn't you?"

Junja nodded.

The old woman squatted down, patting the space next to her. "Sit down and tell me everything you remember."

Grandmother took Junja's hand. The old woman's skin felt cool and dry, like birch bark. The girl squeezed it gently before speaking.

"In my dream, I was married to the sea king. His two ladies-in-waiting were our daughters. Everything was strange and foreign under the sea. I couldn't understand the language of the fishes very well, but I lived in a house as big as a palace and was very rich."

Grandmother grunted to acknowledge that she was listening.

"I lived a comfortable, happy life under the sea for many years. But I still felt homesick for the village. When I could no longer bear it, I begged the sea king to allow me to visit, to see you and mother. The sea king asked why I wanted to return to such a pitiful place when my life with him was so grand. I said I wanted to eat a tangerine, because there was nothing in the sea that tasted like it. He chided me for my lack of gratitude, but he granted my wish. He placed a pink pearl in my mouth and told me to swallow. When it was time to return, he said, the pearl would bring me back."

Grandmother felt Junja's pulse under her fingers, throbbing strong and steady. The girl described how she swam away from the palace toward the sun.

"When I reached the surface, I woke up. And then I got out of bed, went to the kitchen, and found the chicken soup." Junja turned to her grandmother. "So, was it a worthless dog dream?"

The old woman rose out of her squat, using Junja's shoulder as support. "It feels like a true dream to me."

"What does it mean?"

"That you will marry a rich man, move far away, and have two daughters."

"That's what happens in the dream."

"Sometimes what happens in a dream is the same as the meaning of the dream."

"How do you know? What if the dream means something else?"

The old woman shrugged. "The only way to know for certain is to live your life and find out."

☽

While Junja lugged buckets of water from the well, Gongja tended the fire under the iron cauldron. Jin helped Grandmother bring the bedding and clothing out of the house.

"What's the point of cleaning this when it'll just get dirty again?" Jin whined.

"What's the point of eating when you'll just get hungry again? Or waking up when you'll go to sleep again? Please do not speak such foolishness, or else you'll teach your mouth to say only foolish things." The old woman whacked her grandson on his bare legs with the switch she used to beat the quilts on the wooden rack.

"Take off your clothes now! Disgusting Japanese bugs. Jeju didn't have anything like this before those dogs showed up."

Junja poured ashes and lye into the bubbling pot. She remembered running about nakedly while Mother and Grandmother boiled their clothes clean. When it was warm and sunny, she would bathe in the ocean, scrubbing down with fistfuls of wet sand before running back home to be rinsed with fresh water.

After the clothing was laid out on the sand to dry, Junja joined her grandmother, who was braiding Gongja's hair. Jin was waiting, head shaved clean, a pile of hair on the ground next to him.

"All finished, Gongja. Off you go to the beach to bathe. Jin—throw that hair into the fire! Stay to the left of the large rocks and don't wander out too far. Scrub yourselves carefully!" Grandmother's voice broke off as the two scampered away.

The old woman patted the ground in front of her. "Your turn, Junja."

She combed through Junja's hair, squinting and muttering as she worked. "Isn't it interesting how, as I get older, I can see things as tiny as a grain of sand. But those big trees and boulders are blurry, and I can hardly make out the mountain and hills anymore."

Junja said nothing, only half listening to Grandmother, who was now reminiscing about the keen eyesight of her youth. Once the old woman followed her memories into the past, she would wander at leisure before returning to the present.

". . . and that's how I found the first oyster bed, which led me to the second. The sea bought this house for me, as a reward for my sharp vision. Now, even my greatest gift is weakening, like everything else in my body. Aigoo! If it weren't for the strength of the Goh family spirit, I don't think I'd be able to lift a finger."

Grandmother's next words shocked Junja like a bucket of cold water. "Your father is coming for your brother and sister." The old woman's voice was low, to avoid being overheard. "They will live with him and his new wife."

"What?" Junja tried to turn her head, but her hair was wrapped in Grandmother's fist. "Father has a new wife? How do you know?"

The old woman sighed. "I sent him a letter. Of course, there was another woman. That man was too weak to leave on his own."

"Why just Jin and Gongja? Why am I not going too?"

He had only asked for the boy at first. The old woman had written back insisting that he take his youngest daughter as well. Junja would never find a suitable husband while burdened by the care of a sister and grandmother. If he didn't understand that, he might as well throw both his daughters off a cliff with his own hands.

"You're old enough to take care of yourself. And I need you here to bury me properly." The old woman separated Junja's hair into three sections and combed scented oil through each plait before braiding them together.

"I wouldn't leave Jeju even if Father begged me," said Junja, trembling. "Jin and Gongja don't have to go, do they? We have this house, and I make enough to feed all of us." Like her mother and grandmother, Junja was well on her way to becoming a top-rank haenyeo.

Grandmother wound a piece of twine around the bottom of Junja's thick braid. She leaned in to pull the knot tight with her teeth before answering. "He'll be arriving in about two weeks, when the tides are high."

"From where?"

"Busan, where he now lives."

He must have met the new wife during a supply run to the mainland. Junja remembered the last trip he had made, when he was gone far longer than he was supposed to be. When Father finally returned home, Mother had refused to talk to him, and the small house had been bitter with silence.

"Do Gongja and Jin know?"

"Jin knows he is going on a trip, that's all. You can tell Gongja, or I can. Whatever you think is best."

"I'll tell her," said Junja before changing her mind again. "They should stay here with us, Halmung. They don't really need to go, do they?"

Grandmother placed her hands on Junja's shoulders. "Your father has promised to send them both to school. Can you do that much for them? And think about yourself. What man would take in a brother and sister? You wouldn't be able to marry until they left. Do you really want to become an old maid?"

Junja looked down at the ground and bit her lip.

Nine

The morning's cleaning wrung out the old woman, so she went inside to rest. Junja draped the bedding between two wooden racks before spreading coals underneath and covering them with sand. The rising heat would steam out any remaining uncleanliness without burning the cloth. With the sun beating down on the other side, the thick quilts would dry quickly and smell sweet.

The girl thought back to the night she spent at Cloud House Farm. There had been enough clean bedding to spare for a guest. Her blanket had been silk, so light she worried she might be cold, but she had stayed wonderfully warm. Grandmother had explained that though silk batting was lighter, it was both warmer when it was cold and cooler when it was hot. "Even when they sleep, the rich are removed from the heavy cares of the rest of the world."

Junja tried to imagine living on the mountain instead of by the shore. Would her skin grow soft and white from sleeping under silk blankets every night? Would she tire of gosari and crave salty tastes from the sea? Rather than bringing her offerings to the water, she would light candles and incense for the mountain.

A shout from the street interrupted Junja's reverie.

"Hey, you there! Is this haenyeo Goh Sookja's house?" A man in the road was waving a walking stick to attract her attention.

"Yes, this is haenyeo Goh Sookja's house." Junja squinted against the midday sun.

The man ambled toward her. As he approached, his hat slipped and he halted to rearrange it. The man took another step, but a gust of wind pushed the hat off his bushy head. Junja almost smiled when she recognized the constable who had been guarding the mountain road. She half expected cherry blossoms to fall out of his beard.

"I've visited every pigsty between Mosulpo and Seogwipo looking for haenyeo Goh Sookja. Have I really come to the right place at last?"

The constable walked rudely close to peer at Junja. A smoky odor wafted from him. He was taller than she remembered, and his beard more matted.

"Ah, yes. You're that girl. The one who tried to sneak past me without paying the toll. Take me to your mother, the excellent cook." He added a belated 'please' to soften his bark.

"I can't, sir."

"And why not?" The constable puffed out his chest.

Junja's voice quivered. "My mother passed away this spring."

The man stammered. "You're joking, right?"

Junja shook her head, eyes glimmering.

The man took off his hat and threw it into the dirt. "Damn, this dog luck of mine."

When he noticed Junja's stricken face, he bent down to retrieve his hat, muttering. "Please accept my sincere condolences."

The constable eyed the stump Junja was sitting on. "May I sit down, please? I've been walking all day, and your news comes as a bit of a shock."

The girl scooted out of the way. The constable plopped down with a sigh.

He started fanning himself with his hat. "I feel a bit faint. From hunger. You wouldn't, by any chance, have something to eat in your kitchen? I understand it probably wouldn't be as delicious as those rolls your mother made, but I'm so hungry that anything would taste good." He tossed her a coin. "I'd be happy to pay a fair price."

Junja caught the coin. She wiped her nose and stammered. "There's some jook I could heat up."

"No, no, no. Why would I eat porridge when I still have all my teeth? Something more substantial . . ." He rubbed his chin. "How about some rice cakes? With pork belly on the side?"

The man must be daft. Who would have rice cakes and pork at this time of year? "We don't have any pork, sir. And we won't have any rice cakes until harvest."

"What about some kimbop? Do you know how to make that?"

Junja had never heard of that dish before. "I'll do my best to make you something worth eating."

"All right, then. Why don't you try." The constable waved her away, pulling a silk handkerchief out of his stained pants. He blew his nose loudly as the girl ran inside.

☽

Junja considered the options in the pantry: radish, kelp, and fish, all dried; millet, barley, and beans in straw baskets; and in a dark corner, a bowl of mung beans sprouting in water. Outside, spinach, green onions, zucchini, garlic, and lettuce grew in the garden, where crocks of kimchi and bean paste were buried under the shade of a magnolia tree. She decided to fetch an egg.

The chickens squawked so loudly that Grandmother was roused from her nap. The old woman went outside to ask why the girl was looking for eggs when she should have been tending the wash.

"The bedding is drying, Halmung. There's a constable in the front yard who wants lunch. He's already paid for it." Junja showed her grandmother the coin.

"A constable?" The old woman hid her sudden wariness.

"He was guarding the mountain pass the day I got the pig. He looked hungry, so I gave him some bing-ddeok. He said it was the most delicious thing he'd eaten on the island and that he wanted to buy meals from Mother. He's been searching for her ever since."

"You never mentioned that before."

"I never got the chance."

"Of course, you didn't. Such a terrible, terrible day." Grandmother peered around the corner of the house to see the constable readying himself for a nap. After watching Junja gather ingredients from the garden, the old woman decided to roll up her sleeves. "Let's pull some watercress too."

"Won't that be too much food?"

"Not for what he paid. Let's put out some gosari as well. That'll give him his money's worth." Grandmother walked back toward the house. "I'll start the soup."

☽

When Junja and Grandmother brought out the food, the constable was snoring next to the stump, his hat covering his face.

"Sir! Hello, sir?" Grandmother gently prodded him with her toe.

The hat slid down, revealing one open eye. "Who goes there?"

"We brought your lunch, sir."

The man sat up, eyeing the generous meal with suspicion: millet with mung beans; gosari; fish; egg custard; green onion kimchi; seasoned dried radish; and a round shell brimming with dwenjang soup.

"Well, all of this looks very promising."

Junja balanced the board with its dishes on the stump. The constable scooted closer, raising his knee to sit more comfortably. He took a deep sniff of the soup.

"It smells promising, too. But will it be worth eating?" He took a noisy slurp, and his eyes grew wide. He spluttered angrily, "Who made this?"

Grandmother inclined her head, while Junja wrung her hands.

The constable looked visibly upset as he shoved a few strands of gosari into his mouth. He chewed quickly, tasting every side dish twice before putting down his chopsticks. He lifted the bowl of soup again and took a deep swallow before looking up.

"I regret to say this, but your dwenjang soup rivals my mother's. But I'll deny saying so if you ever repeat it." He picked up his chopsticks again, this time eating with gusto.

At the end of the meal, the constable announced his intention to visit as often as possible. He addressed his questions to Grandmother, who, he rightly guessed, bore primary responsibility for the meal. "If I brought you meat, could you prepare it the way I like? Such as trotters?"

"If you pay me properly, I could cook anything you want. Even sausages."

The constable looked skeptical. "My mother's soondae is famous. I couldn't eat just any ordinary kind of sausage."

"Then you'll be able to appreciate just how good my soondae is. Of course, I'll need the proper ingredients."

"I can get whatever you need. Beef, rice, sugar. Even foreign items from the American military commissary."

The old woman narrowed her eyes. "How very interesting. Let's discuss the details over a cup of tea, shall we?" She gestured toward the blankets and drying rack. "Junja, go tend the bedding. The constable and I are going to have a little chat."

Ten

His name was Lee Kyung Ho. He hadn't intended to become a constable, but the political unrest had interrupted his studies at Seoul National University, where he had been hoping to become a classical scholar and poet like his deceased father and grandfather. Convinced that war was imminent, his mother had bribed his way into a desk officer's post to keep him away from the unnatural border that cut the country in half. His knack for bureaucratic prose had led to a promotion down south on Jeju, the island of exiles. It was far from the conflict brewing up north, but too far from his mother's cooking.

"No one speaks proper Korean around here! It's not just an accent you Jeju folk have—it's an entirely different language!" Constable Lee was on his fourth lunch visit in as many days. This time he had brought a bag of finely milled white flour, which the old woman transformed into knife-cut noodles.

"The soft yet chewy consistency of these noodles is remarkable. I'm not sure my mother could match this." Mr. Lee's beard seemed to soak up as much broth as he swallowed.

Grandmother responded from her perch on the front stoop. "I would like to meet your mother someday, as you are quite a talented judge of good food."

"You're right about that." The constable waved his hands expansively. "All my senses are sharp, but my sense of taste is exceptional."

He lifted the bowl to slurp down the dregs. "I keep meaning to ask you something." His eyes narrowed. "Your spoken Korean. It's quite polished. And your accent isn't so distorted. But you're a diver in a hick village. Who are you really?"

The old woman returned the constable's probing stare. "You're more perceptive than you appear, aren't you?" She lifted her chin. "The Goh family is one of the original yangban families of Jeju, known for educating its daughters. I attended school with my cousins in Seoul before the family fortunes took a downturn during the occupation."

"That's why you can cook mainland dishes?"

"I learned in my aunt's kitchen."

"Does that mean you know how to make kimbop? It would come in handy to be able to take a meal to go."

"If you can describe the taste properly, I can cook anything."

Grandmother listened to the constable's enthusiastic praise for the seaweed rolls and determined that the right kind of seaweed did not grow in Jeju's warmer waters. "You'd need to send for some from the mainland." She rummaged in the wooden chest for a stump of pencil. "Do you have any paper for a grocery list?"

Mr. Lee handed her a rumpled piece, soft from being erased many times. "I can send the list to Mother when the passenger ferry comes in from Mokpo."

The old woman looked up quickly. "Do you know when that boat is due?"

"Five days. It was delayed by engine repairs. And now they're waiting for the tides."

"How do you know this?"

"From the radio operator at Jeju Port. I have full access to the logs."

Grandmother twisted the pencil, looking thoughtful. "You're a person of many hidden talents, aren't you?"

The constable returned her stare. "Perhaps as many hidden talents as you."

The old woman glanced around to make sure that none of the children, especially Junja, were close enough to hear her next question. "You wouldn't, by any chance, know which dog beat my daughter to death, would you?"

The constable's expression remained carefully blank. "The girl's mother was taken in for questioning by the military police? That's how she died, the haenyeo Goh Sookja?"

The old woman nodded. "This information is not to be shared, especially with the children. It's safer for them to believe there was a diving accident." She took a breath. "We don't need to attract any more attention from the so-called authorities."

Mr. Lee understood the old woman's caution. His half-lidded gaze opened up. "I'll find out who was responsible. I'm curious: What will you do when you find out?"

Grandmother didn't answer, and the constable knew better than to ask again.

☽

Grandmother was certain that Father would be on the delayed boat from Mokpo, so she allowed her youngest grandchildren to play in the sea as much as they wanted, without reminding them of their lessons. The water was not as soft and warm up north, she explained to Junja as she piled extra helpings of food onto their plates.

"Your father is coming tomorrow. You'll need to gather everything you want to take with you to your new home." Grandmother made the announcement near the end of an especially lavish dinner. That morning, she had traded away a cherished silver hairpin for some oxtail and a fist-sized chunk of beef.

The children looked down at their bowls. Their bulging cheeks stopped moving.

"I'll get more sprouts." Junja rose from the table to hide her face.

Jin swallowed. "Will Father let me take my rocks?"

Gongja wrinkled her nose. "Why would you take rocks to the mainland? Everyone will think you're a stupid country bumpkin."

"But these are special magical Jeju rocks. Right, Grandma?"

The old woman nodded. "The black windstones of Jeju are the teardrops of Grandma Seolmundae's five hundred sons."

Gongja scoffed. "How could a giant grandmother create all of Jeju with just seven shovels of dirt? And if she was so strong, why couldn't she pull herself out of the pot of soup she fell into? It's a silly story."

"Watch your mouth," Grandmother shouted after Gongja as the girl ran into the kitchen. "Why do you think doldam walls work so well to keep out the winter cold? A wall made of ordinary rocks couldn't stop those howling sea winds. Don't offend the spirits with your careless talk."

Junja was wiping her eyes on her sleeves when Gongja burst into the kitchen, sniffling. The two sisters wept silently as they held each other close.

Eleven

"Are you sure that's our father? He doesn't look familiar to me at all." Jin was worrying his bundle, pulling at the ties that kept it closed. All the clothing he owned was wrapped inside, along with several black stones.

"Isn't he handsome? You and Gongja look just like him, except for the gray in his hair." Junja tried to sound cheerful as she rubbed the bristle on her brother's head.

Father had arrived on a hired cart while she and Grandmother were making breakfast. Junja had heard his whistle from afar and remembered how the sound could coax mountain sparrows out of trees. The little things would hop closer and closer as Father chirped, enticing them into a cage with a twig of millet. After he moved away, Mother had stopped feeding the birds, and the fluttering bamboo cage had gone still.

"I can't believe I'm moving to a big city on the mainland." Gongja preened herself in a little fragment of mirror. Junja, who found the shiny shard in the ocean, had bound its sharp edges in cloth before giving it to her sister as a farewell gift.

"Why can't you and Halmung come with us?" Jin started sniffling.

"Grandmother is too old to leave Jeju. And I need to stay here to take care of her." Junja's attempt to be convincing sounded hollow to her own ears.

"W-w-what if Halmung dies while we're gone? How am I going to pay my respects?" Tears streaked Jin's face. "I don't wanna go. I don't wanna leave."

Gongja lifted her eyes from the mirror to frown. "It's bad luck to say things like that, dummy!"

"You're the dummy! Stop staring at your stupid face all the time."

Junja hushed her sister and brother. "Don't fight like this when you're with Father! Please behave, for Mother's sake."

☽

Gongja and Jin ate their porridge while peeking at their father. His face was covered by the bowl as he loudly slurped.

Junja had been surprised by how much her father had changed. His cheeks were thinner, his skin darker, and multiple lines worried his forehead. Everything about him seemed smaller than she remembered, including his thinning hair.

He had returned Junja's stare, unnerved by her resemblance to her mother. "You look just like her on the day we met."

After he recovered from that shock, Father had horsed around with Jin, making the little boy laugh. Junja felt less anxious, seeing them bond so quickly. Sons needed their fathers. The move would be good for her brother. However, Junja worried that her sister would never leave the kitchen, for all purposes a servant to the second wife. Grandmother must have shared her concern, because she made Father repeat his promise to send both children to school.

He smacked his lips as he placed the empty bowl on the table. "My apologies for eating and running, but we need to leave right away. I'm sure you understand."

Grandmother frowned. "Why the rush? It's been six years since you last saw your children."

Father rubbed his brow. "More American ships are expected. Once they land, there'll be no room for the ferry from Mokpo. We need to line up tonight for the morning departure. If we don't make that boat, we might get stranded for weeks before they let a civilian ferry back into the harbor. My funds won't last that long."

Grandmother turned to Junja. "Go help your brother and sister get ready." When the children were out of earshot, she spoke again, in a low voice.

"How many ships are coming to clog up the entire port like that?"

"I don't know. The entire city is on edge, waiting for something bad to happen."

"If too many people think that way, then something will." The old woman grasped at a straw. "Take Junja with you as well."

The man looked down, ashamed. It had been hard enough to convince his wife to accept the younger two. "I don't have money for her fare."

"I can give it to you." The old woman thought of her remaining silver hairpin.

He considered his wife's temperament. "I can't risk it. Besides, there are just as many American troops in Busan. If trouble is coming, no place in Korea will be safe."

The children returned, putting an end to the whispered conversation. Both Gongja and Jin looked subdued. Their eyes and noses were red.

Father reached into his pocket, smiling broadly. "Jin! Gongja! I have a surprise for you." He pointed to his closed fist.

The two youngsters approached their father with caution. Jin pounced first, trying to pry open his father's fingers. His hand opened to reveal two squares of rice candy, wrapped in paper. He gave the sweets to the children while ushering them away. "You kids go wait outside for the cart." He turned to the grandmother. "Could you pack us something for the road?"

Junja remembered that wheedling voice, the one Father would use to charm Mother out of a temper.

"I've already packed your lunches." The old woman gestured to a cloth bundle on the floor. She nodded to Junja. "Say what you need to say. Who knows when you'll see each other again in this lifetime. I'll be outside with the little ones." The front door closed, leaving the two of them alone.

Father cleared his throat. "I'm sorry I can't take you with me." He was holding out something small, wrapped in a scrap of fabric.

More rice candy? Junja pretended not to see it. "I'd rather stay here."

"You're old enough to take care of yourself, I guess." Father took her hand and pressed the object into her palm. "Please, take it. It's not much, but it's all I can give you."

A bit of money, Junja thought, to pay off his obligation to her. She bowed stiffly. "Thank you."

"Well, then. I should be going." He held out his arms for an embrace. When Junja ignored him, he cleared his throat and swallowed.

"Don't forget your promise to send them both to school!" Junja was surprised by the vehemence in her voice.

Father jumped. He avoided Junja's eyes as he walked away. "I swear I'll keep that promise."

☽

Inside the small package from father were several coins and a small pink pearl. Junja showed it to Grandmother after the two of them had stopped weeping. They had stood in the road waving goodbye until they could no longer see the cart.

The old woman wiped her nose before taking the stone. She squinted as she rubbed it between her fingers. "I never thought I'd see this again."

"You've seen this pearl before?"

Grandmother nodded. Junja's mother had found the stone in an area bordered by hidden currents and dagger reefs. She had risked her life to swim through those twin dangers and had discovered a sandy bed hidden by a forest of giant kelp. "Your mother was in Seogwipo to sell the pearl the day she met your father. She must have given it to him as a bridal gift instead. Bad luck to do that. No wonder the marriage didn't last."

There were local legends about the pearls that were discovered when Korea still had a powerful king. Chests brimming with pearls, mandarins, and abalone had once been sent to the royal court in annual tribute. As the old ways were forgotten, fewer divers found such treasures. But Junja had found one, and apparently her mother had as well.

After Junja coughed up the pearl, Grandmother had snatched the stone from the sand. Asked by the other haenyeo what it was, the old woman had shown them an ordinary pebble instead.

Grandmother told Junja to keep her mother's stone a secret, to safeguard it from theft. "Tell no one until the time comes to sell it. Hide it on your body. Pearls must be kept near living flesh, to keep their luster."

"I'll hold onto the pearl forever, Halmung. As a memento of Mother."

The old woman shook her head. "Unless you want to lose a husband too, you're better off selling it. When the time comes, try to sell it on the mainland. It'll fetch a better price there."

Twelve

They went to the burial mound when the hour of the Ox gave way to the hour of the Tiger, as darkness turned into dawn. They arranged the offerings in wooden bowls that glowed with moonlight: millet, buckwheat, tangerines, pears, fish, rice cakes, bean sprouts, seaweed. Junja poured the water. Grandmother lit incense. They kneeled to pray, then prostrated themselves, touching their foreheads to the cool ground while holding their palms up to the heavens.

As the sky started brightening, Grandmother and Junja did the work of remembering. In the spring, Mother's mound had been a bald pile of earth they smoothed with their hands while Junja wept and Grandmother wailed. Now, they were mowing the grass on her grave with the same scythes they used in cutting kelp.

The old woman glanced at Junja, whose eyes were swollen. Far too young to be tending her mother's grave. She wondered how Jin and Gongja were faring, entrusted to the care of their flighty father and a stranger she didn't know.

After the prayers were completed, the old woman and the girl gathered the offerings, placing the food into a basket to take home for a late breakfast. The remainder of the day would be spent visiting with friends and neighbors, sharing treats from the harvest festival.

Grandmother studied the enormous moon, still sharing the sky with the sun. "The water will go out very far this evening. The returning waves will be powerful."

That meant long strands of kelp tossed on the sand, chilled from the deep. Crabs lured out of hiding by the lunar glow. Beds of clams laid bare. Driftwood and glinting scraps from boats lost at sea. Easy pickings, as long as a watchful eye was kept on the incoming tide, which could crush the unwary with a giant fist of water.

Junja nodded. "I promise I'll be careful."

>

The harvest moon burst with light. Waves slapped the sand. Junja darted between the exposed rocks. She scooped up emerald clumps of seaweed while timing the tides, counting under her breath.

She chased the receding wave, following its trail of foam to the rock tower that stood alone, far from shore. Her hands reached down, feeling for the mossy seaweed that grew at the boulder's base. Something tried to squirm away, but her quick fingers grabbed it. Two more wriggling crabs were caught before Junja ran back, just ahead of the surf that crashed behind her, spraying her with mist. The waves washed her ankles.

The bulging bag squirmed. She tossed in several fistfuls of wet seaweed. She studied the water, wondering if she could chance one more trip.

"Junja!"

The girl whirled around. A voice, just audible above the ocean's roar.

A tall silhouette stepped out from the shadows. "Junja!"

The bag slipped from her shoulder.

"Suwol?" She had not said his name aloud since their afternoon among the ferns.

The boy was standing in front of her, pale with moonlight. He was carrying a pack and a walking stick, looking just like he did the first time she saw him. Alongside the boy, Boshi wagged his tail and panted.

"Why are you here and not on the mountain?" In her shock, Junja forgot to greet him. She had to remind herself that Suwol was the first-born son of a nobleman, with a scholar's honeyed tongue. She needed to stay alert.

The girl bowed. "It's been a long time, sir."

Suwol stepped forward, swallowing. The dog rushed back and forth between the boy and the girl. "It's been a long time, yes— much too long. Are you feeling better now? Every time I came to offer my condolences, your grandmother turned me away. She said you were still in mourning."

The girl took a step back. "I was sick for a while. But I'm better now. Thank you for your concern, sir." She bowed again, sinking deeper than she needed to.

"Are you mad at me for leaving without saying goodbye? I tried to, but the other haenyeo wouldn't let me in the house. I waited for as long as I could, but you never came back outside." Suwol's head drooped. "I'm so sorry about your mother."

The girl's eyes glimmered. "You're not at fault for anything. No need to apologize."

The dog nosed Junja's hand and whined. The boy shifted his weight from one foot to the other. "Did you find the gosari where I left them for you?"

Someone had spread the wilted greens on a bank of hot sand to dry. When Junja found the fern buds, they had cured properly, turning dark and shriveled, like strange characters written on the sand.

"So you did that. Thank you." She wanted to look away from the boy's face but was unable to move her gaze.

Suwol took another step forward. Junja stayed put, trying not to shiver.

"I brought you chicken soup from my mother. I tried to stay until you woke up, but there were other people with me, and they couldn't wait." He took another step.

The girl could see the boy's anguish, clear in the moonlight. "The soup was delicious. Please tell your mother that we are very grateful for her generosity, sir. Are you here to pick up the crock?"

Suwol's knuckles whitened around the walking stick. "Why are you speaking to me so coldly? I thought we were friends."

An agony of guilt roiled the girl. She couldn't stop herself. "I should've gone home sooner. What happened to my mother is my fault."

The boy shook his head. "It's not your fault, those d—"

Junja interrupted. "My mother was supposed to go to the mountain that day, not me." Her eyes brimmed. She wrapped her arms around herself.

Suwol put down his walking stick and took off the pack. "You must be cold." He took another step toward the girl.

Junja took a half step back, shaking her head. Tears glistened on her face. "Thank you for your condolences, sir. You can go now."

As the girl turned away, Suwol closed the gap, pulling her toward him. The heat from his body warmed Junja through her wet clothes. Suwol whispered against the back of her ear. "You're too cold-blooded to be human. You really must be half fish."

Junja broke free of his embrace. She turned around quivering, arm raised to strike.

Suwol stopped her hand as his lips fell upon hers.

☽

The moon watched as Junja's bag fell to the sand, spilling open. One by one, the crabs emerged, ragged claws scuttling on sand. They were pushed forward by every wave, toward the open sea, where lights bobbed on the water. On the cuttlefish boats, men held out their nets, waiting for the soft creatures to swim toward the blaze of their torches.

☽

"You taste like the sea." Suwol breathed against Junja's ear.

Junja quivered, though she no longer felt cold. "What does the sea taste like?"

"Salty. Sweet. Wild."

The surf pounded the shore like a drum. The moon made Junja's face glow. She had memorized Suwol completely: his eyes, his voice, his scent, his touch. "You taste like the mountain."

The boy closed his eyes. Junja could hardly hear his question.

"What does the mountain taste like?"

"Mushrooms. And gosari."

☽

The yellow dog nosed the boy, whining softly. The bonfire had long since turned into ashes. Crab shells, roasted and sucked clean, were strewn on the sand. The moon, reaching its bright height, had started its nightly descent.

Junja stood up. "I should go before my grandmother starts worrying."

"Let me walk you home." Suwol tried to take her hand, but Junja avoided him.

"Someone might see us."

"I don't care."

"I'm an unmarried woman. Even if you don't care, everyone else will."

"What if the man holding your hand were your fiancé?" Suwol managed to grab the girl's hand.

At the first prickle of contact, Junja flushed with both pleasure and exasperation. She tried to sound annoyed, but her voice wasn't forceful enough. "A first-born yangban son choosing his own bride? I've never heard of that one before." Junja managed to pull her hand free.

The boy crossed his arms. "I don't believe in those dated, silly customs."

"You're assuming that I would want to marry you."

"Why wouldn't you?" Suwol grinned.

Junja sighed. "Think of your parents."

"People should be free to marry anyone they want. Marriage shouldn't be determined by families."

"That's Communist!"

"Don't you agree?"

Junja looked around her. She had been warned never to talk about politics, not even in jest. Be careful and neutral. Silence was safest. "Mother used to say that as long as the government didn't get in the way of us living our lives, she didn't care who they were or what they believed."

Suwol threw up his hands. "You have to care!" He was speaking in earnest now. "Jeju should be its own sovereign nation. The mainland is just a puppet of the Americans, who keep meddling in our business."

Junja tried to cover Suwol's mouth. "Shh. Someone might hear you." The dirt path had grown wider, and they were approaching the village. Suwol's dangerous words could not be overheard.

Boshi, who had been trotting behind them, stopped and growled. Nose working furiously, the white dog loped over to a dark bulk propped against the shadows of a doldam wall like a pile of logs.

Suwol whistled. The dog ran back, chewing and wagging his tail. "I have to go, Junja. I promise I'll visit you again soon."

The girl frowned. "Where are you going this late at night?"

Suwol squeezed Junja's hands. "Nothing for you to worry about. You stay safe. Don't take too many chances with the ocean, because I want to marry you."

Junja slapped Suwol on the arm. "Shh, stop your crazy talk." She wanted to sound angry, but her heart was thudding with such joy that she had to push Suwol away, to stop herself from embracing him. "Go ahead, get out of here."

The boy laughingly bowed in jest and crossed his fingers, holding them up in promise as he jogged away.

Thirteen

Grandmother was lying on her pallet, listening for Junja and worrying about the wild moon. When she heard the creak of the kitchen door, the old woman closed her eyes. Relief turned into gratitude—she reminded herself to bring an offering to the sea king—before relaxing into exhaustion. The old woman sank into a dream.

She was young again, her body lithe and supple. She marveled at the rush of power charging through her body, nothing at all like the slow trickle that sustained her waking moments. She was walking on the shore, trying to calm the god of the ocean. Waves pounded the sand, but the sea king's fists could not reach the object of his rage, which lay somewhere beyond the mountain.

His immense voice was the howling wind. The sea king issued a warning, a string of gusty syllables that whispered and shrieked. The word unspooled on the gale, a whistling pronunciation of unspeakable pain.

The incoming tide turned red around her ankles.

She stood defiant against the winds that lashed her. She screamed, using the most powerful utterance in every language known to man and beast and god. One word stood between her and the incoming sorrow, one bright twinkle against a rising wall of darkness. That scream withered her muscles, wrinkled her skin, and silvered her hair.

The old woman's eyes flew open. They were running out of time.

Fourteen

When the first man disappeared from the village, no one paid any mind. A foul-tempered bachelor who once killed a pig for snorting at him, he wasn't the sort of person anyone would miss.

When the next man vanished, some people joked that he had run away to join rebel leader Lee Duk Ho, who was rumored to hiding in the mountain. Wagging tongues whispered that the man was shacked up with a woman in another village. His wife, who discovered his absence after diving all day, swore that he was too spineless to join the Communists and too afraid of her to have an affair.

Because no one knew what happened to these two men, they weren't included in the official count of villagers who were rounded up by the military police and jailed in Seogwipo. Seven men had been languishing in those cells all summer. One was released after his wife paid a large bribe. Upon his return, the family packed their belongings onto a skiff to escape to one of the smaller outlying islands. They warned everyone else to follow their example.

The absence of nine men slowed down the harvest and burdened the women, who had to toil in the fields after they emerged exhausted from the water. Everyone looked to Grandmother for advice, but the old woman withdrew into an uncharacteristic silence. Everyone expected her to go into town to broker the men's release. Instead, she ignored the situation.

None of this, however, worried Junja so much as the fact that Grandmother had stopped diving. The old woman let Junja take over her dives, explaining that the girl was skilled enough to take on the added responsibility. In the mornings, Grandmother opened her eyes just long enough to remind Junja to say her prayers before turning over to fall back asleep. The other haenyeo expressed Junja's private concerns out loud.

"Not diving again? Is she sick?"

"Why does she spend so much time with that clown of a constable? If she weren't so old, you'd think they were having an affair!"

Junja held her tongue but watched her grandmother carefully. The old woman now spent most of her days in meditation and prayer, rousing herself only for Mr. Lee's visits, when she would prepare elaborate meals. The two of them would linger over tea for hours, their favorite topic of discussion always the same. As she eavesdropped, Junja wondered how it was possible for them to ignore everything else to fixate so single-mindedly on food. Had her grandmother gone soft in the head?

☽

"The next government shipment into Jeju includes a thousand sacks of rice and a hundred pallets of beer, sent on direct orders of President Rhee Syng Man himself." Constable Lee held out his cup.

Grandmother poured the barley tea. "Is it true he's married to an American woman?"

"I don't know what she is, but she's definitely not Korean. President Rhee attended university in America and met her there."

"Is she as ugly as they say?" As soon as Junja heard her grandmother ask this question, the girl wanted to scream.

"Even uglier."

"He's no beauty either, I've heard." The old woman offered the constable a peeled tangerine, which he stuffed whole into his mouth. "The ugly ones always have something to prove, don't they?" She chuckled before asking another question. "How much of that rice is going to be sent down to the regiments here in the South?"

The constable chewed juicily and swallowed before answering. "Half. And by the time everything changes hands, a lot less."

"We're going to need more grain to make it through winter. It's going to be a bad one." Grandmother glanced at Junja, who was washing the dishes from their lunch and pretending not to listen.

"That reminds me—" The constable reached into his rucksack to pull out a squat tin. "Those fiendishly clever Americans have figured out how to put boiled pork into cans, so it doesn't spoil. It stays good for weeks!"

"What kind of meat doesn't spoil?" The old woman made a face as she took the offered can. "Unnatural."

"It's not bad if you know what to do with it." The constable pointed to a small metal pick stuck to the bottom of the tin. "Pull that off and then thread it on the tab there. As you twist, the can will open. I'm curious to see what a good cook could do with it."

"If that's a challenge, I accept." Grandmother waved Junja over. "Does this smell like pork to you?"

The girl sniffed the can and shook her head.

The constable shrugged. "If you like it, I'll bring more. The Americans eat this stuff all the time. They just slice it up and fry it."

Junja interrupted. "Halmung?"

"Yes, child?"

"Are you going to dive this afternoon?"

The old woman waved her away. "Go ahead without me."

☽

"I'm worried about my grandmother." Junja was holding onto one side of a dripping net full of kelp and abalone while Suwol grabbed the other.

The boy had managed several visits in between mysterious errands that he refused to talk about. Junja had invited him to lunch once, but when Suwol heard that the constable would be present, he declined. The sight of a Nationalist uniform, he told her, made him lose his appetite.

The boy adjusted his grip on the wet netting. "You should be worried. Being friendly with a Nationalist officer doesn't look good."

Junja hadn't thought of that possibility. "It's something else. She isn't acting like her usual self." The girl frowned at the ocean. The sun was only halfway down, and she still had to dig out sweet potatoes. "Maybe I'm imagining it. Because of all the terrible things people keep talking about."

Reports of torchings, beatings, and much worse had been trickling into the village. Blame was being placed on everyone: Nationalists, Communists, and roving bands of opportunistic thugs, depending on who was telling the story.

"Has your grandmother done or said anything that might put you in danger?" Suwol asked.

"I don't think so. She and the constable only talk about food."

"Seems harmless."

"That's the problem. If she were acting like herself, she'd be the first person to investigate these strange reports. She'd lead the village meeting on what to do. But she's done nothing. She doesn't seem to care."

The boy was silent as he considered. Finally, he decided to speak his mind. "Those terrible things you're hearing? They're all true."

"What do you mean? People are actually being killed?"

Suwol hesitated. "I've seen the bodies."

Junja stopped walking to stare at the boy. "What are you doing, to see such things?"

"It's better if I don't say."

"All right, don't. But why would Nationalist soldiers burn down villages in Jeju? We're all Koreans. Why would Korean soldiers kill Korean civilians? For what reason?"

Suwol's voice was flat. "Because the Americans are trying to get rid of Communists."

The girl flushed. "That makes no sense! All we're doing here is living the way we've always lived. How does that turn us into Communists?"

"It's Communist because the Americans say it is."

"That's craziness."

Suwol's voice dropped. "Want to hear something even crazier?"

"I'm not sure I do."

"Hallasan is going to be banned. To rout out rebel leaders Kim Dal Sam and Lee Duk Ho."

"How can you ban an entire mountain?" Junja glared at Suwol. "Everyone knows that Lee Duk Ho isn't a Communist, any more than my grandmother is. He's just an angry farmer with a grudge, because the US military seized his farm for their base."

"If the wrong person heard you say that, you'd be accused of being a Communist sympathizer or worse." Suwol's mouth turned down. "According to the mainland government, Mr. Lee is a heavily armed Communist agent who's receiving orders directly from China."

"The mountain is going to be banned because of some ridiculous lie? Who's making up this madness?"

The boy's face hardened. "Ask the constable. He might know."

Junja bit her lip.

"This is why you have to choose a side, Junja. Being neutral or staying silent won't protect you." The boy added apologetically, "Look at what happened to your mother."

The reminder made Junja flinch. The boy believed that her mother's death had been no accident, but everyone in the village was too afraid to speculate about what had really happened. Whenever Junja brought up the subject with her grandmother, the old woman flatly refused to discuss it. What if Suwol were right? Fear trickled into Junja's gut.

As the dirt path sloped upward, a sudden gust of wind from the sea blasted the boy and girl, as if to push them onward. Junja and Suwol retreated into their thoughts. Near the approach to the house, Suwol put down his end of the netting.

"This is as far as I go. I don't want to run into the constable."

"He's not expected today." Junja looked apologetic. "You should greet my grandmother, though, instead of leaving without paying your respects. She'll be disappointed to hear that she missed seeing you."

Suwol shook his head. "I wish I could, but I'm running late. I'm sorry."

"Are you ever going to tell me what you're doing?"

Suwol studied the ground. "I'm hunting rabbits with friends."

"You're a terrible liar."

Suwol remained silent.

"How long will you be gone this time?"

"Hard to say. A couple days, maybe longer."

Suwol's hand brushed Junja's fingers.

"Please be careful." Junja tried to smile.

"I will. You stay safe, too." The boy looked around to make sure no one was watching before embracing Junja quickly.

As Suwol walked away, he turned around several times to wave. Junja watched his figure grow smaller and smaller until he stepped into a grove of trees and disappeared completely.

☽

"Ah, there you are, hiding in plain sight."

Junja looked up, annoyed, from the patch of sweet potatoes she had been digging. How did the constable sneak up on her without making any noise? The man had left for Jeju City several days ago, when she last saw Suwol. Why had the constable returned, but not the boy? Junja jammed her spade into the earth.

The constable's beard was covered with pine needles, and his clothes were more disheveled than usual. A limp chicken dangled from his left hand. He held it up for Junja to admire.

Junja ignored the bird. "Does my grandmother know you've returned?" She wiped the dirt off her hands as she stood up.

"I just paid her my respects. And showed her this fat chicken I brought as a gift. She wants you to prep it for dinner." He held out the bird again. "While it's cooking, you're supposed to show me the caves."

Junja's eyes narrowed. "What caves?"

"The caves where you villagers store food for the winter. Your grandmother said I should see them."

Junja could not prevent the shock from showing on her face. The caves were a closely held secret, never shared with outsiders. Had grandmother taken leave of her senses completely?

"I'll be right back." The girl took the chicken and strode toward the house.

☽

Junja found her grandmother in the kitchen, picking through a box of dried roots and mushrooms. The girl rushed to the old woman's side. "Did you tell Constable Lee about the caves?" Junja's voice was louder than it needed to be.

The old woman ignored her granddaughter as she pulled out a woody root and shook it overhead in triumph. "I knew I still had a piece of ginseng left!"

"Why would you tell a Nationalist constable about the caves, Halmung?" Junja asked again through gritted teeth.

For as long as anyone could remember, the caves had been used as a secret hedge against disaster. During the occupation, food and women had been hidden inside them, away from grasping Japanese hands. Anxious villagers, alarmed by the stories, had recently begun hoarding supplies again. Revealing the caves to an outsider would be considered an unforgivable betrayal.

Why would Grandmother do something so reckless? Junja could not understand the old woman's behavior. Had she really taken leave of her senses? Was it age? Or did the constable hold some strange sway over her?

The old woman knew that her granddaughter was deeply rattled, but chose to ignore her questions. "When you show Constable Lee the caves, Junja, pay close attention."

"To what?"

"To what sort of man he really is."

"I already know what sort of man he is." Junja's mouth turned down.

The old woman shook her head. "You think you do, but you don't. Mr. Lee wants everyone to see a man who isn't worth noticing."

"Why? He's a Nationalist constable. He's free to do whatever he wants."

"Is that so?"

"He carries a gun, Halmung. That gives him quite a bit of freedom, I think." The girl placed the chicken and a knife into a large bowl.

"Do you really believe the constable is free to do whatever he wants just because he carries a gun?"

Grandmother's quiet tone gave Junja pause. She was being unspeakably rude to talk back to an elder in such a manner and felt embarrassed underneath her frustration. Junja swallowed all the questions that were rising in her throat, choosing instead to close her mouth and obey. "I'll leave the chicken next to the woodpile, Halmung. The constable and I should be back from the caves in an hour." The girl pulled the door shut behind her.

☽

The tide washed over the rocks, trailing foam that hissed as it dissolved. A small crab disappeared behind a rock.

Junja watched the water as the constable stood next to her.

"Why are we standing here?" He scratched his armpit.

The sound of his voice set Junja's teeth on edge. "I need to time the tides. Getting into the caves is more difficult when the water is rising."

"Why are we here? Why not over there? That area looks calmer." The constable pointed to a pool where the water swirled between several rocks.

"You can't get to the caves that way."

"Well, I don't see how we can get to any caves this way either."

"That's why you're following me and not the other way around." Junja knew that she was being impolite, but she couldn't help herself. Grandmother might be fooled, but she refused to be taken in by this man.

As the tide pulled away, the girl rushed to leap onto a momentarily exposed boulder. She then ducked under a low arch of rock, crouched, and swiveled hard to the right while clinging onto a ledge of rock. When the constable mimicked her maneuver, he almost slipped and fell. As he recovered, disappointment clouded Junja's face.

To her surprise, the constable chortled out loud. "What a cheeky girl! Just like your grandmother!"

Junja clambered up a pathway that threaded between several large boulders, moving so quickly that the constable had difficulty keeping up with her. She didn't check to see if he was still following until she reached the opening of the cave. When she turned around and saw him, she didn't bother to hide her displeasure.

The air at the mouth of the cavern tasted cool. The constable took a step into the darkness to explore further, but Junja didn't budge.

"You've seen the caves. Time to go back." Her voice was taut.

Constable Lee rummaged in his pockets before pulling out a matchbook. The tiny flame cast shadows high up along the walls of the cave and illuminated his face, transforming it into an angular mask of dark and light.

The girl's eyes glinted as she hissed, "If someone finds out what we've done, my grandmother and I will be cast out of the village."

The flame sputtered out.

The constable struck another match. "These are dangerous times. Do you really think your grandmother would take such a risk without good reason?

His eyes appeared sad in that light, his mouth grave.

The light flared and then blinked out.

The darkness seemed to press against them as the constable spoke again. He sounded tired. "I understand your worries. If you'd like to go now, we can. And I'll forget I ever saw this place."

Junja did not answer. The silence between them echoed the emptiness of the cave. She didn't trust the constable at all. But she did trust her grandmother.

When she finally spoke, Junja's voice was subdued. "If you have any matches left, sir, we could light one of the candles."

☽

The lower walls of the cave were serrated in layers of gray and jade green. Higher up, the rocky surface broke off at angular intervals, creating ledges and openings that were filled with gourds and clay pots. Irregular columns of rock seemed to drip from the ceiling, while trails of moisture seeped down in shiny patterns between patches of moss.

"How far does it go?" The constable held up the candle, which cast an eerie glow.

Junja knew that the constable was surprised by the size of the cavern. Even with supplies tucked into every nook and cranny, there was enough space here for a dozen people to sit comfortably. She gestured for him to follow her behind an overhang of rock.

They ventured deeper, the way lit by candlelight. With each step the ceiling and walls seemed to veer away as the tunnel gradually enlarged into a domed chamber spacious enough to sleep the entire village.

"Did the villagers make this place?" The constable raised the candle to illuminate the high ceiling.

"No. All of this has always been here." Grandmother used to tell bedtime stories about the giants who had once battled each other for dominion over the earth. The last dragons had gathered in these caves before they launched themselves from the mountain to the heavens, to escape the chaos.

The constable rested both hands on the cavern walls, peering up. "The university scientists say that Hallasan is a sleeping volcano, a kind of mountain that spits liquid rock from deep within the earth." He ran his hands over the ridged walls. "These caves are most likely tunnels formed by those rivers of burning rock. My guess is that they run all the way back toward the mountain itself."

Junja knew that they did.

"It's probably easy to get lost in here, right?"

"Yes."

The constable squinted past Junja, toward a darkened corridor.

"There must be more than one entrance. Those supplies could not have been brought here using the route we took."

Junja's silence was affirmation enough.

"Only the villagers who live here know about this place? No other outsiders besides myself?"

Junja nodded.

"Let's hope you're right."

The candle sputtered. As Junja watched, Mr. Lee shifted his expression, blurring his features. His shoulders hunched, and his belly paunched out. His voice slid back into a lazy drawl.

"My stomach says it's time to eat. We should head back to your grandmother and lunch."

☽

"It pains me to admit this, but this is the most delicious chicken soup I've ever had the pleasure of eating." The constable took loud slurps from his bowl. "Even better than my mama's."

If Junja hadn't witnessed the constable's transformation in the sea caves, she would not have believed that this was a man worth taking seriously.

Grandmother inclined her head modestly. "I'm sure that by the time your mother reaches my age, her cooking will be just as good, if not better."

Junja stared at her grandmother and wondered if she, too, was putting on an act for her sake. Surely her grandmother had seen the constable's other face. Why weren't the two of them talking openly, without any pretense?

"Spoken like a true lady, with a humility that makes me deeply regret the request I'm about to make." The constable belched. "Troops from the mainland will be stationed here in a few days. We need a cook. I've recommended you and Junja. The pay would not be much, but you'd be assured of adequate provisions while you worked for us. Should come in handy this winter. Your skills will be largely wasted upon this lot, but the job is yours, if you want it."

Junja flushed. "Nationalist troops? In our village?"

"Yes. They're coming to build fortifications. Hallasan has been banned. It's a no-trespass zone."

"What does that mean?" Junja hoped that Suwol and his family weren't in danger.

"It means no one is allowed to set foot on it. Everyone who lives on that mountain has to leave." The constable pulled a splinter loose from a piece of kindling and began to pick his teeth.

"The rumors are true?" Junja felt a spike of worry.

"I'm afraid so." Mr. Lee set down his toothpick. "But it's a very large mountain. Enforcing the ban will be difficult."

Junja could not read the constable's expression. She looked to her grandmother.

The old woman's face was also unfathomable. "Can you clean up while Mr. Lee and I finish our tea? When you're done, go pick some kkaennip. The feral patches on the north side have the best flavor. Get two baskets worth. We'll prepare them after the constable takes his leave."

Such a quantity could only mean that they were finally going on a long overdue visit to the farmer's market in Seogwipo. "For trade or for sale, Halmung?" Junja began to collect the dishes.

The old woman knew what her granddaughter was thinking. "These are not for town. We're headed up island to the market in Jeju City." The old woman glanced at the constable. "Mr. Lee will be escorting us."

Fifteen

Grandmother yanked Junja away from a pasty man with gleaming teeth who was waving a slim dark package in the girl's face.

"Hey, beautiful! Want some chocolate?"

"Don't look at the hindoongi!" the old woman hissed. But the girl could not help staring at those exaggerated foreign faces with complexions like cadavers.

They had left the village on a donkey cart. Next, they boarded a military bus that looped the perimeter of the island. Grandmother had grabbed Junja, startled, as the vehicle hurtled past villages that took an entire day to reach by foot. Once they grew accustomed to the bumpy lurching, the two of them had relaxed into the ride. Junja stared out the window, marveling at how quickly the landscape passed by, while the old woman snoozed on her shoulder. They reached Jeju City's outer gate by midday, with plenty of time for the market. Constable Lee took his leave at this point, promising to meet them in the same place at sunrise the next morning. Military business, he apologized, would prevent him from escorting them all the way to market.

Grandmother had waved him away, unconcerned. "All we need to do is follow the stink."

The streets of Jeju City were jammed with bodies, and the harbor choked with vessels. Hulking gray ships with foreign lettering were anchored far out at sea. In port, their smaller tenders towered over wooden skiffs that had squeezed in to drop off the morning catch. Tall, beak-nosed soldiers with blank faces and machine guns guarded the gangways to these vessels.

One of these men was as black as the rocks on the beach. He noticed Junja staring at him and winked. The girl hurried away. When she peeked back at him over her shoulder, he was grinning.

"Halmung, I didn't know Americans came in different colors. That one over there is dark as soot!"

The old woman slapped down her pointing finger. "Didn't I tell you to stop staring at them?"

Junja yelped as Grandmother pinched her. "I'm just looking, Halmung."

"Men take any sign of interest as encouragement. Keep your eyes on the ground."

When the two of them passed a stand displaying photos of nearly naked foreign women, Junja gasped. Grandmother yanked her into an alley where the stalls offered more familiar sights: glinting piles of dried anchovy, squash lashed with yellow stripes, fiery mounds of chili powder, green-and-white cabbages. Black ribbons of dried kelp dangled from the awning of an impressive wooden stand where fish glinted on blocks of ice. The fishmonger shouted, her voice clear above the din.

"Fresh fish! Fresh fish! Just off the morning boat!"

Grandmother stopped, intrigued. "How can you afford to buy so much ice? It's worth more than the fish!"

The fishmonger looked pleased with herself. "I get it from my American fiancé."

"You're going to marry a foreigner?"

"Yes, auntie. And I'm going to move far away from here, to America."

"Is that so?" Grandmother elbowed Junja. "She's a brave one, eh? To marry one of those hindoongi!"

The fishmonger looked at Junja. "If you're smart, you'll get yourself a GI husband too. You're young and pretty. Get out while you can."

Grandmother frowned and walked away, pulling Junja after her. "Never forget you're a haenyeo, a woman worth two men."

After dragging Junja through several side streets, the old woman finally settled on a spot that satisfied her. She squeezed in between a silent basket weaver and a thin woman with a worried face who was selling dried sunflowers, pots of oil, and seeds. Grandmother fell into conversation with the sunflower ahjumma and left Junja to mind the wares.

The girl started shouting—"Fresh kkaennip! Delicious kkae—" when she was cut short by a glare from the basket weaver. Sighing, Junja studied her surroundings. Hardly any passersby here. American soldiers did not venture into this part of the market, which catered to locals. The crowds clustered along the outer fringe of the market, adjoining the port, where the stands were attended by women with painted faces and loud laughs.

"Grandmother, I think I'd sell more kkaennip if I walked around. Could I take one of the baskets and try?"

The old woman did not seem to care about their lack of patrons. She waved Junja away. "Good idea. Go see the sights. Move your legs and get some exercise."

Sixteen

Grandmother watched Junja venture forth. The girl was too distracted to notice the appraising stares of the men around her. The old woman stifled a sigh. She knew well the market's many novelties and diversions.

She had carried secrets then too. But her body had been young, and her hopes had still been high.

Her jaw clenched. To ward against self-pity, the old woman started counting the dead. Her daughter. Her two sons. Her husband. Her friends: Chun-hwa, Ok-ryeon, Deok-ryang, Cha-dong, Gye-seok. Mother. Father. Her three older brothers. Each loss reverberated, part of a familiar dull ache, the only constant in her life.

There was a time, once, when she had been fueled by outrage. Fury, mixed with youth, had given her boundless courage and strength. She and her friends joined the underground resistance during the Japanese occupation, to annoy and torment the invaders. During the day they read Japanese words, sang Japanese songs, and bowed to the Japanese flag. But by moonlight, they prayed in Korean, spit out Korean curses, and sent treasonous messages scripted in forbidden hanggul.

The Japanese seemed to consider everything a crime: a late delivery of seaweed; a cracked pot of bean paste; a slap against a drunken advance. The worst offense, for which no punishment ever sufficed, was being Korean in Korea.

The sheer volume of petty charges against the haenyeo provided a useful distraction, shielding the women's more serious and secret transgressions. How they had laughed at those bow-legged brutes, too stupid to recognize the true danger of women patronized by the lord of the seas.

The first Japanese soldier they drowned had a taste for unripe virgins. After he forced himself upon several young girls, the haenyeo had dragged him into the sea caves, gagged and bound. The mothers of the children he violated had waited with knives. They had taken care that he not lose consciousness, that he feel each caress of the blades. When they finished, he had been thrown off a cliff. Below, in the seething water, sharks completed their vengeance.

The women fit the punishment to the criminal with the care of seamstresses. There was a teetotaling Japanese officer who liked to defecate on the floor and then watch, pleasuring himself, as a woman cleaned the mess on her hands and knees. That monster had been given sweet rice cakes compounded with herbs and his own excrement. He had been shipped back to the motherland in a bloody diaper. The conscripted Korean sailors on that trip—stolen sons and husbands—reported that the man died on the journey, his body tossed overboard on the orders of his disgusted countrymen.

The women had grown careless in their boldness. When they were betrayed, her five closest friends had confessed to everything, to spare the others. At least they had died quickly, executed at gunpoint.

Of her many regrets, the one that pained the old woman the most was her failure to tell her daughter and granddaughter the truth about the shameful things she had done. She had been terribly wrong to believe that the world would right itself once the Japanese finally retreated.

An unnatural light had exploded in the southern skies that late summer day, creating a demonic force that changed the tides and darkened the horizon. The remains of the Japanese militia tried to understand the tattered transmissions from their radios. Why had the emperor surrendered?

The sea answered that question. Bloated fish washed up, bleached an evil white. Returning fishermen described a divine ball of fire annihilating an entire city. Days later, American military ships had sailed into Jeju City to oversee the Japanese withdrawal. They took down the red-and-white Japanese flag and replaced it with their own banner.

Fronted by these hindoongi soldiers, the mainland government had sent troops. Who would have thought your own countrymen capable of such betrayal? The louts treated Jeju like a fiefdom, desecrating family shrines and plundering food stores. The Japanese occupation seemed, by comparison, an idyll. What the bloodsuckers disdained—because Koreans were beneath them—Nationalist thugs seemed to relish. They forced fake marriages upon the haenyeo, to seize their lands and property. Family pigs and horses were seized and eaten, to punish villagers who didn't obey the emissaries of a flag they had never seen before.

The old woman rubbed her face. Her supreme misfortune of living during a time of invasion had overpowered her family luck. The Goh family's wealth had been sapped by the occupation, their proud compound overrun by Japanese officers. She had learned to dive in her girlhood, as a diversion, and so she joined the ranks of the haenyeo, to keep her belly full.

Her fingers lingered over the lines on her face. And what of her personal luck? Her long life and her health were marks of divine favor, to be sure. She had married a man who, though beneath her, was easy to love. She had been blessed with two sons and a daughter. But her husband and the boys had been stolen by the Japanese, taken away on boats that never returned.

The loss of the menfolk in her family did not count against her. It was a common fate, for husbands and sons to be sacrificed in war.

The loss of her daughter, however, had broken something that now rattled like bones inside her.

As Junja disappeared into the crowd, the old woman looked to her neighbor and lowered her voice to a hiss.

"Five hundred additional troops are being stationed along the southern coast. They're building fortifications. All access to the mountain will be closed within the week."

The sunflower peddler momentarily froze. After a moment, she resumed her flower waving. She spoke through a bright smile.

"Are you Goh Okja?"

"Yes."

"My mother is Bu Malja."

"You look like her."

"Mother's health isn't very good. She isn't diving anymore. But she says she will do what she can."

"That's all we can expect from anyone."

"How many soldiers are expected in your village?"

"Several dozen."

"Fully provisioned?"

"That's what I've been told."

"Weapons?"

"Two men for every gun. At least half the group is sympathetic to us."

"What about the other half?"

"Dogs."

"How do you know who's who?"

"I've been hired as the camp cook. I'll figure it out."

"What about your granddaughter?"

"She knows nothing. I promised her mother I'd spare her from all this ugliness." The slightest of quivers in her voice betrayed the old woman's feelings.

After a pained silence, the sunflower peddler finally mustered the courage to speak again.

"Was it really a diving accident?"

The old woman gripped her basket. Her daughter had been the highest-ranking diver in the village. "It wasn't enough for them to lie, to cover up their crime. They had to insult her as well."

The sunflower peddler groaned softly. "Who's responsible?"

"Mainland curs acting on behalf of their American masters." The basket trembled in the old woman's hands. "They wanted her to sign a confession. But the paper was blank. When she refused, they beat her and dumped her body on the beach."

The sunflower peddler cleared her throat. Her hoarse words hardly gave any comfort, but she offered them anyway. "She'll be protecting her daughter, you can be sure of that. You concentrate on avenging her."

The old woman had already swallowed a bellyful of revenge in her life, and she was sick from it. What she wanted now was redemption.

"What is to be done? What do I tell the others?" The peddler waved her sunflower back and forth.

"Hide as much food as you can. Keep anything that could be considered a weapon out of sight. Be suspicious of everyone. If you see signal fires on Hallasan, leave your homes and go into hiding. Do whatever you can do to protect yourselves. Tell as many people as you can."

Seventeen

As soon as she left her grandmother's line of sight, Junja bent down to roll her pants higher, revealing her ankles. She pinched her cheeks to bring out a flush. She copied the smiles of the other women in the marketplace, lips open and teeth bared in both promise and warning.

A tall man with yellow hair shouted gibberish into her face. "Hey, sweetheart, what're you selling?"

Junja looked into his pale eyes and tried out the only English word she knew.

"Heh-roh!"

"Hello, beautiful!" He grinned.

Junja smiled back, bobbing her head. "Heh-roh! Heh-roh!" The man continued to babble, a stream of nonsense. Junja's mouth tightened. The man retracted his smile and walked away.

"If that's all you can say, you're not going to get much. Come over here. I'll help you out."

The fishmonger with the ice was waving to her. Despite Grandmother's warning, Junja was fascinated by this woman, whose shrewd face was softened by the kindness of her eyes.

"Where's your granny?"

Junja tilted her head. "Back there."

"You need to sell to foreigners. They'll pay whatever you ask."

"I can't understand them."

"Let me do the talking. We'll split it fifty–fifty."

When Junja hesitated, the fishmonger appraised the girl, looking her up and down. "What's your name?"

"Junja."

"I'm Yoonsoo. My sister Yoonja's about your age. Eats meat or
fish every day because of me. You can keep all of nothing, Junja,
or you can have half of what I'll get for you. I promise it'll be
more than your grandmother makes, if she sells anything at all."

Junja bit her lip. "You didn't even ask what I was selling. Do
foreigners like kkaennip?"

The fishmonger laughed. "They don't need to like it. They just
need to buy it." Her lips pursed. "We need to do something about
the way you look. Take off that vest."

"I only have my small clothes on."

"That's a lot more than most of the women around here are
wearing."

Junja pulled off her rust-colored vest. Her breasts pushed
against the thin fabric of her shirt in a way that made her think of
Suwol. Her face flushed. Mother would have insisted that she
cover herself back up immediately.

"That's good. Keep blushing. Take out those braids and let
your hair loose."

Junja hesitated. Mother would have left by now, but Grandmother would probably follow the woman's directions, to see
where they led. Junja decided she was curious enough to remove
the string binding her hair. Her fingers combed through the long
strands to smooth them out.

"Foreign men love long, loose hair."

Junja suddenly understood. "I'm selling kkaennip, not myself."
She gathered her hair, trying to tie it back again.

The fishmonger batted her hand away. "I know that. And you
know that. But they don't. We let the men think what they want

to think." The fishmonger paused to help a customer before resuming her conversation with Junja. "Don't worry. No one is going to lay a finger on you. My promise, as a fellow haenyeo."

"You're a haenyeo too?"

"What Jeju woman can afford not to be?"

"But you're selling fish." Not seaweed or shellfish, which comprised the bulk of a diver's daily catch.

"I have my own boat." Yoonsoo was pleased by the look of respect on Junja's face. "Used to be my father's. When he passed, I took over the fishing. A lot warmer and easier than diving."

A foreigner stopped in front of the Junja, looking her over. "How much, gorgeous?"

Junja glanced at Yoonsoo.

The fishmonger smiled. "She sell spicy leaf. Good for mens. Make strong long time. Taste good. Try." She turned to Junja. "Act like you're going to give him a taste."

The man leaned in close. "What's your name?" His teeth were stained brown.

The fishmonger answered for Junja. "She my cousin. She no speak English."

"Tell your cousin I'd love to take her dancing."

To Junja: "He's interested. I think he'll buy something." To the man: "She no dancing. Only selling leaf. You wanna go dinner date?

"I want to go dancing." The man's smile began to slip.

"Maybe I was wrong. Don't think he's going to buy." Yoonja waved the man away. "See you later."

Junja watched the man disappear into the crowd before turning to Yoonsoo. "How did you learn how to speak English so well?"

The fishmonger tapped her head with a finger. "Because I listen and I'm smart. And my American GI teaches me. I'll say it again: get an American boyfriend. Best way to protect yourself from what's going to happen."

"What do you think is going to happen?" Junja thought of the running argument between Mother and Grandmother. Mother had begged the old woman to ignore what was going on and stay out of trouble, while Grandmother insisted that it was their duty to get involved. After what Mother had suffered, Junja found herself agreeing with her grandmother. What was the use of avoiding trouble when doing so could still get you killed?

Yoonsoo gestured with both hands. "Look around. What do you see? Soldiers and guns, most of them foreigners. If you still can't figure it out, then maybe you're stupider than I thought."

"Hey, miss. What's in your basket?" A thin man with curly brown hair and pimples approached Junja awkwardly.

Yoonsoo leaned forward to speak for Junja. "My cousin she sell delicious leaf. Make mens strong."

"What's your cousin's name?"

"Her name Junja. What's your name?"

"My name's Charley." The young man looked at Junja. "Junja, how much are those leaves?"

The fishmonger replied, "She only speak Korean."

"Does she dance?"

"She good girl. She only selling leaf."

The young man looked relieved. "I'd love to take her on a date. Just dinner. No dancing."

"You buy some leaf, I tell her."

"How much?"

Yoonsoo named her price.

The young man reached into his pockets.

Yoonsoo turned to Junja. "This one's a good guy. He's going to buy some kkaenip just to talk to you."

"That's crazy!"

"They're so rich, our money is like dirt to them."

The man dropped the coins into the fishmonger's open palm.

"He wants to eat dinner with you. Do you think you could escape your grandmother for a couple hours? I promise nothing would happen."

Junja frowned as she considered. How far was she willing to go to pretend to be someone else? It would depend on the stakes, she thought. Was a free dinner worth the deception?

"Don't do that! Just smile and nod, no matter what I say."

Junja shook her head. "I don't trust him. And I'm not sure I trust you."

"What if my fiancé and I joined you? We could chaperone. Your granny could come too."

"He'd buy my grandmother dinner too?"

"I think I could set that up. Lemme find out." The fishmonger spoke to the young man. "You wanna double date? My boyfriend Joe from Chicago, me, Junja." Yoonsoo jerked her thumb Junja's way.

"She said yes to dinner?"

As the young American smiled, Junja realized that he was probably close in age to Suwol.

"She say you so handsome and look like good guy."

"You're not pulling a fast one, are you? She seemed upset."

"She feel bad because grandmother lonely. She worry too much. What time you want dinner?"

"I have guard duty tonight, so I can't stay out late. Would five o'clock work?"

"Five oh-clock okay. Go to Yum Yum Café. Over there, with yellow flower. Here, take your leaf." The fishmonger motioned to Junja to hand the basket to the young man.

The man pushed it away, laughing. "I know how this works. You won't translate unless I buy something. She can keep the leaves. I just want to have dinner with her."

"Okay. See you later, Chollie. Five oh-clock."

The young man bowed to Junja before walking away, grinning.

The fishmonger handed one of the man's coins to Junja and pocketed the other one. "Tell your grandmother that the two of you are invited for dinner over at my place."

"He said it was all right for my grandmother to come?"

"This has nothing to do with him. I'm the one inviting your grandmother. Don't forget, five PM at Yum Yum Café."

"What's Yum Yum Café?"

"My restaurant."

"You own a restaurant too?"

"What do you think I do with all the fish that doesn't sell? Throw it back into the sea?"

The fishmonger pointed across the market to a row of splintery gray wooden buildings leaning against each other. "My restaurant is over there, third door from the left. Sunflowers are painted on the sign."

"What if my granny doesn't want to come?" Junja was trying to figure out how to tell Grandmother about the dinner without revealing how she had gotten the invitation.

The fishmonger shrugged. "That would be a first. I've never known anyone around here to refuse a free meal." She picked a leaf out of the basket and popped it into her mouth. As she chewed, she started nodding. "Tell your granny that the fishmonger with the ice invited you, because the kkaennip I bought was so delicious." She took the basket out of Junja's hands and pressed the young American's other coin into the girl's palm. "She'll be my guest."

)

The market shut down in fits and starts, bits and pieces breaking off and dispersing with the receding crowds. The fishmonger was the first to take down her stall and leave. Next, the shop with the magazines was dismantled, bundled up, and carted away. The sunflower peddler left early as well, to start the long walk home. As dusk approached, Junja and her grandmother were among the remaining stragglers. They traded the last of the kkaennip and its basket for some dried squid.

"So where is this fishmonger's restaurant?" The old woman rose out of her squat using Junja for support.

The girl pointed. "Just across the main street, in that row of little buildings. It's called Yum Yum Kah-pey."

"What kind of nonsense is that?"

"American."

"Well, if she has sense enough to judge my kkaennip good, then her cooking might be edible. It would be nice to eat something hot."

"She's very clever, Grandmother. And she seems kind."

"I'll be the judge of that. Don't trust anyone too quickly, Junja. In times like these, people will say or do anything to put themselves first." The old woman noticed two soldiers standing nearby and added, "Beware of soldiers, especially."

)

Despite its shabby exterior, the café was immaculate inside. Four small tables were staggered on the wooden floor. The walls were covered in newspaper, with an occasional glossy picture cut out from a magazine. The scent of frying onion made Junja's mouth water. A large wooden radio sat silent on a table in a corner.

Yoonsoo poked her head through the door connecting the kitchen to the dining room. "You're early! Good. We could use your help, Junja." The fishmonger rushed out to bow to Grandmother. "Nice to meet you again, Auntie. Please, take a seat and make yourself comfortable."

Junja followed Yoonsoo into the cramped kitchen, where a girl was chopping greens. The fishmonger tousled her hair. "Junja, this is my younger sister, Yoonja."

When the girl turned around, Junja had to swallow her shock. Yoonja's upper lip was split in half. Her words hissed and whistled out of an unsightly gash. "Niceth to meet you, Junja."

The fishmonger acknowledged the cleft without pity. "She may be scary-looking now, but when the American doctors fix her, Yoonja will be one of the prettiest girls anywhere." She punched her younger sister's shoulder affectionately. "See how nice her figure is! Even better than mine."

Yoonja grimaced at Junja, who took a few moments to understand that the contortion was a smile. "Did you make the kkaennip? Tho good!"

Junja grinned back. "I helped my grandmother. I'll let her know you like it."

"Pleathe, give her some barley tea." Yoonja motioned to a large kettle.

Junja took a cup of tea out to Grandmother, who was peering at the pictures on the wall, hands clasped behind her back. As the old woman settled onto a floor cushion to drink, the girl noticed an illustration of an American woman with long dark hair. She was kneeling on a beach, wearing an enigmatic smile and scanty small clothes that clung to her body. Did American women work as haenyeo too?

"That's my fiancé's favorite pinup girl. He says she reminds him of me!" The fishmonger joined Grandmother at the table with her own cup of tea. "But my boobs are much nicer, I think." She gestured toward the kitchen. "I'll sit with your grandmother. Why don't you join Yoonja in the kitchen? She'd appreciate the company."

☽

"My sister arranged a dinner date for you?" Yoonja lifted the lid on a boiling pot. The billowing steam hid the lower half of her face. Without the distraction of the harelip, she was indeed a beautiful girl.

"Yeah. She said he was a nice guy." Junja suddenly felt embarrassed about agreeing to the date.

"If Yoonsoo said so, he'll be nice. She's never wrong about people." Yoonja's knife moved evenly, a steady beat.

"Has she ever arranged a date for you?"

Yoonja touched the cleft. "What kind of man would be interested in this?"

Junja reddened. "I'm sorry . . ."

"You don't need to apologize." Yoonja put her knife down. "When I was born, Mother tried to drown me. Yoonsoo pulled me out of the water and hid with me in the woods, until Father came home. Her punishment was to take care of me. Mother was sure I would die because I couldn't suckle. Yoonsoo and Father kept me alive by spooning cow's milk into my mouth."

Yoonja gestured to the pot of salt, which Junja handed to her. "She was only eight years old when she did that. Mother died of a fever four years later, and then Father was taken by the Japanese.

My sister's been taking care of me my entire life." Yoonja nodded emphatically, as if she were agreeing with herself. "You will never meet anyone kinder or braver than Yoonsoo."

As if summoned by her sister's praise, the fishmonger poked her head into the kitchen. "Hey, a couple of soldiers want to order dinner. Can you help them out? I'm busy talking to Junja's grandmother."

Yoonja looked hopefully at Junja, who shook her head. "My grandmother doesn't want me talking to soldiers. And I don't know what you're serving. Better for me to stay here."

Yoonja sighed. She was used to being stared at. She wiped her hands on her apron. "I'll go out, then. You can clean the fish."

Eighteen

Out in the dining area, the fishmonger listened to the old woman air her outrage.

"You know what the mainlanders have been doing under direct orders from your precious Americans?" Grandmother spat out the question as she glared at the two young soldiers who had settled themselves at a table on the other side of the room.

"You can't believe all the crazy rumors. Raids against villages? Communist sympathizers being dragged away for questioning and disappearing? They're just stories to scare people into obeying the curfew."

The old woman's hands clenched around her cup. "My daughter was taken away for questioning and tortured. She died of her injuries."

The fishmonger blinked. "There must have been some kind of mistake. Did you report it to the authorities?"

"Which authorities? The local policemen who dragged her out of the water and threw her in jail? Or maybe you mean the Americans, who work with lying traitors? The monster who killed my daughter used to be a Japanese collaborator. Your precious GIs made him a Nationalist officer."

"I didn't know the situation was so bad outside the city." The fishmonger looked pained.

"It's bad all over Jeju." The old woman stared into her cup.

"The commanding officer in Jeju, General Kim, he seems like a reasonable man. I've heard he's fair and cautious. Not the type to shoot first and ask questions later."

"So I've been told by a Nationalist friend."

"This friend—is he reliable?"

"He has no reason to lie and a great deal to lose if his sympathies were discovered."

The fishmonger considered. "Working in the marketplace and here in the restaurant, I overhear a lot. I've heard soldiers arguing. There's a lot of confusion about what the mainlanders have been sent to do here."

"Most of the high-ranking officers have no decency. Give a man a taste of power, and he'll reveal his true character. Lots of dogs out there."

"If you're right about that, Auntie, then nothing we women do will make a difference. Better to concentrate on saving ourselves, don't you think?"

"The bigger the dog, the bigger the stick you need."

The fishmonger sighed. "Which stick, Auntie? China doesn't feel right at all."

The old woman didn't answer.

"Have you talked to any of the refugees from the North? They say that the Chinese are as barbaric as the Japanese, maybe even worse."

"I guess it's a matter of picking between poisons." The old woman sounded tired.

Yoonsoo shook her head. "The Americans live too far away. It makes no sense. But China? They want Korea back under their thumb now that the Japanese are gone. It's our past, all over again." She sniffed. "China or America—either choice carries a steep price, Auntie. I don't care to find out what it is. Let me help.

I can find Junja a nice man, who'll take her away from here, to America."

"I will not let you prostitute my granddaughter."

"You consider marriage prostitution?"

"It often is."

The fishmonger ignored the barb. "If you change your mind, Yoonja and I will be here in Jeju City until spring. That's when my fiancé's tour of duty ends, and we leave for America. I work the market every day. Yoonja's always here at the restaurant, and I join her at night. If something happens, tell Junja to make her way to the café. I'll do what I can."

Grandmother said nothing, her mouth set in a hard line.

Yoonsoo smiled in apology. "Oh, and don't send your granddaughter empty-handed. As you know, nothing is free. Especially in times like these. She'll need money for tickets and bribes, things like that. She can get room and board if she helps with the restaurant, but she's going to have to pay for everything else."

The old woman nodded. At least the fishmonger had enough sense to leave. She obviously wasn't the sort of person who allowed principles to stand in the way of common sense. To survive this world, a woman needed to know when to negotiate and when to compromise.

And when to run away.

☽

After the dinner date, which surprised everyone by being both delicious and entertaining, the fishmonger offered to rent the floor of the café as sleeping quarters to Junja and her grandmother. The old woman declined, explaining that they had staked a spot in the grove just outside the city walls. Constable Lee would be expecting them there at dawn. After thanking Junja profusely for her help in the kitchen, Yoonja sent the two of them off with several roasted sweet potatoes and a pocketful of chestnuts.

Outside in the brisk night air, the old woman took a deep breath and stretched. People were milling about in the street, despite the chill.

"There used to be a bathhouse nearby. A scrub and a long hot soak would feel wonderful." The old woman sounded wistful.

"How different can it be from a bath at home?" Junja had never gone to a public bath before.

The question surprised the old woman. Her own life at that age had been very different. She had been far more worldly, having lived in Seoul to attend school. At least Junja knew how to write and read. Many of the villagers didn't even have those rudiments. But never to have experienced the pleasure of a bathhouse? The old woman felt such pity for her granddaughter that she decided to be reckless. "Let's take a bath together, shall we?"

At the entrance to the bathhouse, a stout woman with steel-gray hair greeted Grandmother with a deep bow. When the old woman explained that this was her granddaughter's first visit, the baths were offered at half price.

The two of them undressed before squatting down and throwing bowlfuls of water over themselves. Junja copied her grandmother, who slathered a handful of soft mugwort soap over her body before scrubbing with a rough washcloth. She finished by unpinning her hair, soaping it into a lather, and rinsing herself with ladles of clean water. Now clean, the two of them were ready to soak.

The stone-tiled bath was set into the ground, far deeper and larger than Junja had expected. Several women were already lounging in the water, and their heads turned languidly toward the newcomers. Their gazes slid away, and the women resumed their murmured conversations. One woman was as angular as a man, with dark purple nipples on her bony chest. She was talking to a woman who was short and round like a peach, with pendulous breasts. Two grannies with snowy hair and stooped backs sat neck-deep in the water, eyes closed, groaning openly with pleasure.

Grandmother motioned to Junja to sit down. The women sighed as steam billowed up, shrouding them in mist. The warmth settled on Junja's skin, a damp sheen that turned into trickles of moisture. She felt like she was inside a cloud. Her eyes closed.

Grandmother spoke, her voice softer than a whisper.

"Junja, try to remember. What happened when you visited the sea king? What dream did you dream under water?"

Grandmother had not asked this question in such a long time. Junja meant to say that she did not remember, but the words that slipped out of her mouth went their own way.

As the old woman listened, lines of water dripped down her face and ran into her mouth, like tears.

Nineteen

A hand slapped Junja awake. Another hand covered her mouth, while a voice hissed against her ear.

"Suwol is in trouble. We're going back into the city to help him. Don't talk. Nod if you understand." Grandmother was squatting next to Junja's head.

Junja's eyes flew open. Why was Grandmother talking about Suwol? Junja thought back to the market, the dinner, and the bathhouse; there had never been any mention of Suwol. The girl nodded. As she sat up, a branch snapped.

"Hush!" The whisper came from a shadowy bulk by Grandmother's side. The dark silhouette turned, revealing Constable Lee's bearded face. He gestured to the two women, motioning to them to stay silent and follow him.

Junja's thoughts whirled as the three of them picked their way through the leaves, past other sleeping bodies. Why was the constable involved? The half moon hung low, its thin light doing nothing to illuminate the strangeness of the situation.

When they reached the main road, the constable began talking rapidly as his eyes darted about, searching for eavesdroppers behind every tree. "There isn't enough time to explain everything. Just follow my directions exactly."

This was the same decisive man that Junja had momentarily glimpsed in the sea caves. The girl was so startled that she could not help asking, "How do you know Suwol?"

The old woman hushed Junja. "We'll explain later. There's not enough time now."

The constable leaned in. "This is our story: Suwol is your new husband. Your grandmother bribed me to bring the two of you into the city to find him. He disappeared the night after your wedding, four days ago. You came into the city to chase after him because a villager tipped you off about his intentions to go gambling in Jeju City. He disappeared with your dowry—two small gold rings—as well as all the wedding gift money."

"What? That's crazy!" Junja glanced at her grandmother, whose face was unreadable.

The constable turned to the old woman. "Are you sure you want to involve her? You know the risk."

Grandmother's eyes were pitiless as she looked at Junja. "Forget everything you've heard, because I'm going to tell you the truth now: Your mother was beaten by the military police. The same men who killed your mother now have Suwol. What we do next will either save his life or condemn us all to a firing squad. Do you understand?"

Junja's eyes opened wide. Mother hadn't died of a diving accident?

"Do you think you can do this?" Grandmother placed her hands on Junja's shoulders.

Fear and fury collided in Junja's chest. So many questions she wanted to ask. She nodded. "What do you want me to do?"

The old woman pinched Junja so hard that tears sprang into the girl's eyes. "Cry. Make your eyes red and swollen. Think about your mother. Your brother and your sister." The old woman pinched her again. "Our lives depend on those tears."

As they walked, the old woman whispered instructions. "Avoid answering questions that you don't know how to answer. Act stupid. Or cry and hide your face. Faint if you're desperate. Remember, you're a jilted bride who's come all the way to the city to find her missing husband and stolen dowry."

The constable added, "Take your cues from your grandmother. Let us do the talking." He opened a flask, splashing his hand with its contents. After patting his face and beard with liquor, the constable wiped his hands on his clothes and took a large gulp for good measure.

As they approached the city's perimeter, Mr. Lee began stumbling. He sang, tunelessly and loudly, while Grandmother moaned about her granddaughter's shame. The old woman pinched Junja again, a reminder.

The guard at the main entrance of Jeju City was a skinny, pockmarked youth with a bored expression. His helmet was too big for his head, and his hands were red and chapped. Constable Lee waved to him grandly as he tried to stumble past.

"Stop right there." The guard pointed his rifle at the constable. "Market day is over. Why are you out past curfew? Please state your business."

The constable stumbled to the side of the road, where he retched.

The guard lowered his rifle to reveal a disgusted expression.

The constable planted himself before the guard, swaying. "Ish a secret. If I told ya, I'll ruin this girl's honor. We can't have that now, can we?" He hiccupped.

Grandmother's low keening rose into a full-throated wail. "Aigoo . . . aigoo . . . the shame . . ." She pinched Junja, who covered her face with her shirtsleeves.

The guard repeated himself. "You must state your business."

Constable Lee rolled his eyes, clutched his heart, and bellowed, "Our business is love."

Grandmother whacked the constable's head. "Shut up, you drunken fool! Don't you dare ruin my granddaughter's reputation."

Mr. Lee turned to Grandmother, slurring. "I'm a conshtable, auntie. I could have you arreshted for touching me like that. Guard, arresh this woman for accoshing a Nationalish officer."

The guard turned his head away as the constable cleared his nose into the street by pressing one nostril shut and blowing hard out the other.

"Sir, do you have any identification papers to prove you're an officer?"

Constable Lee searched himself. He reached into every pocket, taking out pieces of string and bits of lint and dropping them into the street. "Here, hold this for me, will ya?" He placed a damp and smelly piece of cuttlefish jerky into the guard's hands and wagged his finger, swaying. "Don't you try to eat that! I'm watching!" He unbuttoned the top of his shirt, to grope his armpits. Then he unbuckled his pants and turned around in exaggerated modesty. He pulled out a crumpled piece of paper from under his belt and smoothed it out under his squint. He thrust the paper into the guard's hand as he belched. "Here you go. Constable Lee of Seogwipo. Right there, if you can read."

The guard held the paper close to his eyes. "My apology for detaining you, sir." He bowed to the constable and waved the group through.

The constable stumbled through the sleepy streets, stopping to take sips from his flask. Grandmother moaned and wrung her hands. Junja watched the two of them in amazement until another hard pinch made her cast her eyes down.

Mr. Lee's circuitous weaving led them to a cluster of squat gray military buildings. He began slurring loudly as they approached.

"Time to pay up, auntie. I kep' my end of the deal. Gimme the resh of my money."

Grandmother began thrashing Mr. Lee, who stumbled under her blows. "So you're a cheat as well as a drunk? You promised us you'd take us to him. I don't see him anywhere! I'm not paying you anything!"

The two of them bickered while Junja tried to squeeze out a few tears. When a few passersby stopped to stare at the spectacle, she held her sleeves up to cover her face.

Two men in military uniform emerged from one of the gray buildings and walked briskly toward the ruckus.

"What's the problem here?" The lower ranking officer addressed Constable Lee, who was trying to protect himself from Grand-mother's slaps.

The old woman wailed, "I paid this constable to find my granddaughter's husband, but now he's too drunk to find his own prick."

The higher-ranking officer peered at Mr. Lee's face. "Constable Lee?"

The constable peeked through his fingers. He tried to stand at attention but couldn't help swaying. "Yessir, Constable Lee, sir! I mean, Yessir, General Kim, sir. Constable Lee at your service. Sir!"

The general spoke to the other officer. "You may proceed. I'll handle this."

The officer protested. "That would be beneath you, General. I'd be happy to throw him into detention and escort these women to the city gates."

The general considered. "A tempting idea, but I'm in a bad mood. I'm going to question these people personally. You go about your business, Lieutenant General Song. If I need your help, I'll send a request."

The officer shot a disgusted look at the drunken constable before turning on his heel to leave.

The general began to harangue the constable, who cringed under his superior's angry assault. An older man of average height with silver hair, General Kim appeared close in age to Junja's grandmother. His eyes were hooded, and his mouth a firm line. As soon as the departing officer was out of sight and earshot, the general lowered his tone. The two men stepped away from the women and ducked into an enclave that was sheltered from view. Was the constable still pretending to be drunk? Junja couldn't tell.

When he returned, the constable was subdued. His head was hanging, and he was rubbing his face, as if he had been hit. The general studied the old woman and the girl with an expressionless face. Finally, he nodded to Grandmother, who returned the gesture with a deep bow.

Junja was stupefied when her grandmother started to simper, batting her eyelashes. "I am so ashamed to meet such an important man under these embarrassing circumstances."

The general's face did not move. "Let's go find this husband."

On the walk to the jail cells, Junja puzzled over the situation. If Suwol's situation were so dire, why were Grandmother and the constable going to such lengths to behave like fools? How well did the general and the constable know each other? Did the general strike the constable during their private talk?

The girl knew that her grandmother had carried secrets for many years, secrets so heavy they had bent her back and scored her face. She stole a look at the old woman, who was wringing her hands and muttering under her breath. What else did she not know about this person?

The general stopped at a crude wooden gate guarded by a soldier with a rifle. The young man saluted his superior with a stiff hand.

The general's voice was brisk as he walked by the young man. "Please accompany us to the holding cells. With the most recent batch of arrests."

Junja stared at the guard, whose face was familiar. Had she seen him in the market the day before? The young man's gaze slid over Junja at first, before doubling back when he recognized her too. He winked, grinning broadly.

The group followed the guard along a muddy walkway. The stench made Junja and her grandmother cover their mouths and noses. Junja's disgust turned into horror as they passed cells crammed with people bearing bloody signs of illness or injury. Some of the bodies were lying prone in the muck, unnaturally still.

The young guard stopped in front of a makeshift bamboo cage. "This is the one, sir." He was gawking openly at Junja now, without the slightest shame.

A group of men splattered with mud or worse were squatting on the ground near the back of the cage. Suwol looked up from that group, his white face smeared with black. One eye was swollen shut, and his hands were bleeding. When he saw the young guard, he shrank back, trying to hide his face.

Junja suddenly realized why the young guard looked so familiar: he was the motorcyclist who had given her and Suwol a ride from the mountain. The girl began to shiver, so horrified that her teeth seemed to rattle against each other. Junja glanced at her grandmother, whose eyes were fixed on the general. She looked at the constable next. He was humming as he pretended to sway from drink. No way to warn them that their plan would fail. The general would never believe that she and Suwol were newlyweds, not if the guard said otherwise.

Suwol tried to rise, but stumbled.

With a cry, the girl reached out, before stopping herself. The young guard was leering now, as if he were taunting her. The fetid odor from the cell seemed to thicken, making Junja retch. She turned away, covering her mouth with one hand and reaching for her grandmother with the other. Junja's eyes met the constable's as she suppressed another gag. She swallowed the bile that rose to the back of her throat as the constable rubbed the side of his nose. Had he raised his eyebrow ever so slightly?

We're all going to be shot, Junja thought, even as she heard her mother's voice warning her to put such bad-luck thoughts out of her mind.

General Kim's voice was steel. He aimed his question at Junja. "What relation is this young man to you? If you lie, both of you will join him in this cell."

Junja clenched Grandmother's hand, trying to warn her. She stole another glance at the young guard, who winked at her again. Without a doubt, this young man would expose them. Junja cleared her throat as her thoughts raced. If she told the general that she and Suwol were brother and sister, the guard could confirm their story. Suwol didn't have to be her husband in particular; he could be betrothed to someone else in the village. Junja could say that she and her grandmother had come to retrieve her errant brother along with the dowry and return them all the bride.

Junja opened her mouth to answer the general's question, but no sound came out. Her throat seemed to constrict. Junja took a breath and tried again, but her voice had disappeared. Grandmother's hands clenched around Junja's. The young guard's grin grew wider.

"I asked you a question." The general looked impatient. "Are you incapable of answering?"

Junja muttered a quick prayer. She was about to declare Suwol her brother when the constable lurched forward, spraying vomit onto the guard. The young man cursed as the constable's soiled body slumped against him.

☽

"Both of you, out of my sight!" The general, who was covering his nose with a handkerchief, waved away the young guard, who had lost his own breakfast as well when the reeking contents of the constable's stomach landed on him. Mr. Lee was sitting on the ground rubbing his belly and declaring that he was feeling much better now and could stay for the rest of the interrogation.

The general barked at the young guard as he hurried away with the constable. "Clean him off and hand him over to Lieutenant General Song, who will question him separately. We'll see if their stories match up." General Kim turned his glare to Junja. "I want a straight answer from you, young lady. Who exactly is this boy to you?" He pointed to Suwol, who cowered, head drooping.

Grandmother pushed Junja forward. "Go ahead, tell him the truth. Don't be ashamed."

Junja hesitated, still worried. Since the constable was being interrogated separately, she had no choice but to follow their original plan.

The old woman simpered, batting her eyelashes at the general. "The general is a good man. He's here to help Jeju, just like the constable."

Junja bit her lip. Her voice shook as she cast her eyes down. Her words seemed to disappear into the ground. "That boy is my husband. And he ran away with my dowry."

The general pursed his lips. "You don't sound very sure. Are you telling me the truth?"

Grandmother pushed Junja aside, winking coquettishly. "Really, General, must you press a shy young virgin like that? She's embarrassed enough as it is. Surely you understand what she's too ashamed to say? I don't think she even knows the words for it! Of course, a virile man like yourself has probably never experienced such, ah, shortcomings." The old woman directed her next comments to Suwol. Her lips curled, and her eyes flashed. "Such a worthless man! Just a shriveled little chili pepper with no heat!"

Suwol managed to stand. He hung onto the bars of the cell, looking miserable. "Junja, I'm really sorry. This is all my fault." He begged the general, "They haven't done anything. Please, let them go!"

Grandmother snapped at Suwol, "Don't think you can get out of this by avoiding us, young man. Your apologies count for nothing. You never consummated the marriage, so you must return the dowry." She reached into the bars, trying to slap his face. "Dirty dog, spending my granddaughter's dowry in a whorehouse!"

"Whorehouse?" Junja looked at her grandmother, aghast. "I thought he was gambling!"

Suwol dropped his head. The boy's cheeks were crimson.

Junja hesitated for only a moment before throwing herself against the bars of the cage, screaming all the new slurs she had heard at the marketplace, including one that the fishmonger favored. "Liar! Dog whelp! Thief! Rotting fish guts!"

Grandmother pulled the girl into a rough embrace. She patted her head. "There, there, child. I'm so sorry that you had to learn the dirty truth." The old woman cursed Suwol. "Worthless dog! Look how you've shocked my innocent granddaughter with your godless behavior!" Grandmother crossed her arms as she spoke to the general. "Keep him in jail. We don't want him. Just give us back our money and rings."

The general was prevented from replying by the return of the constable, who was accompanied by the officer they had seen earlier with the general.

"General Kim, sir!" The officer's bow was not as sincere as it could be, but deep enough not to be considered disrespectful.

"Lieutenant General Song." General Kim nodded to the younger man. "My apologies for drawing you into this mess, but it seemed necessary to have two separate interrogations. What have you learned from questioning the constable?"

"According to Mr. Lee, the man you have in custody is a runaway groom." Lieutenant General Song looked pointedly at Suwol. "The jilted bride and her grandmother have chased him all the way to Jeju City to get their dowry back." He cleared his throat. "The constable here was paid a bribe to help find him."

The general's hooded eyes lowered even further. "How do we know that's not a fabrication? The boy was followed. He was communicating with known rebels in Jeju City."

"I wrote the report you're referring to, sir. These rebels often congregate at a popular gambling den near the docks. The place is quite notorious for its . . . um . . . activities. The boy was found in one of the inner rooms, unclothed, in a rather compromising position. The items we confiscated were with him at the time of his arrest."

Grandmother wailed. "The two gold rings! Our money! Give them back!"

Two gold rings? A gambling den *and* a brothel? What exactly was Suwol doing by himself in the city? Junja started as her grandmother gave her a covert pinch, but the girl didn't have to force the iciness of her tone. "You were lying naked with someone in a gambling den?"

The boy's flush deepened. "It's not what you think, Junja. I can explain—"

The lieutenant general interrupted, his voice crisp. "Actually, to be precise, he was found naked with another man."

Junja gasped while Suwol's fellow inmates backed away from him in disgust. The shocked silence was broken by Constable Lee, who was laughing as he clutched his stomach. "Well, that alone is grounds for execution. If he's a rebel too, then we'll be rid of two problems with one bullet." He wiped his eyes, shaking his head. "Why don't we do these two ladies the favor?"

Grandmother pulled the ear of the lieutenant general, who flinched. "Do what you want with that dog, but give us back our rings and wedding money. We need them for a new husband."

Lieutenant General Song extricated himself from the old woman's grasp. "I'm sorry, but the funds have been confiscated on behalf of the Nationalist party. They will be used in service of our glorious new democracy."

The old woman raised her fist, making the lieutenant general step back. "What? You soldiers are going to steal my granddaughter's dowry and rob her of a husband as well?"

The general rubbed his temples with his fingers. His words hissed out through clenched teeth. "Everyone stop talking immediately. I cannot think when there's so much rabble." He turned to the lieutenant general. "Song, let's confer in private for a moment."

The general and the lieutenant general walked far enough away for their conversation to be inaudible. The lieutenant pointed first at Suwol and then at Junja, gesticulating while the general nodded.

Constable Lee muttered under his breath. "Be careful. This can still go the wrong way."

Their discussion concluded, the two officers walked back. Lieutenant General Song opened the door to Suwol's cell with a large ring of keys.

Had he opened the door to release Suwol? Or were she and Grandmother joining the boy in detention? Junja's grip on her grandmother's hand tightened as the old woman held her breath.

The general addressed the group. "My officer has convinced me to release the boy. However, we will keep the bridal gift. We hope you find this a satisfactory resolution."

Junja, who was about to thank the general, was stopped by Grandmother's howl of disappointment. "We want our gold rings back, not him! He's useless!"

The general and lieutenant exchanged looks. At a nod from the general, the lieutenant waved Suwol out of the cell.

Constable Lee placed a sloppy hand on the old woman's arm. "Auntie, I've kept my end of the bargain. Pay up."

In response, the old woman balled her fists and started cursing the constable. She tried to kick him too, but the man managed to duck out of the way.

The general casually spat upon Suwol as he left the cell. "If it were up to me, I'd shoot you. But Lieutenant General Song believes that being sent off with these two women is a more appropriate punishment for the likes of you. Considering your unnatural proclivities, lifelong matrimony may indeed prove a harsher sentence than a quick death by firing squad."

Next, the general barked at Constable Lee, nostrils flaring in disgust. "Constable, it does not befit a Nationalist officer to accept bribes. We are here to aid our countrymen in Jeju, not profit from them. You will not accept any payment from these women. As a reminder of your duties, you will escort this group back to whatever village they came from. Make sure they stay there."

The general did not deign to look at Grandmother as he spoke. "It is my sincere hope that we never see any of you again."

With that last comment, the general brushed his sleeve and walked away.

Twenty

Leaving Jeju City was a sorry crawl. Suwol, who was limping, walked more slowly than Grandmother. The constable kept up his drunken charade, drinking from his flask, singing, and weaving from one side of the road to the other. When Junja tried to speak, grandmother held up a warning hand. She kept Junja close, far away from the boy.

Several hours later, the forest began to grow sparse, giving way to open fields. The constable announced loudly that he was going to take a piss as he ducked behind a tree. When he returned, he was walking briskly, all pretense dropped.

"Thank you, Junja, for giving me the idea that saved our necks back there. I'm curious, though: How did you and the guard know each other?"

Junja frowned. "I don't think I was that obvious, sir."

The constable laughed and addressed Junja's grandmother. "She inherited your cool head." He turned back to Junja. "The guard gave it away, not you. As luck would have it, General Kim never looked at the young man. Who was he, and how did you know him?"

Junja described the motorcycle ride that she and Suwol had taken from the mountain pass to the village. Grandmother clucked over how precarious the situation had actually been.

The old woman stroked her granddaughter's hand. "You did well, Junja. Remarkably well. If I had known about the guard, I would've been too terrified to think straight."

Suwol, who had kept silent, tried to speak. "May I—"

He was halted by the constable's raised hand. "Not a word in my presence. I'm so angry at your stupidity, I could've shot you myself."

The constable looked back at the road they had just traveled. "Best to keep going as quickly as you can. From here it's another four or five hours to the turnoff. If you hurry, you'll make it to the next forest before sundown. You can sleep there and continue on to the village in the morning. I have to part ways with you now."

Grandmother looked concerned. "Is there a problem?"

"Just a few minor adjustments because of what happened with Suwol. I'll join you at the village in a day or so, with the additional soldiers I warned you about." The constable addressed Suwol next. "Now would be the time to act like a true hero. Tell your family to leave the mountain as soon as possible. Yesterday would have been better, but no later than the end of the week."

With that enigmatic remark, Constable Lee ran back into the forest. Grandmother, Junja, and Suwol watched him disappear as they resumed their trudging.

Suwol grimaced. "I don't trust anyone in a Nationalist uniform. He's probably going to shoot us in the back."

Grandmother's lips curled. "Use your head. Why would Mr. Lee go to such lengths to free you, only to shoot you on the road home?"

Suwol glanced at Junja, who refused to look at him. "How did the constable know that I had been arrested?"

Grandmother's reply was curt. "The answer should be obvious."

"He's been following me?" The boy swore.

"You know very little about the constable or his motives." The old woman shook her head. "Don't judge him when you know less than nothing."

"Do you know for certain that the constable was following me? Or are you speculating?"

"How else could he have known?" Grandmother glared at Suwol. "You're not in a position to be asking us for answers, young man. If you want to know why the constable was following you, perhaps you should tell us why you were jailed in the first place. How did that fellow put it? 'Found in a rather compromising position?'" The old woman laughed.

Suwol shut his mouth. Grandmother pulled Junja to her side. She wanted the boy to reflect, undistracted. Had Junja's concern for the boy not been obvious to everyone, Suwol would still be incarcerated, or worse. Of that she was certain.

☽

The threesome had been walking for several hours when a clatter from the road ahead halted them in their tracks. A horse-drawn cart, raising a cloud of dust, rattled around a bend. Suwol, Junja, and the old woman stepped aside to let the cart pass. As it drew closer, Suwol squinted.

"That looks just like—"

"Suwol? Is that you?"

Suwol whooped. "Father!"

Grandmother beamed. "What excellent timing. Never has a horse smelled so lovely."

After introductions and bows were exchanged, Suwol and Junja were given the task of turning the cart around. Mr. Yang explained how he had left the mountain as soon as he heard that Suwol had been arrested.

The old woman startled everyone with the bluntness of her question. "What kind of kinship exists between you and Mr. Lee to make a Nationalist constable keep an eye on your foolhardy son?"

Mr. Yang's face remained blank at first, before creasing into a grin. "Mr. Lee told me to be careful around you. He said you were as clever as his mother and as good a cook. He also said that if the Nationalist army had twenty men like you, we wouldn't be in this terrible situation, where blood is pitted against blood."

The flattery failed to distract the old woman. "You didn't answer my question."

Junja and Suwol listened with growing astonishment. "Did you know that your father knows Constable Lee?" Junja whispered to Suwol, who shook his head.

Mr. Yang rubbed his chin. "Simply put, Mr. Lee is Suwol's first cousin."

Suwol interrupted his elders with a shriek. "A Nationalist constable is my cousin? How is that possible?"

"He's your mother's elder sister's only child." Suwol's father shrugged.

"Mother has an elder sister?"

"Half sister. In Seoul. Your mother's mother was the second wife, not the first." Mr. Yang turned to grandmother. "Apologies for my son's rudeness. I'm sure you understand why he doesn't know much about this part of the family tree." He gestured to the horse cart. "May I offer you a ride, Auntie?"

The old woman took his offered hand and climbed into the cart. Mr. Yang clambered up after her. When Junja and Suwol tried to climb on as well, Mr. Yang held up his hand.

"The horse can't pull all of us. This road's much too steep. You two can cut across the hill and catch up with us at the pass." Mr.

Yang rummaged under his seat and pulled out a carefully wrapped bundle. "Mother packed some food. Should be enough for both of you. Don't dally and be careful."

When the dust from the cart settled, Suwol opened the cloth bundle. He took out two rolls of bing-tteok and gave one to Junja before taking a large bite. "They hardly fed us." He wolfed down another mouthful.

Junja nibbled and chewed slowly to make her roll last. She was hungry too, but she knew that Suwol was hungrier. When he offered her another roll, she declined, telling him that he could have the rest.

When he finished eating, Suwol gulped water from the gourd and belched. "I feel almost human again." He tried to reach for Junja's hand, but the girl held it out of reach.

Junja crossed her arms. "Why don't you tell me what kind of errands you've been running to get yourself arrested in Jeju City?"

Suwol looked away. "Just some pig-related business for my father. It was all a misunderstanding."

The girl sighed. "No wonder they put you in jail. You're a terrible liar."

"Actually, I'm pretty good at lying. But it's really hard lying to you." Suwol tried to take her hand again, but Junja shook him off.

Suwol sniffed the air. "Do I smell that bad?"

"Stop changing the subject. Why is everything such a big secret with you? Just tell me what you've been doing."

The boy sighed. "I've made oaths. I don't want to break them."

"I saved your life." Junja started walking faster. "I think that's worth more than some oath."

By some trick of light, the blue of the sky found its mirror image in the ocean, which was now visible on the horizon. The sudden breeze that ruffled the surface of the water swept the hair off their faces. Junja looked up, sensing the airplane before she could hear it. She watched it approach, mesmerized by its speed.

The machine roared overhead, so low she could read its numbers.

Junja ducked with a cry, and Suwol reached for her hand.

"You're safe. It's gone." His arms closed around her.

"I've never seen one come so close."

"They fly down low like that when they're on search missions."

"What are they searching for?"

"Communist rebels."

Junja raised her eyebrow. "Did they see one?"

Suwol didn't answer.

The plane flew out to sea and then turned, forming a large arc in the sky. It headed back toward land, winging toward the mountain.

"They're not looking for individuals, but large encampments." Suwol felt a prick of worry.

"How do you know that?"

"Because I do."

"What about Cloud House Farm? Do they go there too?"

"Every day. And every day the planes fly lower."

"That can't be good."

"It's not."

"What are you going to do?"

"There's been talk of moving to the shore, like my Nationalist half cousin recommended." Suwol's tone veered on sarcasm.

"Maybe he knows what he's talking about. You could stay in my village."

"Would you like having me closer?"

"That depends on whether you trust me enough to tell me the truth about what you've been doing."

The boy kicked a stone from the path. "You're beginning to sound like my mother."

Junja walked faster, annoyed. Her irritation wasn't with the boy, but with herself and her unruly pleasure in being near him. She thought about the men in the marketplace and the young American who bought her dinner. She had been flattered by their attentions, but they aroused no feelings in her. Suwol, however, affected her in ways that made her blush. She wanted to touch him so badly that she had to clench her hands to keep them from reaching out.

The silence stretched out. When Suwol finally spoke, his voice cracked. "If I tell you what you want to know, would you at least look at me?"

Junja stopped walking. The boy's face lit up.

She took his hand. "Tell me everything. Especially the part about you lying naked with another man."

Twenty-One

Junja's grandmother kept her perch atop the narrow wooden seat by gripping its splintery sides. The motion of the cart on the uneven dirt road pained her, but she was grateful not to be walking. Suwol's father was trying to explain the complicated history that had led to his son being secretly shadowed by his wife's nephew.

Mr. Yang had grown up on the mountain with Kim Dal Sam, one of the alleged leaders of the Communist party on Jeju. A cabbage farmer's son, Mr. Kim had been known for his precocious intelligence. A neighboring nobleman sponsored the young man, sending him to study in Seoul. There, Mr. Kim had met Constable Lee, in a noodle shop popular with students. The two of them became friends over an argument about which kind of meat made the best broth. Their paths had diverged until they unexpectedly crossed again on Jeju, this time on opposite sides of a simmering conflict that neither man had ever imagined would turn bloody.

"And yet blood has been spilled," the old woman murmured, thinking of her daughter.

"It's as if some kind of madness has seized the government in Seoul," exclaimed Mr. Yang. "Jeju has always gone its own way. How does acting as we've always done turn us into Communist rebels?"

"You keep calling Kim Dal Sam a rebel leader." The old woman was trying to make sense of this new information. "Is he a Communist after all?" If the man had attended university in Seoul, the idea was not as far-fetched as she had first thought.

"Kim Dal Sam is leading a group of starving peasants with pitchforks. He's a thorn in the US military's side, so they've labeled him a Chinese spy and Communist rebel. Now, he's a legitimate target."

How horribly familiar this sounded to the old woman. This was how the madness began, with lies that swallowed individuals before devouring an entire country. "It started like this with the Japanese. They showed up on our doorstep, ordering us around and demanding our allegiance. No one took them seriously at first—it was too outrageous."

Mr. Yang thought of his father, who had served in the royal court and witnessed what happened there. "It's a convenient excuse, to blame everything on the invaders. But the kingdom was corrupted from within."

"Of course, it was. The royal court has always attracted the greedy and the unscrupulous. Many of the nobles were traitorous thieves who only cared about themselves and grabbing as much as they could. If the Japanese hadn't been our ruin, then the Chinese would have been. Korea is now playing the bone again between two dogs, this time Russia and America.'"

"Selfish brutes. We should have killed all the collaborators, every single one of them."

The old woman had to disagree. Anyone who believed that violence could be justified had already succumbed to the madness of war. She remembered what it was like, emerging from that delirium, realizing what she had done when she killed those

Japanese soldiers. "You would think a rabid beast like war can't sneak up on you, but it does. Knowing who's gone crazy—that's the trick."

Mr. Yang confirmed what Grandmother Goh had already guessed: Constable Lee was a man who held fast to his moral bearings. Upon his deployment to Jeju as a Nationalist officer, he had contacted Kim Dal Sam, who agreed to meet despite their conflicting circumstances. Mr. Yang, as a relative by marriage to one man and a childhood friend to the other, had been asked to host the secret gathering. It was the first time Mr. Yang had met his wife's half cousin. Constable Lee appeared to be a man of unusual intelligence and empathy.

"Yes, you're right. Mr. Lee possesses a great deal of jeong," said the old woman.

Suwol had been eavesdropping on that clandestine meeting. When Mr. Lee left the room, the boy emerged from his hiding place to pledge his loyalty to Kim Dal Sam and his service to the rebel cause.

"My wife didn't know whether to faint or to beat our son when the boy made his rash promise. She was pulling him away by his ear when Mr. Kim stopped her. He said he could use a good messenger, one familiar with the mountain paths and who wouldn't raise suspicions."

After learning of the arrangement from the boy's distraught mother, Mr. Lee had offered to watch Suwol to make sure he didn't get hurt. The situation was more fraught than Suwol's mother knew: Constable Lee would be playing a double game to justify his movements. He told his Nationalist superiors that he was following Suwol because he believed the boy might lead him to rebel leader Kim. The gambit gave the constable access to privileged information and additional resources but doubled his risk.

The old woman sighed. "That's how the constable knew Suwol had gotten into trouble in Jeju City. And why the general and the constable seemed to know each other."

Mr. Yang nodded, mouth grim. Constable Lee was walking a perilous path indeed.

The old woman looked thoughtful. "Why didn't Suwol recognize his cousin if he's met him before?"

Suwol's father coughed. "How do I say this? The man has a knack for disappearing into his work. He has quite a talent for disguise, one that might have served him well in different circumstances."

A plane roared over the cart, halting their conversation and startling the horse, which reared with a whinny. Mr. Yang jumped down to calm the beast, clucking and stroking its neck. The plane made a slow wide turn over open water before doubling back toward the mountain.

As he climbed back onto the cart, Mr. Yang watched the plane with a troubled expression. "The sooner I get home, the better I'll feel." He turned to the old woman. "My wife will want to thank you for what you did. Perhaps I could persuade you and Junja to join us for a visit? You would be our guests, and I could take you back to the village tomorrow morning."

The old woman considered. She would be able to assess the Yang family's situation while taking the next step in the scheme that she and Mr. Lee had devised. If the plan succeeded, Suwol's safety would be bolstered alongside Junja's security. Two birds with one stone, as the constable liked to say. She wished she could consult him about this last-minute change in plans, but decided to take advantage of the unexpected opportunity. How much of a difference would a night on the mountain make anyway?

The old woman nodded. "I accept your generous invitation. Let's make sure we get to the pass before the children do." She clasped her hands in her lap and hoped that the constable would approve.

Twenty-Two

Back in the forest, Constable Lee gathered pine cones and fallen branches. When the pile of kindling was large enough to last through the night, he built a fire. As the flames roared, he took off the smelly oversized jacket and stained pants that kept people at a preferred distance. Next, he unwound the bindings around his torso that held his spare clothes in place like a pot belly. He spat out the wads of wool that padded his cheeks and threw them into the fire along with the filthy uniform he had just removed.

He went to the creek and removed his underclothes and boots. He polished the boots with leaves and laundered everything else in the water, taking care to scrub out stains against the rocks. As the heat from the fire dried his clothes, he took out a small mirror and a pair of scissors. He stood on the bank, completely naked, as he cut off his long bushy hair and most of the bulk from his beard. He heated a tin of water over the fire and soaked his silk handkerchief before wringing it out and placing the steaming cloth against his face. He unfolded a razor and started shaving, taking care not to nick himself. Finally, he trimmed the hair on his head, peering into the mirror to make minute adjustments.

When he was satisfied with his handiwork, he gathered his hair and threw it into the flames. He paused on the edge of the bank to take a lungful of air before jumping into the creek. His teeth chattered as he scoured his body with handfuls of pine needles. His fingers grew numb as they scrubbed his scalp.

When he could no longer feel his feet, he returned to the fire and wiped himself off with his silk handkerchief, wringing it out as needed. His clothes were still damp, but he put them on anyway. They would dry when he sat by the fire and ate his dinner, a single roasted sweet potato, dug out from the ashes.

Before he fell asleep, he slid on a pair of gold spectacles and studied himself in his pocket mirror. He nodded, pleased, before placing the glasses back into their case. Tomorrow morning, he would pat perfumed oil on his cheeks, return to his true self, and live like a human being again.

☽

When the military truck drove by at dawn, a trim, bespectacled man stood erect by the roadside. The driver rolled down the window and smelled orange blossoms. Two soldiers ran outside from the rear of a truck. They pointed rifles at the man while the driver recited the first line of a script he had been given that morning.

The man with the spectacles rubbed his clean-shaven chin before responding with the correct phrase and code word. The driver nodded to the men with the rifles, who saluted before returning to the back of the truck. The driver raised his hand stiffly but smiled. "An honor to meet you, Lieutenant Lee. Third Platoon of the Fourteenth Regiment reporting to duty, sir."

Lieutenant Lee, formerly the constable, acknowledged the greeting with a slight dip of his combed head. The scent of orange blossom grew sweeter.

"Where are we headed, sir?"

"A little seaside village on the outskirts of Seogwipo." Lieutenant Lee sniffed as he dabbed his nose with his silk handkerchief. "But, first, a slight detour." He folded the handkerchief into a neat square and tucked it into his front pocket. "We need to find a cow."

Twenty-Three

Junja's grandmother faced Suwol's mother over a dinner table graced by some of the finest cooking the old woman had ever tasted. Junja's presence, along with the crowd of women and children at the communal gathering, prevented her from talking frankly to the boy's mother, so the old woman resorted to easy pleasantries while studying her surroundings. The Yang compound was impressive, with its high walls and bird's eye view of the ocean. She was pleased to observe, however, that it did not surpass her family's estate, which now lay in ruins, torched by the Japanese as they fled.

A marriage between her granddaughter and the eldest son of the Yang family would restore a Goh woman to a household worthy of her lineage. Her village hut was fine for hiding in, to make the world think she was an ordinary person, but this arrangement would better suit her ancestors and her sensibilities.

When Junja was led out of the dining room by a crowd of little children, Grandmother seized her chance to speak in private with the boy's mother. She shifted her position on the floor cushion, drawing up a knee and making herself comfortable.

"I've eaten well." She could have been warmer in her praise, but she wanted Mrs. Yang to know that she did not find their wealth intimidating.

The younger woman dipped her head, deep enough to acknowledge the elder's advantage of years. The old woman's smooth accent, she guessed, spoke to an expensive education on the mainland. "I am immensely grateful to share a meal with the woman who saved my silly son's life." The boy's mother smiled, dimples flashing, disarming to anyone else. Her voice, like her complexion, was soft from many years of comfortable living.

The old woman laughed out loud. "What a relief! You're not one of those uppity, sneering types." Her abrupt candor startled her hostess, who adjusted her own response accordingly.

"Why would I give myself airs? We're all equal in the eyes of God."

"So you're a Christian, eh?"

"Yes."

The old woman's golden-brown eyes glinted. "I believe in the gods of Jeju, not one who arrived in a book carried by foreigners."

"You talk like an educated person."

"I went to school in Seoul."

"The Christian missionaries run a college for women there. Have you heard of it?"

"I'm quite familiar with Ewha."

Suwol's mother started. "Did you go there?" If so, the old woman knew more about Christianity than she did.

"Long enough to conclude that the hindoongi religion was not to my taste. The son of an almighty God nailed to a cross for the likes of us?" The old woman's eyes flashed. "For a haenyeo, it's more practical to pray to the god of the seas."

Suwol's mother blushed. "I have to confess that I still ask the mountain god for help when I'm looking for gosari and herbs." She leaned forward to pour tea into her guest's cup. "My family owes you a great debt for what you did in Jeju City. Such a clever ruse to pretend that Suwol was your granddaughter's wayward husband." She kept her eyes respectfully lowered.

The old woman smiled, grateful for this easy opening. "Actually, your nephew Mr. Lee deserves credit for that idea." She blew on her tea. "He also recommended that we turn that lie into truth, given the graveness of Suwol's situation."

The boy's mother looked up quickly. "I'm not sure I understand."

"Mr. Lee says that Suwol is being watched by other Nationalist agents as well. It's the only reason his life was spared, because they believe he will lead them to the rebel stronghold on the mountain. The more your son behaves like a newlywed, the safer he will be." The old woman took a loud slurp of her tea. "I don't think this will be too much of a strain for him."

"Are you saying that something has already happened between my son and your granddaughter?" Suwol's mother kept her voice smooth, though her dismay was obvious.

Junja's grandmother chose her words with care. "There seems to be a mutual interest that will make our task less onerous than it could be. The sooner we act, the better off your son will be."

"And your granddaughter—she'll be better off too." Suwol's mother did not soften the edge in her voice this time.

The old woman's mouth turned down. Marriage to Suwol might improve Junja's future prospects, but at great risk to her present safety. "Though it pleases me to have my granddaughter marry into a yangban family like my own, Junja will be linked to a foolish boy whose ties to Kim Dal Sam have almost gotten him killed. I will be placing my granddaughter in grave danger to protect your son. These are not circumstances I'd willingly choose for her. I'm sure her mother wouldn't have either. We do what we must in dangerous times."

The boy's mother looked away, chastised. She was all too aware of her obligation to this woman, but she could not concede right away. It would be unseemly, considering the difference in their status, to agree too quickly to such an arrangement. Suwol, as the first-born son of a yangban, was far more than the girl deserved, were circumstances normal. Unfortunately, nothing about the world seemed normal anymore. The old woman's jab about Junja's mother hit its mark, reminding her of their long-standing friendship.

Suwol's mother took a deep breath. "Your daughter will have to live here, on the mountain, with us."

"And she will." The old woman understood the reasons for this woman's posturing. The rest of the conversation, however, had to be forthright. "But not until it's safe. For now, both of them must live by the sea. The mountain will be banned soon. You don't want to move under those circumstances."

The expression on the small woman's face flickered. Planes had been flying past the compound almost every day, making several passes with each visit. "God will protect us."

"Gods are not shields to be used at your beck and call. You know better than that."

Suwol's mother wrung her hands. "I can't bear to think of what will happen if we leave."

The old woman thought about the last time she had seen her family home. "Better for your children to sleep in a strange village than to die in their own beds."

Suwol's mother looked Junja's grandmother in the eye. "I will agree to the marriage on one condition. We hold the wedding here on the mountain."

The old woman pretended to mull over the prospect. She had to restrain herself from revealing her satisfaction. The conversation had played out more smoothly than she hoped, with everything proceeding in the manner she and the constable had planned. All they needed now was the cooperation of the gods.

☽

"Tomorrow?" Junja's voice stopped just short of being a scream. Did she just hear her grandmother correctly, that she was supposed to marry Suwol the next day?

The old woman flinched. The two of them had been given a very comfortable room with ample privacy. Still, the girl's voice was loud enough to have been heard by people in the main house.

"Keep your voice down."

She and Suwol's mother had consulted an astrological calendar and agreed upon the closest propitious date. The boy's parents were telling their son of the arrangement at this very moment as well.

Junja's voice lowered to a hiss. "Halmung, as much as I like Suwol, I can't marry him tomorrow!"

The old woman sighed. Choosing who and when to marry were luxuries denied to most women. Not only was Junja of age, she even liked the boy. Why was she making such a fuss? "If you want to keep Suwol safe, you two must marry. We have to make that story we told in Jeju City true."

"How will the general know? Is he coming here to check that Suwol and I are living in the same house? Doesn't he have more important work to do?"

"Constable Lee told us that soldiers are going to be stationed at our village. Any one of those men could be reporting back to the general in Jeju City."

Junja bit her lip. "Why tomorrow, Halmung? Why not a week or a month from now? Anything but tomorrow!"

"We don't have much choice, Junja. You heard the constable tell Suwol to leave the mountain before the end of the week. His mother insisted on having the wedding here. She and I agreed on the date after much careful consideration."

Even so, why had such a significant decision been made without consulting her first? Junja clenched her hands.

Grandmother laid her palms on Junja's fists. "Now you understand what being a woman means. The world will determine your path for you, without any regard for your abilities or your desires. At least you are a haenyeo on Jeju. We have more say about our lives than most women."

The old woman closed her eyes, wrung out by the frenzy of the past few days. "Had you not cared for Suwol, I never would have agreed to this. You should thank me for considering your preferences." She gave Junja a gentle push. "Let's go. They're waiting for us."

Junja stood up. She cared for Suwol, more than she wanted to admit, and the boy had been declaring his affections for her since the day they met. Everyone was moving faster than she could bear. What did Mother always say about unknown waters and unfamiliar situations? Watch, before wading in. No matter how much she tried, Junja could not fathom Grandmother's motives. Surely another way could be found to ensure everyone's safety, one that wasn't as drastic as a last-minute marriage. The girl wiped away her tears of frustration. Mother always knew how to work her way around the old woman's stubbornness. Junja sniffed, willing her tears to stop as she followed her grandmother toward the main house. No need for Suwol and his parents to know that she had been crying.

☽

Suwol's mother had instructed an auntie to find a suitable han-bok for the girl's grandmother. The old woman had demurred at first, saying that all eyes would be on the young bride, not the grandmother. When the small woman put her foot down, Grand-mother Goh stopped resisting. The woman's hospitality was fault-less, and she had no desire to look like a pauper at her granddaughter's wedding, no matter how hastily arranged.

She ran her hands over the gray silk skirt and jacket, hoping that her granddaughter's future would be as smooth and soft. Her breath caught, snagged by a familiar pain. She rubbed the right side of her belly. Something had been stirring under the surface there, fed by her anguish over her daughter's death. Instead of pulling out that weed, she had let it grow. Now its roots were reaching into the core of her being.

Had circumstances been different, she would have denied this intrusion. She would have walked up Hallasan to meditate and pray, before asking the shaman to expel the darkness with a proper ritual. But there wasn't enough time. Soon, this plant of sorrow would consume her body.

She sighed. She had to rest if she was going to make it through tomorrow's ceremony.

The door slid open a crack. "Halmung?"

The little one. The old woman smiled. "Yes, child?"

Peanut opened the door wider. "If Junja becomes my sister by marrying my brother, does that mean you'll be my grandmother too?"

"Would you like that?"

Peanut nodded. "The pigs would like you to be their grand-mother too."

"Really? How do you know?"

"They told me."

The little girl was serious. The old woman studied her bright eyes and decided to give her a gift. "Come in, so I can tell you a story."

Peanut scooted inside.

"This tale is about a warrior princess from a long time ago, when our country had a different name. She reminds me of you."

The little girl grinned as she made herself comfortable on the floor.

"The princess lived way up north in a mountainous region so wild and barren that in the winter the white clouds that people breathed out would freeze into sparkling bits of ice and fall to the ground. Because of the harshness of the land, a woman from that place was twice as tough as any male warrior from the south. The princess could shoot arrows from horseback and fight with a sword."

Peanut's eyes grew round.

"Like you, the princess understood the language of animals. She could hear the whisperings of falcons, who could sight game from high up in the sky. And she understood her horse's warnings about snakes and other dangerous animals. Because of her ability, the princess was a better hunter than any of her thirteen brothers and became her father's favorite.

"Every day, the princess rode out with her horse to go hunting, bow slung over her back, where she could reach for it quickly. One afternoon, a strange sight stopped her horse in its tracks: a crying tiger with its head bent over a stream.

"The princess positioned her bow, pointing an arrow at the beast. It had a magnificent coat that would make a splendid gift for her father. She studied the tiger carefully before deciding to target the tiger's eye.

"As she drew her bow, the tiger turned his golden gaze toward her and spoke: 'Have you come to take away my misery, princess?'

"The princess was startled, but she stayed still, bow drawn. She had never talked to a tiger before, so she didn't know what to expect. The tiger continued to talk as if it were human, telling her how grateful he would be for his life to end. As he talked, his silvery tears dropped into the stream, hissing as they merged with the water.

"'Are you giving me permission to kill you?' the princess asked the tiger.

"The tiger answered, 'I am begging you. Because I've been enchanted, the only way I can die is if your arrow pierces one of my tears before it falls into the stream.'

"The princess studied the gleaming tears as they fell. They were large and glowed like moonlight. She let her arrow fly . . .

Peanut pounced on the old woman. "And did she hit a tear?"

"No, she did not. She took another arrow from her quiver and missed again. And again. Until only one arrow remained."

Peanut covered her mouth. "That's not good."

"Yes. The princess realized that the tiger had tricked her. He stopped crying and stood up slowly, as if he were struggling to control his body. His eyes swirled, sometimes human, sometimes beastly. When she saw the powerful muscles of its haunches ripple, the princess understood that the tiger would cross the space between them in one leap.

"Everything happened in an instant. The tiger pounced, the princess leapt, and the horse bolted. Just as the princess felt the tiger's teeth sink into her neck, she heard it cry, 'Forgive me, princess!' That's when she thrust her last arrow deep into the tiger's eye, piercing one of its tears."

"Please don't tell me the princess died. I don't think I like this story."

"Yes, she died. But the tiger accompanied her into the next world, where both of them were reborn as a queen and king."

Peanut, who had crept slowly onto the old woman's lap as the story was being told, jumped off. She stood in front of the old woman, quivering with indignation. "What kind of terrible story is this? Did you make it up?"

"It's a story my grandmother told me and that her grand-mother told her. If you think about it, the story isn't that terrible. Just a little bit sad."

Peanut shook her head. "All sad stories are terrible. I don't understand why the princess and the tiger became queen and king in the next life. That would mean they loved each other and got married. Why would the princess love the tiger that killed her?"

"Because he was a prince spellbound in the form of a tiger. When they got to the next life, the princess was able to see that." The old woman smoothed the hair on the little girl's head. "Make sure you keep listening to what animals tell you. Unlike people, they are incapable of lying."

Peanut nodded before rapping the side of her head with her knuckles. "I almost forgot! Ummung told me you needed to go to bed soon because of all the work you did. I could help you fall asleep by rubbing your back. Ummung says I'm better at this than everyone else!"

"I'd like that very much."

As the old woman settled into her bed, the child sat down, crossing her legs. Breathing deeply, she rubbed her hands together briskly.

The old woman closed her eyes as Peanut massaged her back in a slow, circular motion. So precocious, this little one. She sighed. A feeling of warmth trickled down her spine. Her body eased into the mat.

The little girl continued to comfort the old woman long after her breathing slowed and she fell asleep.

Twenty-Four

Junja stared up at the darkness, feeling trapped between her grandmother's snoring and her impending nuptials the next day. Would she never fall asleep easily in this house? She turned over and punched the neck roll.

Perhaps some fresh air would help. Taking care not to rouse her grandmother, Junja slipped out of their shared comforter and crept along the floor. She slid the door open, pausing when Grandmother groaned and turned over. When the old woman's rumbling deepened, Junja shut the door.

The girl shivered and wrapped her arms around herself. The sky above her roared with light. The great heavenly river streaked across the darkness, a glowing path that divided the starry canopy in half.

How old had she been when Mother first told her the story of the weaver and the cowherder? Junja remembered how sorry she had felt for the lovers, who could only meet once a year, when magpies and blackbirds flew to heaven to form a bridge over that milky expanse. Junja blinked, trying to remember which star was the weaver and which the herder.

"That one's me. And that one's you." Suwol's voice could have been a whisper from the trees. He was pointing to the two stars Junja had been gazing at.

The girl smiled. "How long have you been outside?"

Suwol shrugged. "Not long. I was hoping you'd show up and decided to wait."

"Are you having trouble sleeping as well?"

"Who wouldn't on the night before a last-minute arranged marriage?" The boy sounded rueful.

Junja wondered if he had overheard her protesting to her grandmother. Then she wondered if he had done his own share of protesting as well.

"We don't have to go through with this, you know. Not if you have any doubts. If you're marrying me just to obey your grand-mother, we shouldn't get married at all." As Suwol ran his hands through his hair, the girl noticed again how long and graceful his fingers were.

"What choice do we have?" Junja was genuinely curious.

"I don't know. I could run away, maybe. Or go into hiding. I didn't really have a plan when I decided to talk to you."

Junja felt a rush of warmth toward the boy for considering her feelings. She wanted to return the favor. "What about you? How do you feel about getting married tomorrow?"

Suwol swallowed. "My opinions shouldn't influence you in any way."

The girl persisted. "But I want to know: If you had to marry me tomorrow, would you be doing so against your will?"

Suwol pointed up to the sky again. "That cowherd up there? He waits an entire year for just one night with his wife. You'd be surprised what a man is capable of when he's in love."

Junja's heart thumped. The boy's words made her feel like she was soaring.

Suwol's voice was shy. "I've wanted to marry you since we picked gosari together."

That morning among the ferns had been the happiest hours of Junja's life. They had been perfect, marred only by their proximity to the worst hours of her life.

Junja shivered. "I've never been as happy as I was picking gosari with you."

Suwol reached out for her hand. "We could pick gosari together as a married couple, if that's all right with you."

Junja looked at his outstretched fingers, which trembled as they waited for her to touch them. "We'll have to figure out a way to make it all right."

The boy and the girl stood, holding each other's hands, under an arch of stars.

Twenty-Five

When the sun rose the next morning, everyone agreed that the day promised to be glorious, with ideal autumn weather for a wedding. The air was brisk, but not painfully so, and the brightness of the sun made everyone feel warm. Even the children behaved, attending to their chores without having to be asked and playing among themselves without bothering their busy mothers.

In the kitchen, women chopped and mixed. The various dishes tasted exceptional, and everyone looked forward to gorging themselves at the wedding banquet that would stretch late into the evening.

The men were busy too, bringing down a barrel of makgoli that had been chilling inside a cave where giant blocks of ice from the mountain lake were stored, blanketed by thick layers of wood shavings and leaves. After several rounds of tasting, the fermented rice wine met with everyone's enthusiastic approval.

☽

Junja looked down at the dress that Suwol's mother was measuring against her. The bridal hanbok was a dainty, embroidered concoction the color of dawn. The girl shook her head regretfully, and the small woman was forced to concede that it was impossible to alter the dress to fit the girl, who stood a head taller. Mrs. Yang's murmured instructions to an auntie led to the presentation of several other silken options, all of them far more luxurious than anything Junja had ever owned. The only dress that came close to fitting was an antique dance costume. One of the aunties had dug it out of a dusty wooden chest, a forgotten legacy from a relative who once danced for the royal court.

While the jacket top was respectable, the yellow skirt was scandalous: gauzy and transparent, more appropriate for swirling about and beating drums than for a formal wedding. Suwol's mother looked pained when one of the aunties piped up that these were modern times after all and that at least the dress was an appropriate color to be married in.

"This is so pretty." Junja fingered the intricate needlework on the jacket sleeves.

"It's an old-fashioned dance costume—doesn't that bother you?" Suwol's mother was more distressed than Junja, who was sincere in her admiration.

"Not at all." Junja smoothed the skirt with care.

"It's too short. The tops of your socks will show."

"I don't think Suwol will mind." Junja looked down at her feet, which were sticking out, bare. A cousin had promised to loan her white dress socks and silk shoes for the ceremony. "If I bend my knees just a bit, the dress will hang perfectly."

Grandmother had emphasized the importance of showing just enough gratitude without fawning. Junja understood: they were not just fisherfolk, but yangban stock of old. In her grandmother's eyes, this was a marriage between social equals, so Junja had to hide her feelings of inadequacy.

"Well, even if we have to make do with the dress, the other wedding preparations will be done properly." Suwol's mother threw up her hands. "I'll take you to the bathhouse."

☽

The small woman pointed to the washing area and soaking tub and handed Junja a small lidded crock. "Please, use this special oil. It will make your hair very soft and fragrant."

The girl bowed. "Thank you very much."

"I've got to hurry back to the kitchen." Suwol's mother ran several steps before stopping in her tracks. She called out over her shoulder. "I almost forgot: one of the aunties will be coming by to give you a scrub."

As Junja soaped and rinsed herself, she looked around the bathing room, which bore obvious signs of recent use. Most likely Suwol had visited this space before her. What must he be thinking? Her heart thumped. Tonight she would be sharing a room with him, alone.

Like she did before a dive, the girl quieted herself, emptying her mind. She climbed into the tub, pausing to take a breath before sliding under the water completely. She sat on the bottom of the tub, weightless and surrounded by warmth. When she felt a tingling sensation between her brows, she opened her eyes.

Above her, the water was as smooth as glass. A woman with blurry features was looking down, her face framed by the round edges of the wooden tub.

She was probably the auntie who was going to scrub her. As Junja nodded, the woman nodded too, like a reflection. Junja closed her eyes and then opened them again. The woman was still there, staring back. She looked so familiar, as if Junja had seen her many times before.

The women reached her hand out with urgency, her mouth forming words that Junja could not hear. The girl reached out at the same time, thinking that the woman was offering to pull her out of the bath. When Junja's fingers broke the surface, the water rippled, and the woman vanished.

Junja burst out of the water, gasping. Breathing heavily, she looked for the woman, who was nowhere in sight.

"Auntie? Auntie? Where did you go?"

A squat woman with powerful shoulders rushed into the room. "Just got here, miss."

This was not the same woman. "Where did the other auntie go?"

"Other auntie?"

"The one who was just here."

Junja was visibly shaken. The stout woman had heard that the girl's mother recently died. Not surprising, if she was seeing ghosts.

"Whoever you saw is gone now, so no use fretting. I promise a scrub will make you feel much better." The auntie held out a thick hand to help Junja onto the table.

"Lie face down." The woman threw several bowlfuls of warm water onto Junja's back before picking up the scrubbing mitts.

Junja grabbed onto the sides of the table, grimacing as the auntie seemed to flay her skin. She thought about that other woman, whose familiarity haunted her. Her inability to recognize the woman's face made Junja feel oddly bereft, as if something she needed had slipped out of her fingers just when she had it in her grasp.

☽

When the plane passed over the compound, no one paid it much mind because it did what all the other planes had done, swooping down to thunder overhead before rising up to circle the top of mountain. The women setting up the wedding feast in the court-yard continued to arrange the platters without a single glance up. The men hanging lanterns for the evening's festivities kept astride their ladders, hardly noticing the roar of the engine.

No one saw how low the silvery machine dipped, skimming a cluster of trees. No one witnessed its elegant arc as it swooped back up, trailing a plume of white smoke.

But everyone heard the explosion.

☽

Inside her room, Junja was rocked by a thunderous boom. She was wearing the yellow dress, with its rippling skirts, and her hair was pinned up with silver. Her lips and cheeks were rouged, but her feet were still bare. She ran outside.

A dark silhouette was blotting out the afternoon sun. The plane flew toward Junja in a gale that scattered leaves and whipped her yellow skirts into a froth. A small object was thrown out of the plane. The glinting package seemed to hang in the sky, as if suspended by strings, before it started gyrating, tumbling through the air.

Someone yanked Junja by the arm, pulling her out of the courtyard and into the surrounding trees. A flash of heat pushed her forward, making her fall facedown into leaves and dirt. The man covered her body with his own.

Junja tried to take a breath, but the air seemed to have been sucked out of the forest.

☽

When she returned to her senses, the man was gone. Junja blinked as smoke stung her eyes. She stumbled back into the courtyard, which glowed with an uncanny orange heat.

A giant fire demon was sitting astride the main house, licking the tile roof with its forked tongue and tearing the wooden pillars with its claws. The beast panted, loud and hoarse, throwing balls of flame upon the straw roofs of the surrounding homes.

Women and men were battling the inferno with buckets and bowls of water, hurling the shining liquid into the air. The drops of water enraged the monstrous fire, which reared up and roared. The wrathful bellow rattled a man astride a ladder, who fell into the blazing chaos of the demon's belly.

"Do you remember where the spring is?" A man made of soot shook Junja out of her trance. She tore her eyes away from the searing flames and tried to speak. Her mouth was so dry she could only nod.

The blackened man thrust a cooking pot into her hands. "Go get as much water as you can!"

While she was running up the mountain path, Junja looked down. The yellow skirt was hanging in soiled tatters, and her feet were slathered in ashes and gore. That man of soot, she thought, was supposed to be her groom.

☽

The girl had always known water to vanquish fire, but this demon flame seemed unquenchable. Only the ocean could tame such an unnatural beast. Junja prayed to the dragon god to come to their aid. Every time she looked, however, the sea stayed in its place, a distant glitter on the horizon. As the sun fell, she gave up waiting for a divine wave to rise up and save them.

☽

A tendril of cloud wafted toward the half moon. Perhaps that gray mist was the last of the smoke, drifting heavenward. The beams of the main house had turned into glowing coals as large as boulders. Wisps of ash floated up, dark snow falling backward. Scattered on the ground were the dead, covered with makeshift shrouds.

Junja paused to watch, pot in hand, as a black silhouette walked by, holding a tiny figure.

There's another one, the girl thought, wondering when the bodies would stop coming. She rubbed her face. She should be crying, shouldn't she? Perhaps her eyes were scorched.

She ran back up the mountain for more water.

))

Junja dropped the bucket, wishing she could sink into the dark coolness below.

She pulled the bucket back up, feeling it lighten as water sloshed over the sides. She reached for the handle. A grimy hand stopped her.

She looked up. Suwol's eyes were two holes in a black mask. He tipped the bucket into Junja's pot before hurling it away.

The bucket hit the water with a splash and bobbed for a moment before tipping over.

Suwol yanked the bucket up again so quickly that all the water fell out. He threw the bucket and yanked it back up.

He did this again and again, throwing the bucket with such force that Junja could hear it crack against the water. As Suwol readied himself for another attempt, Junja stopped him.

He let Junja take the bucket before he sank to a crouch against the stone wall.

He covered his face as his entire body shook. "This is my fault. All of this."

Junja reached for Suwol's hands, but he pulled them away. "Don't touch me. My stupidity might end up killing you too."

Her eyes stung, but no tears came. Junja blinked. She couldn't help noticing that the heavenly river still coursed with light.

Which star was the weaver and which the herder? Why couldn't she remember?

Suwol tried to stand but lurched and fell back to his knees. "I have to fix this. I have to do something."

Junja put her hands on Suwol's shoulders. "You need water. And rest."

The boy nodded. The look in his eyes pierced the girl. "Could you give me a drink of water, please?"

Junja dipped the ladle and gave the water to Suwol. He gulped it down and asked for more.

Junja watched the boy drink. When she reached for the ladle again, Suwol flinched.

"Sorry. My nerves . . . they're not right."

Junja looked at Suwol's trembling hands. "You need to eat something. I'll go find some food."

Suwol nodded. He leaned back against the stone well.

Junja murmured that she would be right back. She rose from her squat, stifling a gasp at the pain in her feet. Suwol closed his eyes. She told him to rest until she returned, and he nodded. Twice, the girl looked back as she walked away, worried she might see him lying in a faint on the ground. Suwol stayed hunched against the well, eyes closed, as if in surrender.

When Junja returned, Suwol was gone.

Part Two

————

The water on Hallasan gathers a thousand leaves
The water in the harbor gathers the rot of a thousand ships
This heart dissolves into bitter tears
Go over the mountain with my song
Go over the sea with my song

—from "The Songs of the Jeju Haenyeo," recorded by the Haenyeo
Museum

Twenty-Six

PHILADELPHIA, 2001

Dr. Moon tried not to squirm as the pastor paused his questioning to offer a brief homily about everlasting life and a Samaritan woman at a well. He stifled a yawn and glanced to his left, where Junja usually sat. Instead of his wife, their eldest daughter, Hana, sniffed into a soggy tissue. Okja, their youngest, sat stone-faced on his right.

Whenever he was asked about the funeral arrangements, Dr. Moon paused, out of habit, so that Junja could answer. When she didn't, he would look beside him, only to be reminded again of her absence. Even now, four days later, he kept expecting her to return at any moment, as if she had just stepped out to the bathroom. How had the doctors in the emergency room described her sudden death? *An act of God.* Dr. Moon had to stifle a giggle, remembering that phrase. Of course, the divinity had attended to his wife personally. She would have expected no less.

The pastor inquired whether he had a burial plot, and Dr. Moon shook his head. He and Junja had done nothing to prepare, though they had long ago reached an age when death was no longer a surprise visitor, but familiar company. Only Junja would have known which Bible verse to engrave on her marker, which hymns should be sung, and whether her casket should be open for viewing.

Dr. Moon found himself wishing that he had passed first, if only to avoid all these decisions. It was worse than being trapped in a shopping mall. He scratched his forehead, struck by a thought. Flowers, limousine, reception menu, guest list, program, music—a funeral had the same parts as a wedding, except for the coffin. Reminded of the weddings that Junja never got to plan, Dr. Moon glanced at his daughters and winced.

The good pastor repeated himself. He was used to the distracted attention spans of the bereaved. "Will the service be Korean style or American style?"

Dr. Moon consulted his daughter's expressions. Hana was dabbing her eyes; her hands looked just like her mother's, square and strong. Okja's grimace reminded him of his grandmother, who used to frown just like that before whacking him with a willow branch. Though both of them were Korean in appearance, the girls didn't seem very Korean at all. Growing up in a land where people ate too much and laughed too loudly had turned his own offspring into foreigners.

Dr. Moon finally answered, in a soft rasp. "American style because of my daughters."

They would mourn in black instead of white. His daughters, if they ever married, would do so in white rather than the rainbow hues of a traditional Korean wedding. No wonder Americans divorced so much. They cursed their unions by draping the bride in the pale shade of death.

Dr. Moon could almost hear Junja chiding him. *You old-fashioned hick! Everyone in Korea gets married in white these days!*

The pastor steepled his fingers before addressing the daughters in his groping English. "After service, you must give some speech. Eulogy. If you devout Christian like your mom, you can talk about some Bible story or verse. Or you can talk about her sacrifice coming to America for you. Something like that."

Dr. Moon sighed. Their American daughters understood nothing about sacrifice.

☽

While the coffin was lowered into the rectangular pit, the mourners sang a sprightly hymn that had been intended to lighten the mood. Dr. Moon, who was tone-deaf, mouthed his "hallelujahs" soundlessly, as his wife had directed him long ago. Junja's portrait stared at him, a stern reminder to stay silent. He coughed to tear his gaze away and looked down at the coffin. His eyes traced the dark swirls in the glossy wood and lingered over the polished brass trim. The shininess of the coffin bothered him in a way he couldn't explain. Was it wrong to bury something so new?

After the prayer was delivered and the roses tossed into the grave, Dr. Moon stood stiff as he acknowledged the bows of friends and acquaintances. His daughters flanked him, bending awkwardly. Was he imagining it? Or could he really hear the loud, pitying thoughts of his fellow church members?

"They don't even know how to bow properly!"

"Poor woman, dying before her daughters got married."

"What will he do about those two spinsters? Aigoo!"

As custom dictated, Dr. Moon would treat everyone to lunch. They, in turn, would slip him discreet envelopes to defray the costs of the burial and service. This was how the community bound its members to each other, even past death. Junja had always joked that the ones who died first saved a fortune in funeral gifts, while those who lived long would go broke with no one to mourn them.

Dr. Moon looked around the restaurant, wondering how many of these people would be present at his own burial. He jumped as an echo of his grandmother's long-silenced voice answered that question: *"A long, long life for you because the spirits guarding you are so noble! You'll find another wife to cook for you soon!"* Her quavering voice was so clear, she could have been whispering in his ear.

Everyone praised the delicious food, but Dr. Moon worried whether Junja would have approved his choice of restaurant, an all-you-could-eat Korean buffet. He chewed and swallowed as the church ladies brought him plates, encouraging him to eat more to keep up his health. His jaw started to ache, and every mouthful stuck at the back of his throat. He put down his chopsticks.

"Eat more! That's not enough!" Grandmother again. Dr. Moon scowled. Why was she in his thoughts after so many years? He turned to his neighbor and began chatting.

After thanking the last departing guest, Dr. Moon drove home with his daughters. He asked for their opinion on the food and funeral. He fretted about the coffin, hoping that their mother did not find it too fancy. Because Junja would have prodded him to, he mentioned the eligible bachelors at the buffet. A doctor and a widowed lawyer, both men were an appropriate age and willing to consider either one of them as a prospect.

He's in shock, the two daughters thought as they listened to their father prattle. Surely, he would retreat into his habitual silence soon.

The next day, as the sisters sorted their late mother's clothing to donate to the church, Dr. Moon followed his daughters around, chattering. When Hana lifted the plastic film off a lavender wool crepe suit, he rushed over to stroke it. "Your mom made this. She copied from pictures of Elizabeth Taylor when I was in medical school. One of you must keep."

Hana set the suit aside. She pulled the lid off a box. Inside, wrapped in tissue paper, was a shiny green purse made of lizard skin.

"This is real crocodile," said Dr. Moon. "From Florida. Very valuable because crocodile is illegal now."

Okja grabbed their father's arm. "Dad, I need your help in mom's sewing room." As soon as he left, Hana buried the suit and the purse under the donation pile.

Inside Junja's workroom, plastic bins filled with bright bolts of cloth and a rainbow of spools had been stacked against a wall. The sewing machine and its stand were already gone. Dr. Moon had been shocked by how quickly the church ladies descended to clear out Junja's belongings. Ignored on a side table, travel brochures that the two of them had been collecting for his retirement still lay where Junja had left them, organized by destination: Hawaii, Australia, China, India, Greece.

"I can throw these out, right?" Okja didn't wait for her father's answer before tossing the brochures into a garbage bag.

Dr. Moon pulled them out again. He studied them, looking mournful. "Your mom only want to go to beach. No mountain. Only beach."

Dr. Moon continued talking as Okja took the boxes and bags to the hallway. He told her that in Korea a person was never very far from the shore, except in the far reaches of the North, which he had escaped as a teenager. Okja knew this much from her mother, but her father had never talked about what happened.

His voice was a monotone as he continued. He described how their cart had been stopped at the border, at a military checkpoint. Soldiers were bayoneting the pile of straw on another cart, killing a family of four. He and his mother had trembled in their hiding place under the farmer's seat, listening to the screams. Because the bayonets found only straw on their cart, he and his mother crossed the border, alive.

Dr. Moon wiped his nose as Okja swallowed her shock. She was wondering what to say when her father looked out the window and saw a blackbird sitting in a tree. The bird turned its bright eye upon him and opened its beak.

"When was the last time you visited your mother's grave?"

"Why have you been gone so long?"

"Time to go back, time to go back! Caw!"

Dr. Moon jumped. The brochures dropped from his hands, fluttering to the floor. "Did you hear that?" He pointed to the blackbird, which flew away.

"Hear what?" Okja looked at her father with concern. "Are you okay, Dad?"

Dr. Moon shook his head. Surely it wasn't what he thought. He was in America, after all. Such things didn't happen here.

☽

That night, lying in bed, Dr. Moon listened to doors slam and toilets flush, the sounds of his daughters readying themselves for the night. Junja would have admonished them to be quiet. He hoped that sleep would silence the murmuring that filled his head. Grief? he wondered; or was it guilt for being alive when Junja wasn't? Either way, the voices followed a strange script: they muttered and complained, a restless mob.

"When will someone bring us food?"

"My throat is parched."

"How long do we have to wait?"

The clamor grew so loud that he turned on his CD player and raised the volume. Bach, he was certain, would quell anything unreasonable.

Safely boxed inside a Brandenburg concerto, Dr. Moon managed to fall asleep. Inside his dream, snowflakes fell, sparkling white hexagons that shifted and whirled with the notes. As the music ended, the blizzard ebbed, revealing a snowy mountain. Dr. Moon was standing in a parking lot where every car was capped with white pillows of snow. He studied the RVs, wondering if he and Junja should rent one to drive across the country. The snow started falling heavily again, and it grew colder. Shivering, Dr. Moon walked to a small coffee stand on the edge of the lot.

A woman was standing behind the counter, attending to various machines. She was surrounded by a cloud of white steam. Dr. Moon coughed politely to get her attention. The woman turned around, revealing a pleasant face.

"I'd like a mocha, please." He spoke in his native tongue because the woman was obviously Korean. She nodded and began to prepare his drink.

Something didn't feel quite right. Dr. Moon began chatting about the weather, but the woman still didn't respond. Such a strange, unsocial person shouldn't be running a coffee stand, he thought indignantly.

When she turned around to give him his drink, the woman was smiling. She's quite attractive, Dr. Moon observed, before feeling a pang of guilt. He didn't have to feel guilty, though, because . . . As he reached for the reason, it escaped him.

The woman began talking, her smile revealing very white teeth and crimson lips. She joked in a flirting manner that relaxed Dr. Moon enough to make him blurt, "I think my wife would really like you! You should meet her!"

The smile dropped from the woman's face. As she stared, her pupils enlarged, engulfing the whites and transforming her eyes into black pits. The woman's face distorted, lengthening and graying as her skin sagged away and her mouth mawed open. The figure loomed up, stretching tall and vaporous, before it plummeted toward him. Bony fingers stretched out like talons for his heart.

Dr. Moon awoke with a gasp as his hands pushed something away from his chest. His eyes opened wide to darkness and the racing thud of his heart. He pulled the blanket up to his chin and shivered, unable to deny the truth any longer.

He was being haunted by ghosts.

Twenty-Seven

As she lay dying, Junja observed her failing body with a calm detachment. She had almost drowned twice before, so the accelerating panic was familiar. The shock of it happening on dry land, while she was still breathing, was an unexpected twist. While her body ceased its struggle, her fear was replaced by curiosity. She had come this far before; she was about to go even farther. Her heart stuttered, four final beats, as her thoughts unplugged from her brain.

Junja's awareness burst outward, euphoric in its escape from her body. She hovered high above her hospital room, looking down at the machines that surrounded her bed like miniature props in a dollhouse hospital. To her changed perception, the physical plane now appeared as limited and flat as a picture on a TV screen.

A blunt buzzing jerked Junja's attention back to her body, which arced up and dropped back down. Jagged lines of electricity were jolting her heart, which pulsed red before fading again. She was being jumped like a stalled car. Medicine seared through her blood vessels as oxygen from a machine inflated her lungs. Each breath burned, turning her lungs white-hot, but the sparks did not catch. Machines screeched warnings in vain while masked doctors and nurses swarmed around the bed, trying to reanimate a corpse.

Junja pushed away from that scene in disgust. She expanded her awareness toward the waiting room, where her husband and daughters sat frozen in poses of worry. Okja was praying, though she never went to church. Hana was clutching a scrap of tissue to her red nose. Her husband was holding his face in his hands. Was he crying? Junja tried to lift his chin to look, but her hands wafted through his face.

A doctor entered the waiting room. The two girls and Dr. Moon looked up. The doctor cast his eyes down, as if in shame, before he began to speak. Dr. Moon's face dimmed. Junja could feel her husband's shoulders hunch as his body absorbed the blow. She tried to grab him as he toppled over, but he felt insubstantial, like air.

Dr. Moon lay on the floor, eyes closed. Junja tried to stroke his cheek, but her hands passed through his face. She leaned in to listen to his heart, which skipped and faltered. With so much sorrow in their past, how much more could his heart endure? Junja wrapped her awareness around him, willing him her strength. She had failed her future grandchildren by dying too early; they could not be deprived of a grandfather too. As her tears sank into his face, Dr. Moon opened his eyes and blinked.

Junja felt a familiar memory tug at her, like a fish at the end of a line.

She drifted away from the hospital, searching for that memory. The gossamer strands that tethered her to the physical plane now trailed behind her like shiny tendrils. She floated past the tall spires of Philadelphia, feeling the days of her life eddy around her in patterns she had never perceived before. Everything that ever happened belonged to a vast ocean of time. Each moment was a wave, connected to every other wave. Junja could sense how the present turned into the past, like the shallows became the depths.

She saw her husband and daughters in the minister's office, answering questions about her service. She pushed onward, to her funeral, drawn by the sound of singing. That joyful hymn seemed more like dirge, when sung alongside a burial pit. Inside the rectangular hole, her casket gleamed, garish. If the worms didn't care, she wouldn't either.

When Junja tried to push forward, for a glimpse of her grandchildren, she couldn't see more than forty-nine days past her death. Her attempts to communicate with the living were distorted, like radio signals broken by static. Sometimes, her husband could hear her quite clearly; at other times, he seemed to be deaf. When she finally managed to capture his attention, he didn't recognize her at all.

The forgotten memory tugged at Junja again, insistent on being noticed. She followed the urge, wondering where it led. She skimmed over decades of days, which fluttered together in bright flocks. One year stood out, more vivid than the rest. She and Dr. Moon were newlyweds, new to the United States. They had lived in a red-brick building in the Bronx, and she had been pregnant with Hana.

Junja followed the memory to its source, to the hospital where Dr. Moon had worked. Her husband—so young!—was in his scrubs, walking in the hospital cafeteria. He was lifting a glass of water to his mouth when his hand stalled halfway. The glass started shaking so hard that it rattled against his teeth. The water leapt out like a creature possessed, escaping in every direction. As the glass splintered around him, he had landed on the floor.

Shadows from their past had risen up, dragging him down like an anchor. Junja, who had shared that burden, had already succumbed to its weight. She could still hear the clamor of those forgotten souls, begging for remembrance.

Why fear something she had already survived? Junja steeled herself to act. She had to lighten the load that her husband now carried alone, but she could not do it without his help.

Junja allowed her awareness to expand. She plumbed deeper, into the depths. A riptide of memories rushed through her, carrying her back toward a shore they had fled, so many years ago. What had been forgotten about the mountain must now be remembered, and what had been taken from the sea must now be returned.

Twenty-Eight

Two days after his wife's funeral, Dr. Moon phoned his eldest daughter Hana, who had returned home to Brooklyn. When she didn't answer, he called her younger sister in Chicago. Okja picked up on the second ring.

"Hi Okja, I am going to Korea day after tomorrow. Don't worry. Everything is fine."

"Uh, Dad, did you just say you're going to Korea?"

"Yeah, I buy the ticket today."

"Are you okay, Dad? This is kind of sudden."

"Everything is okay. This is just the Korean way when someone dies." Dr. Moon nodded at the phone, satisfied he had fulfilled his obligation to his daughters. There was no point in telling them about the ghosts, which were a private matter. He was about to hang up when Okja's tinny voice reached out.

"Dad? Dad? Are you still there?"

Dr. Moon brought the receiver back up to his ear. "You tell Hana, okay? I will come home soon. Two week."

Then he hung up.

))

Dr. Moon filled the kettle with water and set it on the stove to boil. He needed to put something soothing in his belly. Both his daughters had called back multiple times, with complete disregard for the expense. Their nasally words grated his ear. "Why are you going back to Korea so suddenly? You and Mom told us you never wanted to go back!" The interrogation had exhausted him, because he had to explain himself without mentioning the ghost problem, which he couldn't translate into English properly.

He blinked at the instructions before tearing open the instant ramen package with trembling fingers. Junja would have known what to tell them. She had studied English as a second language at a community college for five years, earning straight A's.

Dr. Moon filled the noodle bowl with boiling water. The tremor of his hands had become more noticeable since the funeral. Junja had been so strong and healthy that he had always assumed he was going to pass first.

"Silly man! Don't you remember what the fortune tellers told you? You'll live long enough to have two wives!"

Was that Junja's voice? Or his grandmother's? He waved his hand to indicate that he had gotten the message.

Perhaps being away from the ocean for so long had dried up something vital in his wife, sapping her body of its vigor. They had lived only an hour's drive away from the Atlantic Coast, but the water there never felt right to Junja. Maybe she would have lived longer in California, next to the Pacific.

She had often reminisced about the fish she ate as a girl, especially when she served mackerel for dinner, simmered in a spicy sauce to disguise the stink of its long-frozen flesh. *"Nothing at all like the fish of my girlhood. We could eat it raw, because the taste was so clean and delicious. Not like this smelly thing."* She would frown, poking the dull silver skin with her chopsticks.

Dr. Moon did not share his late wife's nostalgia for brine. Instead, he longed for the soft sweetness of peaches, their fuzzy skin bursting under his teeth as the sun-warmed juices dribbled down his chin. His boyhood home had been nestled against the bottom of a hill too small for a proper name. Summer there meant peaches and plums, followed by the crisp bites of fall: apple-pears and persimmons. He had climbed the smaller trees, their rough bark scraping his fingers as he plucked the fruit for his mother, who was always smiling back then.

"You need a new wife to cook for you. You can't eat that junk!"

Dr. Moon studied the curly things floating in the plastic bowl as if they were some kind of exotic creature. These mass-produced noodles didn't taste anything like the ones he'd eaten as a child. Such a rare treat wheat noodles were, eaten a few times a year after Father traveled to Seoul and returned with the dusty flour sack hidden safely in his shirt.

"Go fetch an egg," Mother would order. He would snatch the warm egg away from a sleepy hen and come running back. Mother would mix the precious flour with water, egg, and salt, adding ground buckwheat to bulk up the dough. After she rolled out thin circles with a wooden dowel, she'd slice them into strips and drape them over the fence rail. He had to guard the noodles as they dried, fanning away the flies. *"We don't want maggots to hatch in our bellies!"*

Dr. Moon could almost smell those noodles, bubbling in a broth of soy and mushroom. His mouth watered, and he glanced about, worried. Hearing voices was bad enough. What if something grotesque made an appearance? Did ghosts look like they did while they were alive and happy? Or did they resemble their appearance at the moment of their death? Junja, he knew, would not be pleased by the latter.

Dr. Moon pushed the instant ramen away and decided to eat lunch at the Korean restaurant near the university. He paused by his late wife's empty chair, putting his hands on its back for support. As he walked to the front door, he passed his suitcase. He had already packed everything he needed for his return to Jeju Island.

)

On the red-eye to Los Angeles, Dr. Moon was squeezed in between two men wearing red and green jerseys who drank beers while arguing about sports all night. Each time he managed to nod off, he was jolted awake by a stray elbow or a sharp laugh. When the plane landed, Dr. Moon was so tired that he stumbled like a sleepwalker onto his connection with Korean Air.

He sighed as he sank into his seat, grateful that no one was sitting near him. After observing the person across the aisle take off his shoes and turn his seat into a recliner with the push of a button, Dr. Moon did the same. He pulled the scratchy blanket up to his chin and covered his eyes with the sleeping mask that came bundled in a bag with earplugs, a toothbrush, and a shoe horn.

The last time he had traveled such a distance was forty years earlier, when he and Junja took their first plane ride while moving to America. He had sat rigid in his chair, not wanting to disturb Junja, who had fallen asleep on his shoulder. When she woke up, the two of them had surreptitiously eaten the rolls of kimbop she had packed, hoping no one was bothered by the smell. The first meal they were served on the plane had tasted so bad that they had to force themselves to finish, to avoid offending the stewardess. The next time she offered them food, they had smiled politely, shaken their heads, and rubbed their bellies, pretending to be full.

Now, he was flying back in business class on a Korean airline with flight attendants who spoke in Korean, offering a selection of Korean or Western food once the plane reached cruising altitude.

He had chosen the Korean menu with relief, grateful such options now existed. Though he was alone this time, he could feel Junja beside him, urging him to eat. With every bite, his dread began to shift, turning into a wary hope. Perhaps everything in Korea had changed so much that his memories would be altered, transformed into something he could examine without fear.

Dr. Moon reached into his jacket pocket to make sure that the small package he had slipped there for safekeeping was still there. He whispered as he patted it. "I don't know what you want, but I'm taking you home." He waited for a response from his invisible companions, expecting them to start their noisy babble. The only noise he heard was the dull roar of the plane engines, which lulled him into a deep sleep unruffled by dreams or voices of any kind.

> ☽

Dr. Moon blinked as he walked through the terminal at Incheon International Airport. Was this really Korea? Everything was so modern and new. He could have been in America still, except that the signs were all written in hangul, with English translations below.

The novelty of seeing so many faces like his own distracted Dr. Moon, who bumped into a soldier wearing a red beret and cradling a semiautomatic rifle. Dr. Moon gasped, leaping away as his bag clattered to the floor.

"Are you all right, sir?" The young man looked with concern at Dr. Moon's terrified face. He reached down to pick up Dr. Moon's bag.

"Run away!"

"They're coming after us!"

Dr. Moon clapped his hands over his ears. The soldier pushed the bag toward him. Dr. Moon took the handle and backed away, bowing. The soldier nodded in sympathy. Lots of war trauma in the older generation. The strangest things would set them off.

The panicked clamor that only Dr. Moon could hear subsided, ebbing into a low murmur as he walked to the baggage carousel. He took out a slip of paper. He was supposed to find a pay phone and call his friend from here.

"Hey there!"

Dr. Moon glanced up, then looked back down at the paper. Damn ghosts, trying to distract him again. He squinted harder.

"Hey there! Have bugs eaten your ears, you rascal?" A hand grabbed his shoulder.

Dr. Moon looked up into the eyes of an old man with a familiar grin. The shine of his round head was interrupted by a few strands of black hair that had been combed and pressed in place. Bright eyes peered at him through a pair of wire spectacles. The man pulled Dr. Moon into a rough embrace.

"Gun Joo, you look exactly the same, you handsome jerk. Except your hair has gone silver."

"Kim Dong Min! Aigoo, is it really you?" The words stopped in Dr. Moon's throat. "What are you doing here at the airport? Wasn't I was supposed to take a taxi to your house?"

"I haven't seen you for a hundred years! Did you really believe I'd make you take a taxi? I was joking!" Dong Min chuckled as his eyes turned shiny. "I'm so sorry you had to come back alone by yourself, without Junja." He gripped Dr. Moon's hands while his mouth trembled.

☽

As the car needled through traffic in a metropolis he didn't recognize, Dr. Moon remembered the first time he'd met Dong Min, on the ferry landing at Mokpo. They were both new recruits but he had come alone, while Dong Min had been accompanied to the dock by his mother. When the round woman noticed the boy standing alone, her broad face had burst into a smile. She dragged her son over to make the introductions.

"Dong Min-ah, this boy here will become your best friend. If you stay near each other, both of you will survive what is coming. Young man, what is your name?"

He had been so startled that he dropped his bundle, which spilled open. As he picked his belongings off the ground, Dong Min had crouched down to help him. The fat boy had whispered, "My mom's a shaman. Just nod and agree with whatever she says, no matter how weird it sounds."

As soon as they reached the military processing center, he and Dong Min had been herded into a tent, where their hair was buzzed short. They had exchanged their homespun clothes for smooth green uniforms and were told to wait in line for their assignments.

He remembered how he had peeked into the green rucksack, dazzled by its gleaming contents: a personal aid bag, a canteen, and a metal mess kit. All made in America, just like the stiff black boots he had left untied until another soldier showed him what to do. Dr. Moon could still remember how shiny those boots were, the first pair of leather shoes he had ever owned.

The sergeant who was handing out the assignments closed his notebook when the two boys approached him. Dong Min had cleared his throat loudly before asking for their orders.

"You'll have to wait until the next boatload comes in." The man didn't bother to look up.

"When will that be?" Dong Min did not hesitate to talk to strangers, while Dr. Moon, with his stutter, had been the complete opposite.

"Day after tomorrow."

"What are we supposed to do until then?"

The man had spat. "Do I look like your mommy?"

All the boys ahead of them in line had received their assignments and were officially soldiers. They would sleep in bunks and eat in the mess hall that night. He and Dong Min, however, still had to fend for themselves.

Dong Min had said he was hungry—some things never change, thought Dr. Moon. The fat boy noticed the buildings near the docks and suggested that the two of them wander over to find something to eat. Too ashamed to admit that he had no money, he had given Dong Min one of the rice balls he had packed for himself.

Dong Min had taken an enormous bite from the ball, which didn't last very long.

"That's pretty good." The fat boy had licked his fingers. "What about that other ball? Aren't you gonna eat it?"

Dr. Moon remembered how he had lied, saying that he would eat it later. "I'm not very hungry right now."

"I'll eat it, then. Before it spoils." Dong Min was about to grab the remaining ball, but Dr. Moon had snatched it instead, cramming it into his own mouth.

The fat boy had stared at him. "If you're so hungry, why did you say you weren't?"

When he didn't answer, Dong Min had crossed his arms. The expression on his face had been stern. "You just gave me half your food, didn't you?" Then he grinned.

That moment had marked the start of a friendship that spanned more than fifty years. His relationship with Dong Min had outlasted his marriage to Junja. Why had he not visited his friend in all that time? Dr. Moon felt an ache in his throat, remembering how Dong Min had laid his arm across his shoulders to draw him close.

The fat boy had leaned in, whispering so he couldn't be overheard. "My mom gave me a lot of cash. Just in case. Because you shared half of all your food with me, I'm gonna share half of all my food with you."

Twenty-Nine

JEJU ISLAND, 1948

As she taught Junja about the sea, Grandmother had taught her about the rest of the world. The entire universe was an expression of eum yang, the divine energies that gave shape and form to every object, being, and action. These energies expressed themselves as opposing forces that swirled around each other in an unceasing cycle: dark and light, moon and sun, woman and man.

Taking breath into the body was yang. Breathing out, eum. Land was yang; water was eum. Diving into the ocean was safer for women, who were creatures of eum like the fish and plants they gathered. Even so, a diver had to gird herself with every element to enter the watery realm of a god that did not welcome humans kindly: the lungful of air, the heat of the fire, the weight of the stone, the metal knives and picks.

Grandmother liked to boast that as the favored playground of eighteen thousand eum goddesses and yang gods, Jeju was irresistible to such lower divinities and spirits as gashin and dotchebbi. "Gods, goddesses, fairies, and goblins are everywhere on Jeju, watching and listening. Heed what you say and do!" When she was younger, Junja used to imagine these ethereal creatures hiding behind trees and rocks to keep an eye on her.

Were the gods still watching? Or had they diminished into such shadows that they could scarcely be considered gods anymore? After what she had witnessed on the mountain, the girl hardly knew what to believe.

Junja and her grandmother had left Cloud House Farm while smoke still drifted from its embers. As the Yang family mourned, one of the aunties had brought them a bundle of food in lieu of a proper farewell. The woman didn't need to explain that the surviving remnants of the uneaten wedding feast now furnished the altars for the dead. Junja and her grandmother had been invited to stay for the three days of funeral rites, but the old woman demurred with regret. They had to return to their village before soldiers closed the pass.

Junja had been shocked by how slowly her grandmother shuffled, the stoop of her back more pronounced. The old woman had fallen to her knees when the shroud was lifted off the smallest body. She knew who lay there before the child's own mother did.

Peanut had been found in the pigsty, arms wrapped around the dog, whose yellow fur was singed off. Boshi had clung to life to guard the little girl's body; he died, whimpering, as she was pulled away. The girl's mother had gone out of her mind when she couldn't rouse her daughter and had to be sedated with a strong brew of herbs.

The small body had been prepped by two aunties who sobbed while they sponged the burnt flesh. Peanut's right fist had been curled shut around a white pebble that glistened against her chubby palm. Grandmother made the aunties promise that the child would be buried with the stone.

When Junja and her grandmother reached the pass, Suwol had emerged from the trees like an apparition. He was in the same tattered clothes he had been wearing at the well. Soot still blackened his unwashed face. Strapped to his back was a bulging pack.

"Someone is coming to give us a ride to the end of the foothills." Suwol's voice was flat. "Soldiers are everywhere, guarding the blockades." The whites of his teeth and eyes looked eerie against his charcoal skin.

Junja didn't dare ask why he wasn't in mourning, and Suwol didn't offer any explanations. When he vanished at the well, she had screamed out his name until her voice clogged with smoke. Where had he nursed his agony, alone like a beast? Sorrow still cloaked him, a shroud too heavy for her to lift. Junja held her hands by her sides, clenched into fists.

A pock-faced man arrived on a cart bristling with pitchforks and hoes. Suwol helped the two women up before climbing on himself. Junja faced the boy, who hung his head as his shoulders slumped. The scholar's band was gone, and his hair dusty with ash. His hands dangled, limp and dirty. The journey was too short for words, the silence full of everything that couldn't be spoken.

When the cart stopped moving, Suwol looked up into Junja's eyes. The girl opened her hands as he moved close. He pressed a small object into her palm. "This is all I can give you now."

Suwol's long fingers slid out of her grasp. Junja looked down at the dark smudges he had left behind, along with the small brass lighter.

After helping Junja and her grandmother off the cart, Suwol climbed back on. He didn't look back and he didn't say goodbye. Junja stared at the back of Suwol's head as she tried to remember how to breathe.

Grandmother had stood rigid beside her until the cart rattled out of sight. Then the old woman turned, took a step, and collapsed.

☽

The cool depths of the ocean were a relief to Junja, who could still feel the heat from the devastated village radiating from her skin. She had carried her grandmother home on her back, wearing a scowl so forbidding that when they approached the blockade, none of the soldiers dared interrogate them.

The old woman clung to her granddaughter, whose fury made her think of her own anger, long extinguished. She begged Junja to make an offering to the god of the sea.

"Where was the sea king while Cloud House burned?" Junja demanded.

Grandmother had sagged against her, exhausted by Junja's seething emotions. "The mountain is its own god and has its own ways. Please, promise me you'll visit the sea king's shrine."

Junja was keeping that promise, but not out of piety. She felt sorry for her grandmother, who believed in divinities that were impotent or cruel. Despite her continuous praying, the old woman had not been able to rise from her bed since their return home. This woman who could name every god, great and small, could no longer prostrate herself before them. Her body lay like a broken shell.

With her first dive into the ocean, Junja's temper had cooled, out of habit. Water work required complete mindfulness in the depths to guard against deadly mistakes. Now that she was alone, the other divers gone, she was left to reckon with the sea by herself. She held onto her gourd as she floated, forcing herself to remember. The falling bomb. The demon fire. The tiny body. And Suwol by the well, black drops falling from his eyes. When she couldn't bear any more, she screamed out her rage and grief before diving down toward the sea shrine.

An outcropping of black rocks jutting up from the sea floor, the shrine resembled an altar, hidden by a curtain of undulating kelp. Upon its flat table a profusion of corals grew, looking like offerings of exotic foodstuffs. Fish of varying sizes drifted above this table in a slow-moving halo lit by beams of sunlight. The shrine had once been home to an eel, so enormous that its girth matched the span of a young girl's waist and so ancient that it had turned translucent, more spirit than flesh. Some haenyeo claimed that the eel was actually the sea king in one of his many guises, because the creature was always flanked by two large prawns that waved their antennae and rubbed their claws just like the preening attendants of a royal court.

The shrine seemed to glow as Junja plummeted, arms outstretched. She stopped short of its rocky table, hovering for a moment before floating down to kneel on the sand. She dropped her offering, a large abalone, next to a flame-red piece of coral. As she bent her head and pressed her hands together, small bubbles clustered by her nose.

Silently, Junja chanted the words that she had been taught, words that she once believed would summon the gods, who would respond. This time, doubt burdened her prayer. Were the gods listening? Did they care?

An unexpected clamor in her lungs distracted her. She had been diving all day without incident, so she ignored the warning. As soon as she dismissed the sensation, she realized her mistake. Trying to quell her panic, Junja kicked off the ocean floor, swimming up as fast as she dared.

Midway, a dark desperation surged through her body. Her heart drummed in her ears while blackness dulled the edge of her vision. She remembered these sensations from the first time she ever dove. She had survived that terrible dive, but her young friend had not.

Just as it did then, Grandmother's voice came to her aid: *"Do not succumb to doubt. Keep moving and do not stop. Even if you faint, your body will return to the surface, where the others will find you."*

Junja fixed her attention on the rippling sun that was guiding her back to the realm of light, heat, and air. She flew up through the depths, swooning just as she surfaced. When her head rose above the water, she did not scream or gasp. She floated, silent, head lolling, eyes rolled back.

Thirty

2001

Dong Min chattered about his family throughout the drive, which ended in the subterranean car park of a large apartment complex. He had five grandchildren: a boy and two girls belonging to his eldest son and Dr. Moon's namesake, while both his daughters each had one son.

Dr. Moon was surprised by the sadness that welled up at the mention of those grandchildren. Junja had never felt guilty about their lack of sons; she was very much a Jeju woman that way. The failure of their daughters to marry and have children, however, had bothered her more than she ever admitted.

"I'm sorry I never came back to visit you. We made plans a couple times, but something always came up."

Dong Min punched Dr. Moon in the arm. "Hey, I'm equally to blame. You make a long list of all the things you want to do when you have the time and money . . . and then before you know it, you're out of time, even if you have the money! I haven't gone back to Jeju since the two of us left. It's a popular honeymoon destination now, the Hawaii of Korea. Can you believe that?"

The two men strolled the grounds so that Dr. Moon could get some fresh air before dinner. Dong Min proudly pointed out all the features of the development to his friend, whose lukewarm reaction made Dong Min shake his head. "You don't remember any of this, do you?"

Dr. Moon glanced again at the buildings, all recently constructed during his long absence from Korea. He peered at a large hill in the background, which looked vaguely familiar. "What am I supposed to remember?"

"This is where my mother's house and gardens used to be!" Dong Min pointed to an enormous tree shading one of the entryways. "That tree was in the center of the outer courtyard. Don't you recognize it?"

Dr. Moon walked toward the large chestnut tree and placed his palm against the gnarled bark, looking around in shock. "This is Samseong-dong? What happened?" Dr. Moon remembered open fields and groves of trees alongside the occasional building and modest homes. The Buddhist temple had dominated the area.

Dong Min chuckled. "My old neighborhood is the ritziest part of Gangnam now. Welcome to the Beverly Hills of Korea, my friend."

The last time Dr. Moon touched this tree, he and Junja had joined Dong Min and Yoonja to sit under its branches on a warm autumn night. He was in scrubs, and Junja was wearing a dress she had made while working in his aunt's sewing shop. Yoonja and Dong Min were still in the aprons they wore at the restaurant they had started with funds from Yoonja's sister, who ran a sandwich shop in Chicago with her GI husband. The four of them had talked about their day while gazing up at the green spiny nuts, wishing they were ripe enough to roast.

The round man looked around to make sure no one was in earshot and leaned in close, pitching his voice low. "We held on until after the Olympics. Land prices had already gotten crazy by then, but they went up even more after that. When we sold, we became millionaires overnight."

Dong Min thumped the tree affectionately. "All my children and most of my grandchildren are upstairs, waiting to meet you. We're gonna have a huge feast, in your honor. I told Yoonja to cook all your favorites. Just pretend they are even if they aren't, okay?"

"How is she?" Dr. Moon remembered how stoic she had been at the American hospital in Busan, where military doctors had stitched together the separate halves of her upper lip.

"Can you believe her cooking has gotten even better over the years?" Dong Min patted his belly. "Look at me! That woman could make dirt taste delicious. Her soup got better, too—hard to believe, right?"

Yoonja's red seaweed soup had been the unlikeliest of love potions. During their first night on Jeju, before they were posted to Junja's village, Gun Joo and Dong Min had gone to the Yum Yum Café for dinner. As he listened to her recite all the items they could order, the fat boy had stared at Yoonja so earnestly that the girl turned bright red, convinced he was repulsed by her harelip. But Dong Min hardly noticed the girl's disfigured mouth. He later claimed that he had fallen in love with her spirit, which he swore he could taste in her food.

"I'll never forget that dinner she made at your mother's house, when you first introduced them." Dr. Moon's stomach rumbled. "Some nerve, making your girlfriend cook for your mother on the first day they meet!"

"How else was I going to convince the old witch that Yoonja had to be my wife?"

"The look on your mother's face would've turned anyone else to stone!"

He and Junja had accompanied the hopeful couple to the imposing house. The three of them had waited outside in the large courtyard, with its vegetable beds, fruit trees, and rock gardens. After greeting Gun Joo more effusively than her own son and complimenting Junja upon her attractiveness, Dong Min's mother had glared at Yoonja's bandaged mouth with her disapproving lips pressed tight.

When the formidable woman finally spoke, her voice sounded like cracking ice. "Did you bring this girl to my home because you have some sort of interest in her?"

Dong Min, who was kneeling alongside Yoonja, had lowered his forehead to the floor. "Yes, mother. I would like your permission to marry her."

"What happened to her mouth?"

"She had surgery to fix a cleft palate."

"You want to marry a woman who has nothing but a very obvious flaw? Why can't you find someone like her?" Dong Min's mother had gestured to Junja, who was pretending to examine a chestnut tree.

Dong Min had gulped before blurting out, "Mother, can you please allow her to cook dinner for you? You'll understand everything then."

"Typical man, relying on your lower half to make decisions for you." The expression on her face had been fearsome, but Dong Min's mother had allowed Yoonja inside her kitchen.

"Wanna hear something crazy? Mother willed everything directly to Yoonja and not to me!" Dong Min tried to sound indignant, but pride warmed his voice. "She told me that marrying Yoonja was the smartest thing I ever did. And then she told Yoonja that she had to die after me, so that I would always be well cared for. What kind of crazy mother wants her son to die before her daughter-in-law?"

Tears stung Dr. Moon's eyes. "When did your mother pass?" After their escape to the mainland, the generous woman had cooked more meals for him and Junja than his own mother had. Dong Min had been more like a brother, sharing his mother so easily.

"Last year. She would've been so happy to see your handsome mug again! She had a good long life. Who gets 98 years these days? She told me the night before she died that she was going to stop doing shaman work and take a vacation. Said she wanted to see Hawaii. The next morning, she was gone."

Dr. Moon swallowed. What was he going to do now? He had come back to ask for her help. It had never occurred to him that she might not be able to. "You've never gone back to Jeju? Not even once?"

The portly man shook his head. "No. But Yoonja has. Says everything's changed so much I wouldn't recognize it. Swears I'd really like it. But I just can't."

"I don't want to go back either, but I think I have to."

"Why do you have to?"

"I wish your mother were still alive. She'd know what to do."

"Wait, what's wrong? Do you need to see a shaman?"

Dr. Moon rubbed his nose, feeling self-conscious. He crossed his arms and stared up at the chestnut tree, as if searching for the right words. When he finally responded, he was stuttering. "It's g-ghosts, Dong Min. Ever since Junja passed, they t-talk to me and won't leave me alone."

The fat man sighed with gusto. "What a shame you missed my mom. Ghosts were her specialty."

Dr. Moon relaxed, relieved that Dong Min didn't think he was crazy. "When I confided in a Korean friend in Philadelphia, that person recommended that I see a psychiatrist!"

"We went through some really hard times because of that kind of limited thinking." Dong Min shook his head. "When Western medicine became fashionable, Mother had to put up with all sorts of nonsense. People would cross the street to avoid her. One time, when she was at market, one of those pious Christians spat in her face and told her she was working with the devil."

Dong Min frowned, remembering. "The seventies were the worst. Mother had to go into hiding then because the government was putting shamans in jail! Crazy, right? When I think about it, my blood still boils. People changing their beliefs overnight like they were changing their underwear!"

Dr. Moon squirmed. Junja had done the same, and he had followed. They were living in America, after all.

Dong Min crossed his arms. "Turns out Western medicine couldn't fix everything after all. The work of healing, Mother always said, had to start with forgiveness first. Slowly, her customers started trickling back. Those pious Christians showed up, too, disguised in scarves and sunglasses. Broken hearts, cancer, toothaches—it was all the same to Mother. She always got results."

Dong Min interrupted himself to squint at his watch. "Yoonja will kill me if we're late for dinner. I'll think about your problem while I eat. That's when I do my best thinking."

☽

Dr. Moon lowered himself onto the sleeping mat in the guest bedroom that used to belong to Dong Min's mother. He could hear Yoonja cleaning up the dishes from dinner, helped by her two daughters. He loosened his belt and sighed with exhaustion, noticing for the first time that he hadn't heard any voices since entering Dong Min's home. Surely, they were going to start up again. He cocked his head to listen.

A loud rap on the door made him jump.

"I'm coming in," Dong Min announced as he opened the door. He settled himself on a floor cushion with a groan. "Yoonja did some research. Apparently, all the best shamans live on Jeju. Convenient, eh? She got a recommendation for someone who should be able to help you with your problem."

"Thank you." Dr. Moon squeezed his friend's hand.

"I can't let you go by yourself, though." Dong Min took off his glasses to clean them. His face looked strangely youthful without the wire frames.

"What do you mean?"

"I'm going with you."

Was that a ghostly cackle? Dr. Moon nodded absently.

"Hey, are your ears going bad? I just told you I'm going too!" Dong Min grabbed Dr. Moon's hand and held their clasped hands up high. "You and me, together on Jeju, just like old times. Whaddya think of that, my friend?"

Dr. Moon looked up. "Really? You're serious?"

Dong Min lowered their arms, grinning. "After everything we survived down there, I can't let you go by yourself. Yoonja would never let me hear the end of it." A sudden frown creased his wide forehead. "This time, however, we're flying. No more ferry crossings for me."

☽

While the plane circled Jeju to land, Dr. Moon scanned the shoreline, wondering where the old boat landing used to be. Fifty-three years earlier, Jeju City had been a modest seaport with wooden buildings. He and Dong Min had arrived in October; seven weeks later, they took the same ferry back to the mainland. Dong Min had somehow convinced Yoonja to join them while her sister helped Junja sell a silver hairpin to an American soldier for an exorbitant sum. A winter gale had ambushed them on open water. As the boat bucked on the roiling waves, he and Dong Min had lain in the hold, retching and shivering, while the girls braved their way to the deck to beg the sea god for safe passage. They all survived the crossing, but Junja never prayed to the sea god again.

The taxi deposited the two men at an intersection where someone's laundry rack full of kitchen towels was drying in a patch of sun, ignored by passersby in the street. Yoonja had reserved a hotel room for them inside the shaman's quarter, which the driver refused to enter because he had a fare on the other side of town.

"Did Jeju City have a shaman's neighborhood back then? Or is this something new?" Dr. Moon was trying to ignore the pain in his right heel, which twinged with each step.

Dong Min stopped to dab his forehead with a handkerchief. "Back then, the entire city used to be smaller than this neighborhood. Don't you remember?"

Dr. Moon stumbled on a cobblestone. Everything around him seemed to shimmer, like a mirage. The echoing vastness of Junja's absence expanded, even here, in this place that no longer resembled anything they once knew. They had walked by each other's side for so many years, crossing an ocean and a continent of time together. He had circled back, alone, to the place where they started their journey. He had hardly known Junja when he last stood on these shores. Now that he was back, he hardly knew himself, without her beside him. How could he remember anything without her?

A sensation swelled in Dr. Moon's chest, surging toward his throat. He tried to speak but could only manage a gasp. The words he wanted to say were obliterated, washed away by the tears he had been holding back since the funeral. Dong Min, seeing his friend sob in such a forsaken manner, started to cry as well. The pedestrians walking by the two weeping men turned their heads and pretended, out of respect, not to notice.

☽

After a short stroll through the neighborhood to stretch their legs, Dr. Moon and Dong Min ate dinner in a small restaurant with five tables.

"You know, whenever I eat anything made with beef, I remember that cow we had to walk all the way to Lonely Rock Village. Remember how we had to camp outside with nothing to eat but sweet potatoes?" Dong Min slurped a long tangle of noodles and stuffed some spinach into his mouth. "I like to believe that all the pleasures of my old age are a kind of payback for the suffering I had to endure in my youth."

The two of them had ridden their first motorized vehicle together on Jeju Island: a large green military truck. They had whooped with excitement as it rumbled down the road with thrilling speed. At their second stop outside the city, an officer had climbed into the rear of the truck to ask if anyone had experience with cows.

Dr. Moon wasn't going to admit that he knew more about cows than he wanted to. He and his mother had worked for a wealthy farmer shortly after their harrowing experience crossing the border in a straw cart. They had milked the beasts, cleaned stalls, and harvested hay from the fields, among other lowly tasks. At the end of the season, the farmer had refused to pay them, saying that the milk they had drunk for lunch had been deducted from their wages.

Dong Min had poked him, asking in a whisper if he knew something about cows. As soon as he nodded, Dong Min's hand had shot up. The officer, who wore gold spectacles and smelled like oranges, introduced himself as Lieutenant Lee. After interrogating the two boys, the lieutenant assigned them the task of walking the beast he had just acquired to its final destination, Junja's village.

Dr. Moon crunched on a cube of pickled radish as he remembered that two-day trek. His feet had started bleeding in the new leather boots, and the pain had grown excruciating with each step. Just when he thought he couldn't bear it any longer, a numbness had crept over his feet, and he had continued walking.

"I've never been able to wear boots since that time." Dr. Moon tilted the bowl and swallowed the broth.

☽

The shaman's home was a small hut with a corrugated tin roof and stone walls. A strip of garden dense with foliage and cluttered with black volcanic stones formed a green buffer between the busy street and the modest home.

"Must be an ancient crone who cooks everything the old-fashioned way." Dong Min gestured toward a basket of sweet potato slices drying in the sun and a clothesline heavy with dried mackerel.

The owner of the noodle shop had directed them to the place, dismissing the name Yoonja had given them as a fraud that only out-of-towners consulted. This shaman came from a venerable family and was a favorite with locals. "The best shaman on Jeju. Doesn't take shortcuts and respects tradition."

Dong Min sniffed as he studied the modest surroundings. "If she's so good, why does she live like this?" He gestured at a pile of wood. "Still using wood to heat her house and cook? That's beyond traditional—it's crazy backward." He nonetheless spoke politely as he shouted through the front door.

"Hello? We've come to see the shaman!"

A middle-aged man with a comb-over opened the door. His voice was pitched low. "Do you have an appointment?"

"We came from the noodle shop. The owner recommended this place."

The man nodded. "My sister is with another client now. Please, come inside and wait."

The two men ducked as they stepped through the low door-way. They took off their shoes and put on faded plastic slippers from the shoe shelf. A faint muskiness clung to the air, a familiar scent that Dr. Moon couldn't place.

Dong Min whispered, "This place feels sorta spooky, doesn't it?"

Dr. Moon nodded, feeling anxious.

☽

A slight sparrow of a woman with white-streaked hair was kneeling in front of an altar. Multiple strands of wooden prayer beads were draped between her fingers as she rubbed her palms together in supplication. When the shaman finally looked up to acknowledge them, the two old men gasped. Her startling beauty, so unexpected in this modest setting, made her seem far younger than the shapeless ahjumma clothes she was wearing.

The woman studied Dr. Moon as she spoke to Dong Min. "Your mother sends her greetings." Her voice was a delicate murmur.

The fat man's eyes widened and then narrowed. "Can you ask her where my wristwatch is, please? I can't seem to find it."

The beautiful shaman laughed, a silvery bell. "In the same wooden box as always, silly boy. Don't save it; wear it!"

Dong Min grabbed Dr. Moon's hand. "She's the real thing!" He turned back to the shaman. "We're here because he has a ghost problem."

The shaman stared over Dr. Moon's shoulder, her pupils enlarging and darkening. She nodded. "You are carrying spirits that need to be returned to their proper places."

Dr. Moon gulped. "Can you help us?"

The shaman's eyelids drooped, fluttering in place so that the whites of her eyes occasionally flashed. When she looked up again, her gaze was moist. "Both of you need more strength for this task. You must go to Hallasan. To Yeongshil Pass. Make an offering to the Mountain God. Pray for energy and guidance. While you get yourself ready, I will make the necessary arrangements."

"Are you going to recommend a kut?" Dong Min suspected that the shaman was going ask Dr. Moon to host a ceremony for the dead, just as his mother would have done.

The shaman stood up from the floor, brushing off her baggy pants. "The spirits have something to say, and he needs to listen."

"How much will it cost?" Dong Min suddenly looked wary.

The shaman named a price that made Dr. Moon gasp.

Dong Min raised his brows indignantly. "That's highway robbery!" The fat man tugged at Dr. Moon's sleeve, indicating that they should leave.

The woman shrugged, a graceful lift of her shoulders. She adjusted one of the candles on the altar. "A bargain for what I do. You won't find anyone to do a proper kut for less anywhere else on Jeju. Perhaps you should ask around first and come back when you're ready."

Dong Min countered at half the price. The shaman didn't deign to respond.

Dong Min pulled Dr. Moon into the hallway and gestured for him to put on his shoes. Just as they were walking out the door, the fat man turned around one last time. "Your original price, but with a ten percent discount because he's traveled all the way from America."

The beautiful shaman looked amused. "I suppose the spirits can take that into consideration."

☽

Dong Min left the gray rental car idling on the sidewalk while he ran into a twenty-four-hour convenience store. An outraged pedestrian shook her cane at Dr. Moon, who cowered in his seat. His friend returned with a bulging plastic sack that he handed to Dr. Moon, who peered down at the contents.

"Plastic bowls. A sack of rice. Beef jerky. Candles. Oranges. Apples. And two bottles of liquor? When did the shaman tell you to get all this stuff?"

Dong Min glanced at the side mirror. "She didn't have to tell me anything. If we're going to pray to the Mountain God, we can't go empty-handed. The gods expect treats, especially the booze." He swerved the car straight into moving traffic, tires squealing.

Dr. Moon thought of the collection plate at church, where offerings were always made in cash or checks, sealed inside envelopes. The shaman's price for the kut had made him gasp, even though Dong Min crowed that they had gotten a bargain. The spirit world seemed to operate like the mundane world, with payments in exchange for services. Was there a god that didn't require tithes or a religion not based on transactions?

Dong Min cursed at a car that cut them off. "When's the last time you made an offering?"

Dr. Moon knew that Dong Min was not talking about those collection plate envelopes. "My mother and I visited the temple for Father a few times . . ."

"What about your mother, the widow who raised you? Don't tell me you haven't paid your annual respects to her."

Dr. Moon's brow furrowed. He had paid for her funeral and observed the proper rites at the time, but he had never held a jesa after moving to the States.

"Things were different when we got to America. Junja was very enthusiastic about being Christian." Every Sunday, he had accompanied her to church, a habit more social than spiritual he had often thought, but never dared say out loud.

"In Korea, even Christians still honor their parents on the anniversary of their deaths!"

"Are you trying to make me feel guilty?"

"Of course, I am! Living in America doesn't make you less Korean. You can't leave Korea behind like a pair of old shoes."

It was not for lack of trying, thought Dr. Moon with a pang. He remembered all the times he had pretended he couldn't hear Junja crying in the bathroom. Every Fourth of July, for the sake of their daughters, they had watched fireworks that reminded them of gunfire. Despite the Christmas presents and holiday festivities, they had always dreaded winter with its annual ambush. The first snowfall gutted them, every time. Junja would go to bed early. He would sit in the dark, listening to Brahms with a glass of Scotch.

Memories of Korea, sudden and sharp, like splinters. Their life in America had ached with them.

☽

As the small gray rental car shuddered up the mountain road to the trailhead, Dr. Moon looked out the window at a landscape that looked so familiar that he asked Dong Min several times whether they had been in that place before. At every bend in the road, the trees seemed to be reaching out, urging him to remember.

Dong Min clenched his hands on the steering wheel as he glanced out the window. "Are you asking if I drove this road earlier? Or if we passed this way back then?"

"Back then."

"Most of the roads we've been driving didn't exist then." Dong Min took a deep breath. "However, Seogwipo is behind us that way, and we're headed up the mountain. Even if we aren't taking the same road . . . yeah, we're in the same general area we were back then."

A sense of tightness constricted Dr. Moon's chest. The pressure did not start easing until they reached the gully at Yeong-shil Pass. Dong Min stepped over the sign and lifted the rope, urging Dr. Moon to move quickly before anyone noticed them straying from the path. The two men gingerly picked their way through a dry stream bed, following the gravel spill into a wide gully surrounded by enormous craggy boulders. The two men gazed up at the looming rocks, which seemed to be guarding the peak beyond. Had they stayed on the trail, Dr. Moon and Dong Min could have walked to Hallasan's peak, a half-day's journey away.

"Feels like the Five Hundred Generals are watching over us," Dong Min muttered. "Kinda spooky."

Dong Min took the food out of the plastic bag, heaping the rice into a plastic bowl and arranging the oranges and apples in pyramids of three. He opened the soju and makgoli bottles, filling the paper cups to the brim. Dr. Moon looked behind them to make sure no one could see them from the trail, where a sign warned hikers to stay on the marked path at all times.

"We didn't pass a Buddhist temple back then, did we?" The tightness in Dr. Moon's chest seemed to relax.

Dong Min studied their surroundings. "No, we definitely didn't come up this far." He looked down at the small makeshift altar and held out a matchbook. "This is your duty, I think."

Dr. Moon's hands trembled. He wondered if the ghostly voices would comment, but they kept silent. He tore off a match and struck it. The breeze that had been stirring the trees died down. The birds ceased chirping, and a cloud passed over the sun, dimming its light. As Dr. Moon touched the flame to the candles, the entire mountain seemed to hold its breath.

Thirty-One

1948

Lieutenant Lee was standing on the beach, surrounded by women dressed in skimpy clothing that clung to their wet bodies. Gun Joo turned his eyes away, but Dong Min brazenly admired the view.

The fat boy whistled. "Would you look at that! We had our fill of wind and rocks walking that dumb cow. At last, we get more of what Jeju's really famous for: the women!"

Gun Joo had heard about the haenyeo, the women divers of Jeju who foraged for food in the sea. He hadn't realized, however, that some of them would be grandmothers, while others were girls close in age to himself. Unlike Dong Min, he was unable to stare so openly and studied his boots instead.

Lieutenant Lee was holding forth about a new invention, a contraption consisting of a mouthpiece connected by tubes to a tank of bottled air that allowed a diver to breath underwater. American soldiers using the device could stay submerged for almost an hour.

The two boys waited respectfully while the lieutenant talked. Some of the women doubted his story; others wished they could buy such a device to simplify their work. Several of the younger divers noticed the boys and pointed to Gun Joo, giggling.

Dong Min leaned in to whisper, "Looks like those gals have their eyes on you!"

Lieutenant Lee returned a scythe to one of the divers and thanked her for letting him examine it. When he finally addressed Gun Joo and Dong Min, his voice was a lazy drawl.

"I trust your trip wasn't too difficult."

"It was fine, sir!" Dong Min stood straight and saluted.

"Where's my cow?"

"Tethered at camp, sir!" Dong Min answered again.

"How's her condition?" The lieutenant turned to Gun Joo, but Dong Min responded instead.

"Same as we found her, sir!" He scratched his chin. "Well, maybe a little fatter now."

Lieutenant Lee turned to Gun Joo. "Cow expert! Why haven't you got anything to say?"

Gun Joo stuttered, "B-b-because my friend is better at talking, sir!"

The women laughed.

"Are you a smart aleck? Or are you saying that he's the brains while you're something else?"

Gun Joo studied the sand as his face grew hot. "I didn't m-mean any d-disrespect, sir!"

The lieutenant took off his glasses to wipe the sea mist fogging the lenses. "As long as you're here, why don't you two lads help these women bring their harvest back to the village." He turned on his heel and bowed to the haenyeo. "Excuse me, ladies, but I must go check on my cow."

☽

The older haenyeo embarrassed Gun Joo with their flattery, patting his arms and peering at his face. The younger divers hung back, but their compliments were loud enough to be heard by Dong Min, who rolled his eyes.

"Such fine pale skin!"

"Look at his long eyelashes!"

"That's a mouth made for kissing, right there!"

When Gun Joo offered to help carry their bundles, the women refused him, insisting that he not dirty his uniform.

Dong Min, who was staggering under a large basket of kelp, bumped into Gun Joo's side. "Help me out, pretty boy."

"Hey, don't bother him, fatso. He's not the one who needs the exercise!" The haenyeo flicked water at Dong Min, who wiped his face with his sleeves.

Red-faced, Gun Joo took the other end of the basket while Dong Min fumed.

The boys made several trips, helping the women carry their harvest back to the village. With each return to shore, more divers would stagger from the water, dragging nets bulging with shells and writhing with tentacles.

The loads were heavy, but Gun Joo dared not complain. Dong Min also kept his mouth shut. Neither boy wanted to admit that these women, who laughed as they casually hoisted baskets above their heads, were stronger than they were, even after diving in the water all day.

When it seemed that the last diver had swum in with the tide, the elder in charge of the fire circle began chanting out names. Each haenyeo responded when her name was called, except for one. Her name was repeated at the end of the roll call.

"Goh Junja."

There was still no response. The elder looked around. "Who was diving with Junja?"

The young girl who raised her hand was defensive when she answered. "We were. She told us to go ahead. We thought she'd be here by now."

"Where were you diving?"

"Near Lonely Rock."

The elder turned to Dong Min and Gun Joo. "You'll do us a big favor if you look for her. Scramble past those rocks over there and walk along the cliffs. Look for a large boulder out in the water. The trail down to the beach is slippery, so be careful. When you find the girl, please tell her it's time to come back."

☽

The two young soldiers stood on the edge of the high bank, scanning the shore. Dong Min, who saw the girl first, pointed. The two boys watched the girl rise up through the water. When she reached the surface, she didn't scream and she didn't move. She didn't do anything they had seen the other divers do. She simply bobbed on the water like a piece of driftwood.

"Something's wrong with her. We have to do something." Gun Joo hesitated just long enough to remove his boots before rushing down to the beach.

Dong Min began to untie his boots as well but stopped when he remembered that he didn't know how to swim. He half ran and half slid down the steep path as he followed his friend.

Gun Joo splashed out to the prone diver, whose body was floating limp on the waves. He swam as fast as he could, but his awkward splashing made him lose sight of the girl. He lunged when he saw her bob back up, but his hands grabbed empty air.

"She went under over there!" Dong Min was gesturing wildly from the water's edge.

Gun Joo gulped some air and dove. He swiveled in the water, limbs churning, looking for the girl. How could she have sunk so quickly? He took another half turn. Out of the corner of his eye, he glimpsed her plummeting down toward the depths.

Gun Joo returned to the surface with a gasp. He panted as his arms flailed against the incoming waves. His legs were tiring, but he pushed away his exhaustion. He was about to dive under again when the girl surfaced beside him with a whistling exhalation.

"Why are you in the water, soldier?" She seemed to spit out the last word.

Gun Joo stared. Water glistened on the girl's skin, making her sparkle like an otherworldly creature. Her beautiful glare shook out a stuttering response.

"You d-d-didn't m-make any n-noise, and you were j-just floating."

Junja didn't want to admit that she had blacked out just as she surfaced, almost drowning. "A Nationalist soldier rescuing a haenyeo?"

"Are you Goh Junja?"

"Yes, I'm Goh Junja." She tossed her head and took a deep breath, readying herself to dive.

Gun Joo managed to grab the girl before she went under. He held her by the wrist as she spluttered in outrage. "Goh Junja, we were sent to get you. You have to come in now."

☽

The women who had come running when they heard the ruckus were standing by, shaking their heads as Junja resisted the divers who tried to bring her back to shore. The girl was standing rigid in the shallows, screaming out a volley of curses that made Gun Joo blush. He didn't know that a woman could know such words or contain so much fury.

"What did you do to her?" Dong Min studied Gun Joo's face, which was raked with scratches.

"I grabbed her arm to stop her from diving again. When I told her she had to come in, she started attacking me."

Dong Min grunted. "Crazy wench. Looked like she was trying to drown you."

"If those other divers hadn't shown up when they did, I think she would have." The two of them had been struggling in the water when the other women separated him from the girl's pummeling fists and clawing fingers.

The elder appraised the marks on Gun Joo's face and apologized. "I don't understand why she's acting this way. I'm truly sorry for the trouble."

Gun Joo was embarrassed about making such a scene. "I'm at fault, ma'am. It wasn't right of me to grab her arm. I'm a stranger, after all."

The elder shook her head. "If she was going to dive again, what choice did you have? No, the fault is hers. And mine for sending you. Please forgive us."

When Junja's screams cut into the conversation, the elder shooed them along. "It sounds like she's not going to come out while you're standing here. If you two boys head back to camp, it will be easier for us to calm her down."

☽

As dinnertime approached, soldiers began returning to the camp, some carrying shovels or axes, others pushing wheelbarrows. A few of them had blood-stained bandages wrapped around their hands; all of them looked exhausted. As they passed Gun Joo and Dong Min, who were setting up their tent, a couple of them muttered that some guys had all the luck.

While Gun Joo and Dong Min had been ambling alongside a slow-moving cow, the other soldiers had spent the past two days in backbreaking labor, moving rocks and shoveling earth.

Despite their exhaustion, the young soldiers readied themselves for dinner with obvious excitement as they rinsed their faces and combed the dust out of their hair.

"I think I need to wash my face and hands before we eat," Dong Min was feeling sweatily self-conscious. "You wanna come too?"

Gun Joo shook his head. "I already took a bath in the ocean, remember? I'll finish setting this corner up and meet you in the mess line."

$$\supset$$

The young woman standing next to Junja poked her in the side. "There's the one you attacked. Behind the short fat one."

The other girls gasped and punched Junja on the arm.

"Ohmanah! Look at the scratches on his handsome face!"

"Why'd you do such a thing?"

"I hope you didn't leave permanent scars!"

"Keep your eyes down, girls." The village elder in charge of the mess line inspected each spoon and ladle with suspicion. "Remember, don't give too much, but don't give too little either. One scoop of millet or sweet potato, but not both. And no second helpings, no matter how nicely they ask. Understood? Lieutenant's orders."

As the soldiers moved through the line with their mess tins, whispers and giggles followed them. Some of the bolder boys made direct conversation with the young women, while others were more discreet. Dong Min watched one soldier push his tin forward for millet, along with a small piece of bark. The girl who took both glanced at the attending elder to make sure she hadn't been seen before tucking the secret scrap of communication up her sleeve.

Dong Min whispered to Gun Joo. "I guess our fellow soldiers have spent the past couple days flirting at mealtime. Every guy here has his eye on someone."

Gun Joo blushed. The girl who had tried to drown him was standing by the sweet potatoes, wearing the same expression of contempt that he'd seen in the water. She glared down at the mound of potatoes, looking up just long enough to dump food into the proffered tins. She ignored everyone's attempts to make small talk.

"Millet?" The pretty plump girl who was scooping millet tried to catch Gun Joo's eye.

Dong Min answered for his friend. "Yes, he'd like millet, please."

Gun Joo covered his tin. "Actually, I want sweet potatoes."

Dong Min tried to move Gun Joo's hand. "He doesn't know what he's talking about. We've been eating nothing but sweet potatoes for two days. He wants millet."

Gun Joo's hand didn't budge. "I really like sweet potatoes."

"You're crazy!" Dong Min squinted down the line. When he saw Junja standing by the bowl of sweet potatoes, he repeated himself. "Yup, you're completely nuts."

Dong Min shook his head as he watched a silent Gun Joo choke down sweet potatoes while stealing glances at Junja. The girl had not looked up when she served him, but her serving spoon had struck his tin with an especially hard clang.

Dong Min threw a utensil at his friend. "Stop eating with your fingers and use the *pork*, like the other guys." He waved his hand in front of Gun Joo's face. "And stop staring at that girl, you pathetic fool."

"I'm not looking at her. I'm looking at the sweet potatoes to see how many are left." Gun Joo batted Dong Min's hand away.

"No second helpings, remember? Besides, you can't fool me. I know exactly what's going on." The fat boy sighed as he scraped his empty tin.

"Oh yeah? What's going on?"

"You've fallen for her."

"No, I haven't."

"Yes, you have. I should know, having recently fallen in love myself."

"I'm not 'in love.' I'm just interested."

"Well, you're not the only one who's 'just interested.'"

Two fellow soldiers were attempting to engage Junja in conversation. Though the girl ignored them, Gun Joo felt a jealous flush warming his face.

"She's attractive, no question about that. But she's nuts." The fat boy tried to pick his teeth with the tip of his fork.

"Why do you keep saying that?"

"Because I saw her attack you. She was trying to drown you!"

"That's because I grabbed her arm."

"And that justifies what she did?"

"From her point of view, yes."

"You know what? She's perfect for you."

"You really think so?"

"Yeah. Because you're just as crazy as she is." The fat boy stood up. "Come on—let's wash these things and finish setting up our tent.

Later that night, as Dong Min snored beside him, Gun Joo smiled up at the darkness. He finally understood what his friend had seen in the harelipped girl because he had seen the same in Junja.

Thirty-Two

2001

After concluding their prayers with three prostrations, Dr. Moon and Dong Min scattered the rice, throwing large fistfuls around them. Next, they hurled the liquor in wide silver arcs in all four cardinal directions. They left one orange and an apple on a rock before placing the bowls, empty bottles, and remaining food back into the plastic bag. Dr. Moon followed Dong Min's lead as he bowed deeply in farewell, hands clasped together in thanks.

As the two men walked down the gully, Dong Min stopped to pick up litter, muttering about careless hikers.

"Maybe we should walk up the mountain for a bit. Not too far—just enough to see the view." Dr. Moon offered the suggestion tentatively, in case his portly friend rejected the idea.

Dong Min thumped his chest. "You know, I feel so energized by this place that I think I could do something crazy like that. But we have to go slow, okay?"

Dr. Moon nodded. "Can you walk in those shoes?"

Dong Min stamped his sneakered feet. "Of course. My feet can walk in anything. I'm the one who should be asking you that question. Can you walk in those shoes?"

Dr. Moon stamped his orthopedic walkers in response. "This is the first comfortable pair of shoes I've ever worn in Korea. Let's see how my feet do."

A steady flow of hikers streamed by the two old friends in both directions as they climbed the trail. Some folks were dressed as they were, in casual everyday clothes, but the majority were wearing hiking boots, mountaineering vests, and sporty brimmed hats. These professional-looking climbers planted their poles with a rhythmic speed that spurred Dr. Moon and Dong Min to walk faster.

"I think we missed the memo for the dress requirement." Dong Min chuckled as another couple passed them, clad in identical, color-coordinated hiking gear.

"Remember the young guy who passed us earlier? The one who was carrying a huge backpack with a teddy bear tied to it? Where do you suppose he was going?" Dr. Moon wished he had stopped the fellow to ask.

"There's a lake at the top. People camp overnight there, even though it isn't technically allowed." Dong Min wiped the perspiration off his face with a handkerchief fished out from his pocket. He folded the handkerchief over to reveal a fresh side and handed it to his friend. "It's considered a sacred spot. Of course, Mother always said that all mountaintops were sacred."

As Dr. Moon blotted his nose and forehead, he caught sight of a large bird wheeling over the deep valley alongside the trail. The bird floated over the Five Hundred Generals, the craggy boulders that stared out to sea from their airy perches.

"The scenery's amazing, isn't it?" Dong Min scooted over to let a group of determined hikers pass. "But the trail's as crowded as Yoonja's favorite shopping mall during a sale!"

Dr. Moon pointed. "There's a viewing platform. Let's stop when we get up there."

☽

"Did this happen to you in America as well?" Dong Min crammed half a roll of kimbop into his mouth and spoke through bulging cheeks. The two of them had waited for a large group of young, sociable hikers to finish their picnic before taking their places on the viewing platform. As they left, the hikers offered their remaining seaweed rolls to the two old men, who happily accepted.

"What are you talking about?" Dr. Moon was savoring his kimbop, which surprised him by being exceptionally delicious.

"People giving you food for free. It always happened back then too."

"I don't remember anything like that."

"How can you not remember? In the mess line, girls would always slip you something extra. A heaping scoop of millet while everyone else got level scoops. They always saved the biggest piece of fish for you."

"They did? I never noticed."

"Wow. You must have been really distracted by Junja."

Dr. Moon considered. "I think you were just as obsessed with Yoonja."

Dong Min laughed. "No, I was more obsessed." He studied the glittering ocean, breathing deeply. "We were so distracted by our hormones that I don't think we appreciated how beautiful Jeju was back then. Much more beautiful than it is now, with no highways or large hotels."

A deep voice interrupted. "I sincerely agree with you. Jeju used to be much more beautiful."

A wizened man in baggy gray pants and a shapeless gray jacket was standing on the trail, leaning on a walking stick. Under his wide-brimmed straw hat, his head was clean-shaven. A monk, whose face seemed etched by a permanent smile. The man gestured toward the platform. "May I join you?"

Dong Min rose to make room for the monk, bowing as he did so.

The monk took off his pack to settle in alongside them. "I always make it a point to stop here because it's one of the few places left on Jeju where the view hasn't changed too much from the old days. If you block out those buildings over there with your hands, it's like traveling back in time fifty years."

All three men raised their hands to reframe the view.

"That's much better," sighed Dong Min.

Dr. Moon put down his hands to address the monk. "You were on Jeju fifty years ago?"

The monk nodded, smiling. "I've lived on Jeju my whole life, mostly right here on this mountain. I was born here, and I've never left, not even to visit Seoul. I'll die here too."

Dong Min counted his fingers and looked at Dr. Moon. "Were we here fifty years ago?"

"Fifty-three years exactly this October," said Dr. Moon. He added, "But the date is different if we use the lunar calendar."

The monk nodded. "Time moves differently with the moon." He scratched his head. "Judging from your accents, I don't think you two are Jeju-born. You must have spent time here as soldiers."

Dong Min glanced at Dr. Moon before answering. "Would you say we were actually soldiers? Maybe more like trainees . . ."

The monk's next question startled both men. "Are you here to ask for forgiveness, perhaps?"

When neither man responded, the monk smiled into the awkward silence. "My apologies. I didn't mean to suggest that you two had done something wrong."

At first, Dr. Moon's words stuck in his throat before loosening and tumbling out. "The Nationalist troops did terrible things. We were here. We saw what happened."

Dong Min quickly added, "But we didn't take part in any of it."

Dr. Moon's voice was so quiet that the monk had to lean in to hear. "We didn't stop it either."

Dong Min looked up at the sky. "If we had tried to, we wouldn't be here today."

Dr. Moon hung his head.

The monk, who started bobbing his head as he listened, continued to nod. "You've come to the Mountain to ask for forgiveness. Just like I have."

Dr. Moon and Dong Min didn't know what to say. They could hardly fathom this smiling monk doing anything that would need to be forgiven.

The monk pointed his walking stick toward the foothills. "See that hillside just below us? The one with the large clearing in the trees?"

An abrupt emptiness interrupted the green of the forest.

"Fifty-three years ago, there used to be a village there. Until it was fire-bombed by an American plane. The fire was so hot that the village burned for an entire day and night. For a long time, the earth there was barren, and even now the grass still struggles to grow."

The monk closed his eyes. "Dozens of villages on the mountain were destroyed, but I witnessed that one happen. I was on this trail. I saw the plane and the explosions. When I reached the temple, the decision had been made to evacuate. My fellow monks and I, we took the fast route off the mountain when we should have stopped to help." He cast his eyes down in shame.

The monk looked back up, his expression sad. "I've been praying for all the lost souls of the mountain ever since."

The two old friends looked at each other as an unspoken communication passed between them. Dr. Moon nodded to Dong Min, who spoke.

"Well, you see, sir . . . there's something you don't know."
Dong Min cleared his throat. "The truth is, we . . . uh . . .
we . . ." His shiny face reddened as he turned to Dr. Moon. "I'm
not sure that—"

Dr. Moon interrupted. As he spoke, the stutter that had been
left behind in Korea when he moved to America returned. "He
and I—we r-ran away from the N-N-Nationalists. We're
d-d-deserters."

There. Their shameful secret had finally been confessed.
Besides the three of them on the mountain, Yoonja was the only
other person who knew, now that Junja was gone.

The monk's face crinkled again. "What an interesting coincidence that we've met like this on the mountain. The three of
us"—he gestured to Dr. Moon, Dong Min, and himself—"we're
all deserters."

Dong Min shook his head. "What you did wasn't desertion.
That was common sense. And I don't think that what we did
counts as desertion either."

"We may not consider it desertion, but the government would."
Dr. Moon looked stubborn. It was obvious that the two men had
had this discussion before.

Dong Min raised his voice. "But we were following orders!"

The monk interrupted. "Orders? From who?"

Dr. Moon answered. "Our commanding officer, Lieutenant
Lee. He told us to leave Jeju. He ordered us to run away."

Thirty-Three

1948

"Please, sir, I'm begging you. Let me go to the mountain." Junja trembled. She had to go to the mountain as soon as possible, for Grandmother's sake.

The girl was kneeling with her head bowed before Lieutenant Lee, who was leafing through a stack of paperwork presented to him by the private serving as his communications secretary. Despite her posture, Junja's voice did not convey any humility. She sounded like she was trying not to bark out an order.

"Hallasan is forbidden." Lieutenant Lee glanced at the girl through his spectacles.

Junja tried not to glare. The lieutenant had not inquired even once about her grandmother's poor health during the weeks that his troops had been stationed at the village. The girl understood his need to maintain appearances, but surely he could have found a way to help without compromising his cover.

"I know . . ." Junja added the honorific after a delay, ". . . sir."

"Then why are you wasting my time?" The lieutenant wondered how the girl would respond. Only Junja and her grandmother knew about his true alliances. As far as his soldiers were concerned, he was an eager lapdog of the Nationalists and their American overseers.

"My grandmother is very sick. She needs mushrooms and roots that can only be found on the mountain." The lieutenant had to grant this request, thought the girl, with some desperation. Grandmother had shrunk to half her size and was now unable to eat.

"It's too cold for mushrooms." The lieutenant signed the document that the secretary presented, with a flourish of his gold pen.

Junja unclenched her jaw to speak. "Not the kind I'm looking for. These mushrooms become part of the tree. They're hard as wood." Junja decided to prostrate herself, stretching out her hands in supplication. "I beg you, sir, please have mercy on my sick grandmother. Please allow me to gather medicine from the mountain." She tried to make her voice deferential and meek; instead, it sounded like something was stuck in her throat.

Lieutenant Lee turned to the secretary. "What do you think, Woon?"

Secretary Woon possessed small, shifty eyes and an even smaller, shiftier heart. He had tried to talk to Junja several times in the mess line, but the girl always rebuffed him. Woon sensed an opportunity now. "Sir, I think you should allow the girl to go, but send her with an escort."

Lieutenant Lee didn't trust this young man, which was why he kept him close. "I think that's far too lenient. What's the health of a granny to our proud new republic? She's going to die of old age anyways."

Junja quivered but kept her face pressed down to the ground. She had to remind herself that she knew the lieutenant when he was Constable Lee. There was nothing straightforward about this man, whose every word seemed to serve a larger purpose.

Secretary Woon saw his chance with Junja slipping away. "We must treat our countrymen with compassion, sir, even when they are wayward Communists. I could accompany the girl, sir, to make sure she does exactly what she says she's going to do."

The lieutenant looked unconvinced. "How about sending a wire asking for official permission?"

Secretary Woon knew, as the lieutenant did, that the request would be denied. "Might I suggest, sir, that I record this matter as a matter of daily camp business? Perhaps the girl could be foraging for additional provisions?"

Lieutenant Lee appeared to lose interest. "I'm too busy for such trivial matters. How about I leave everything in your capable hands, Woon? I'll sign off on whatever you decide."

☽

Dong Min and Gun Joo were digging a trench on the outskirts of the village when Junja, Lieutenant Lee, and the communications secretary walked around the bend. Junja and the secretary were carrying baskets.

"Junja, the lieutenant and that rat Woon are headed this way." Dong Min suppressed a laugh as Gun Joo's grip on his shovel slipped.

Lieutenant Lee stopped to examine the trench. "I came to see if more hands were needed, but you two seem to be finished already. Excellent work, lads!" He turned to Woon and Junja and waved them along. "Please hurry back once you've found your mushrooms. I'm expecting an important wire this evening."

Gun Joo did not like the thought of Junja being alone with Woon. He pulled his shovel out of the trench and rested it on the ground. "Excuse me, sir, but isn't it too c-c-cold for m-mushrooms?"

Dong Min swatted his friend. "Not for the hard kind, dummy. Winter freezes are best for those."

"Oh, yeah. I forgot about that k-kind." Gun Joo tried to think of something else to say, but couldn't, so he started digging again, a little too vigorously.

Lieutenant Lee pursed his lips before shouting to Woon and Junja, who were several paces away. "Come back you two! I need to ask a question!"

Woon and Junja trotted back. The secretary tried to hide his irritation under a smile. Why was the annoying lieutenant delaying his afternoon diversion?

"What do you know about these mushrooms, Woon?"

"Not much, sir, but I'm sure the girl could tell me everything I need to know, sir."

Lieutenant Lee rubbed his hands, smiling. "How fortunate for us, secretary, that we ran into our resident cow experts just as they were finishing up this trench. Apparently, these two country boys know all about mushrooms too!" Lieutenant Lee placed his arm on Woon's shoulders. "You're an educated city man like myself, so your time is far too important to waste on mushrooms. We can let these two escort the girl to the mountain instead. You and I can return to camp and attend to another mountain . . . of paperwork." He laughed loudly at his own joke before pitching his voice low for Woon's benefit. "I'm thinking of that important transmission from headquarters. It would be better for you to stay in camp in case it arrives earlier than scheduled."

Secretary Woon couldn't think of a valid objection. He thrust his basket at Dong Min, inwardly cursing the two bumpkins for thwarting the romantic afternoon he had anticipated with a naive country girl.

"Excuse me, sir, but how are we supposed to go to the m-m-mountain if it's b-banned?" Gun Joo could hardly believe his luck at being ordered to spend time with Junja, whose face was unreadable.

Lieutenant Lee snapped his fingers. "That's right. I almost forgot. Clever Woon here made a special pass. It will identify you as Nationalist soldiers on a secret mission." He pulled the paper out of his pocket and frowned. "Did you know, Woon, that there's no name or date on this pass? How did I not catch that earlier? Bah, it'll probably work just fine. Woon is very clever with these kinds of things. I have no idea what I'd do without him."

Woon's smile was more of a grimace. The knuckles on his fist grew white.

Lieutenant Lee noted these details while continuing his chatter. "Well, then, be quick about your mushrooming, lads." He turned to Woon. "Let's go back to camp and have a quick drink before we get back to work that really matters." When he thumped the secretary's shoulders, he noticed the gun holster, which gave him another idea.

"Boys, I think you should borrow Woon's weapon so that both of you are armed. You're heading into enemy territory, after all. If you run across some Communists hiding in the mushrooms, make sure you shoot to kill."

Thirty-Four

"Stop walking so fast!" Dong Min was gasping as he tried to keep up with Junja and Gun Joo, who were walking side by side at a brisk pace.

The three of them had gotten a ride from the village to the foothills of Hallasan from a passing farmer with a team of horses who was heading into Seogwipo to look for work at the American base. When the man saw the two boys in uniform walking alongside the road with Junja, he stopped to ask where they were headed and had given them a ride without asking for compensation.

"Please pass word to your officer that I helped you!" the farmer said, making them promise not to forget the favor. The man sat in the cart, bobbing his head, and looked relieved when the three of them stepped off.

"Why do you suppose he gave us a ride for free?" Junja finally broke her silence.

"Because we could have taken the cart and the horses away from him." Dong Min patted the handgun in its holster. Firearms were too scarce for every soldier to carry his own, so Lieutenant Lee had divided the weapons and ammunition between partnered pairs. Today had been Gun Joo's turn to carry the handgun, but because the lieutenant had given them Woon's revolver, both of them were now armed.

"Why would the farmer think we'd take his horses?" Junja shook her head. "That's crazy!"

The fat boy pointed to his weapon. "Because of this."

Gun Joo swatted his friend. "That's wrong! Stop it!"

"Calm down, Gun Joo. I didn't say it was a good thing that we could have taken the cart, just that the farmer knew we could have."

The three of them fell silent. Terrible rumors were circulating through the village about torched crops, seized animals, and people disappearing, as if snatched by ghosts. The elderly blamed the Communists while the young blamed the Nationalists. Those who refused to take sides pointed their fingers at the American military, which sent orders to every police station and constabulary force on the island. "Don't blame the dogs—look at the ones yanking their ropes!"

Among the soldiers stationed at Junja's village, there were disgruntled mutterings about Lieutenant Lee's leniency toward the civilians. Instead of commandeering the village stores as he could have, the lieutenant had installed a strict system of rationing. Hunger darkened everyone's mood.

The chill prodded Junja, Gun Joo, and Dong Min to move briskly. Junja's handmade leather shoes slipped against the occasional stone. Gun Joo stayed close, ready to grab her if she stumbled. He was grateful for how surefooted he was in his boots, though they remained painful to wear.

"Damn, it's cold." The fat boy blew out a white plume. He slapped his gloved hands together. "I can't believe you were diving a couple weeks ago."

The start of winter had closed the official harvest season. Because of the food shortage, Junja knew that she would have to brave the frigid waters again. She wrapped her arms around herself, shivering at the possibility. "I don't think that was the end of water work for me. Not with so many mouths to feed." The ocean, always dangerous, was much more deadly in winter. Only the young and strong worked the water during the cold months. Elders, with their waning heat, did not endure such trials.

Dong Min shuddered. "I don't know how you women do it. I can't even bear to put my hand in the water."

"We have to eat," Junja said. "What choice do we have? Anyways, we don't dive deep. We just gather what we can close to shore."

As the path grew steeper and more slippery, the three of them stopped talking, to pay attention to their footing. The leaves of summer lay on the ground, frozen into a brown mat that covered the narrow path winding through the forest. Sunlight streamed through the stark branches, and patches of frost powdered the ground. The trickling stream and the crunch of leaves under their feet were the only sounds they heard as they climbed the trail.

"*Gaw, gaw!*" A large blackbird fluttered overhead, settling on a tree to cock its head. Another one landed alongside the first.

When a third stopped to perch, Dong Min started jumping up and down and waving his arms. "Go away! Get outta here!"

A fourth blackbird stopped to add its cackle to the eerie chorus. "*Gaw, gaw! Gaw, gaw!*"

The fat boy's shoulders slumped. "Four blackbirds. All of them telling us to leave. We should turn around. I have a bad feeling about this."

Junja, who was also spooked by the quartet of birds, shook her head. They were almost there. Silly to let a bit of superstition turn them around. She jumped when Gun Joo touched her on the hand.

The boy apologized, pointing. "Over there, near the stream. A lot of birch trees. Probably a lot of mushrooms."

The three of them scrambled down into the ravine while the blackbirds followed, flitting from branch to branch. Water was still trickling, but patches of ice clogged the rock bed. Junja and the boys studied the trees and found what they were looking for: large, protruding scabs of wood. The two boys copied the girl's motions as she scraped the knobby growths with sharp rocks. The four blackbirds watched, eyes glittering.

"I think this should be enough." Dong Min glanced nervously at the birds. "We should head back down."

Gun Joo looked at Junja. He would follow the girl's lead.

Junja took a breath. The sun was blinding. Nothing bad could happen under such a blue sky. She decided to take the chance. "I'd like to pray to the Mountain God."

Dong Min nodded, looking around nervously. "Sure, why not? This seems like a good place. Gun Joo and I will duck around the bend to give you some privacy. Better yet, maybe we should pray too. It never hurts to remember the gods."

Junja shook her head. She wanted to see if Suwol was home. She couldn't go to Cloud House with two Nationalist soldiers.

"The proper place is higher up, about an hour's walk. I'll be fine by myself. You two go back."

Dong Min shook his head. "Sorry, but you're our responsibility. We have the guns and the pass. You might get mistaken for a Communist."

Gun Joo held up his hand, motioning for them to be quiet as the birds started making a ruckus.

"*Gaw, gaw! Gaw, gaw!*"

Off in the distance, shouting. And a faint keening noise, as if someone were crying.

The blackbirds repeated themselves, urging them to leave. "*Gaw, gaw!*"

Dong Min whispered. "Smells like trouble. I think we should take cover." He pointed to a rocky overhang on the opposite bank,

which was pocked with openings, many of them large enough to
crawl into.

The three of them moved swiftly. Gun Joo took Junja by the
hand, leading her over the slippery rocks of the stream. Despite
his help, she almost lost a shoe when her foot became wedged
between two boulders. One of the caves plunged deep into the
hillside and was large enough to hold all three of them. Gun Joo
motioned for Junja to crawl in first. He and Dong Min slid in
afterward, taking up watch on their bellies.

The approaching voices grew louder and more distinct. A man
was cursing at someone, telling them to move faster. Children
were wailing.

Dong Min rubbed dirt onto Gun Joo's cheek, hissing. "Cover
your face with mud, pretty boy, unless you want everyone to see
your white face glowing up here."

Dong Min had already smeared his brown face. Gun Joo took
off a glove, grabbed a fistful of dirt, and spat into it.

In the back of the cave, Junja felt faint. She tried to calm herself. An hour's walk up the trail would have led her to Suwol's
home. Who would be coming down the path from that direction? Why were they shouting and crying?

When Gun Joo noticed the white cloud of breath coming
from his mouth and nose, he wrapped the lower half of his face
with his scarf. Dong Min did the same. The fat boy raised his
eyebrow and pointed to his holster. Gun Joo nodded. Both boys
took out their handguns and readied them.

The approaching group of people grew louder. Two voices were
distinguishable above the weeping crowd. One of the voices
belonged to a foreigner. The other spoke both Korean and English.

"How much longer to go?" The foreigner sounded like he was
whining.

"Two more hour to main roads, sir."

"Some of these people won't last that long."

"The American says that these people will not last another hour."

A third voice entered the conversation. "Then let's pull off here, into this ravine."

"Where are we going to put all these people? The holding cells are full. And where are all the men?" The foreign words sounded harsh and nasally to Junja's ears.

"The American wants to know where the men are."

"Why does he keep asking the same question over and over? Is he an idiot? How should I know? The women claim they're all dead. But they'll say anything at this point."

"They say all mens dead, sir."

A large group of people were scrambling through the trees to enter the ravine. Gun Joo could see that most of them were women and children, dressed inadequately against the bitter cold. A few children were clutching their mothers' hands. A small woman carried a barefoot child whose head lolled back and forth against her shoulder, like a limp doll's.

Gun Joo smelled something burning. He craned his head to see a dirty column of smoke in the distance.

A child's voice pierced the forest. "Mama, I'm cold."

"Hush."

"Why did they shoot all the pigs?"

"Shh. Don't talk."

Five soldiers herded the group toward the stream, using the points of their rifles as prods. At the back of the group, two women held up an old man, whose stick-like legs were exposed and whose feet were bundled in cloth. The women flanking him stayed close, trying to shield his body from the cold with their own. A soldier at the rear shouted and pushed them forward with his rifle. One of the women stumbled and fell. Gun Joo closed his eyes, sickened by the sight. Next to him, Dong Min stifled a gasp.

He scooted over to whisper. "Gun Joo, this is wrong. We have to do something."

"What can we do? We wear the same uniform they do. If we announce ourselves, they might make us do something we don't want to do. We should keep hiding and stay quiet."

Junja could not bear to stay at the foot of the cave any longer. She shifted position, pushing aside the boys' legs, so that she could squeeze in between. She had already covered her face with dirt, and her head wrap was covering her nose and mouth. Gun Joo sensed her warmth and was grateful that his flushing face could not be seen. He pressed against the wall of the cave, trying to give the girl more room.

Junja stared down at the shivering women and children, who were trying to warm themselves by huddling close together. She shook her head and pressed her fist against her mouth.

"Do you know them?" Gun Joo could smell the musk of her head as he leaned in close to speak.

"I think so." Her anguished whisper brushed his ear.

The foreigner spoke again. "Why are we stopping here?"

"The American officer wants to know what we're doing here."

"Tell him we're following his general's orders, just like he is."

The people were prodded into a shivering mass by the stream. Someone started moaning. Two of the uniformed men were conferring, helmets close together. Nationalist soldiers, like Gun Joo and Dong Min, but in combat gear. The two men moved apart, and one of the men walked to another soldier.

Gun Joo wished he could hear what they were saying. The helmeted soldiers moved into position next to each other. After a moment, both men lifted their rifles.

Three more soldiers followed suit and raised their guns, pointing them at the terrified villagers. A slim man in green walked in between the rifles and their targets. A Nationalist officer, he paused to light a cigarette before addressing the shivering group.

"Where are the men hiding?" He exhaled smoke.

No one dared respond.

The officer took another draw from his cigarette. He sounded bored. "Do I have to shoot someone to get a response?"

A small woman stepped forward. Her face seemed to flash white. "The men are dead."

A low moan escaped Junja. The woman sounded like Suwol's mother.

Gun Joo covered her mouth with his hand.

"If you continue to lie, we will shoot each and every one of you until someone tells the truth."

"We've already told you the truth, but you won't believe us. If you're going to kill us, then do it before we freeze to death." The small woman raised her fist.

The officer struck the woman with such force that her head whipped sideways, and she fell to the ground.

He shouted, "How dare a woman speak like that to a man? I asked a simple question. Where are the men? I will spare whoever tells me the truth."

The weeping grew louder. A commotion started at the back of the trembling group of villagers. The old grandfather was slowly making his way to the front by holding onto the shoulders and arms of the women he passed.

"Father, please!" a woman sobbed out.

The old man tried to stand straight but couldn't. He leaned on the women as he spoke in Japanese, his voice shaking with age and chill.

"Jap-loving gehsekki scum. I'm the only man left alive. You want to kill me? Then kill me. Only cowards threaten women and children."

The Nationalist officer walked over to the old man and spat into his face. He responded in Japanese. "You're already more dead than alive, old man. A bullet would be wasted on you."

The American turned to the translator. "What are they saying?"

"They speaks Japanese."

"Why? Are they spies?"

The translator didn't answer the man's question, pained by his ignorance. Were these foreigners unaware that their handpicked Nationalist officer had once been a notorious Japanese collaborator? Or did they simply not care that they were working with traitors?

The translator swallowed before turning to the former collaborator, who was now his commanding officer. "The American wants to know if you and the old man are Japanese spies."

The officer laughed, a sharp bark. "The American doesn't care about any of that. He just wants a good excuse for his conscience. Tell him what he wants to hear."

The translator hesitated. He wanted to stop what was going to happen, even as he despaired that his English was adequate to the task. "He say they not spy. Nobody spy. Nobody Communist."

"Where are all the men? It doesn't make sense, a village filled with women and children, when the mountain has been banned. The men are obviously in hiding because they're Communist spies. The orders are clear."

The translator felt sick to his stomach as he translated.

Up in the cave, Junja shook her head, horrified. Surely, the translator had made a terrible mistake. She desperately wished she could understand what the American had actually said.

The collaborator threw his cigarette butt into the sluggish stream, where it floated for a moment before disappearing under the slush. He shouted to the five soldiers positioned around the huddled women and children.

"Shoot the senile fool. Shoot them all. We've wasted enough time here."

One of the soldiers dared to speak. "Sir, what about the children?"

"You know the orders. There's nothing about making exceptions for Communist children."

A woman started sobbing, beseeching the gods. Children began wailing. Their mouths were clapped shut by their mothers, who began imploring for the little ones to be spared. The five soldiers raised their weapons. Junja wanted to scream for them to stop. Gun Joo, sensing her agitation, grabbed her hand and shook his head.

The soldier who asked about the children lowered his gun. Junja held her breath.

The Nationalist officer was lighting another cigarette. The translator looked at the American, hoping he would stop this madness. The American, not wishing to witness anything unpleasant, turned around and began climbing out of the ravine. For the official record, he would write that the day's mission had successfully cleared a mountain enclave of Communist insurgents.

The soldier who lowered his gun dropped to his knees, head bowed. "Sir, I cannot shoot innocent women and children. Please, spare the children at least."

"So that we create another lot of hungry, sniveling orphans?" The Nationalist officer spat out smoke. "You think these people are innocent? Fool. They're Communists, who are trying to deceive you. Obey orders or die with them."

The man hesitated before laying his rifle on the ground. He prostrated himself. "I beg your forgiveness, sir, but I am a Christian. I cannot kill them. Please forgive me, sir."

The officer blew smoke into the face of the disobedient soldier. "The Christian god serves the Americans, you pious fool. These orders come straight from General Brown, who's been going to church longer than you." He shouted at the other four soldiers. "Strip him of his gear and put him with the group. He's obviously a Communist agent."

Junja began shaking so hard that Gun Joo had to wrap his arms around her to keep her still. He covered her mouth when she began to gasp.

As his comrades removed the stunned soldier's weapons, a woman began keening. She was summoning ancestral spirits, begging for help. The old grandfather collapsed into the arms of the women behind him. The mothers and their children stood next to the icy stream, shivering with cold and dread. The mist from their breathing rose up, a white cloud.

The three witnesses pressed themselves to the floor of the cave. Gun Joo kept his hand on Junja's mouth to quell the girl's rising hysteria. Dong Min huddled at the back of the cave, covering his ears and closing his eyes.

The officer tossed his half-smoked cigarette into the stream and snarled at the four remaining gunmen.

"Start with that noisy bitch. Her voice makes my head ache."

☽

The sudden silence stung with smoke. Junja's mouth was still covered by Gun Joo's trembling hand, which was wet with her tears. Dong Min remained curled in a ball.

Steam rose from the bodies, which were lying in ragged heaps that looked like piles of dirty clothes. An occasional arm or foot stuck out in a random manner, as if some giant had swept up a pile of discarded human limbs and dropped them next to a mountain stream.

The four soldiers put down their weapons. The officer lit another cigarette. The translator, who had followed the American, shouted from the road. "The American officer says we need to hurry up and go."

Gun Joo had not been able to stop himself. Counting was a compulsion, especially when he was under duress. He had counted every time the four soldiers fired their guns, even when those sounds overlapped. The shots were sharp and distinct, so he knew his counting was precise. Four soldiers had discharged their weapons a total of a hundred and four times, with pauses to reload. At least three bullets per person, with the exception of the first woman, who had been shot by all the soldiers at once. Four bullets for the wailing woman, who had cursed her murderers as she dropped to her knees and toppled forward.

Thirty-Five

As he listened to the two boys describe the massacre on the mountain, Lieutenant Lee stared at a dark spot on the wall of his tent.

"Can you describe the man giving the orders? Not the American, but the Korean officer." The lieutenant wondered if the dark spot was a stain or a flaw in the fabric.

The man had been of average height. He smoked cigarettes. And he spoke fluent Japanese. Too many officers fit that description, and the boys had been too far away to see his face clearly.

"Sir, those men wore the same uniform we do. But I couldn't help thinking that they were the enemy." Gun Joo bowed his head in confession.

Lieutenant Lee stood up from the camp stool and walked to the spot that bothered him. He peered at it. It was a flaw in the fabric. He ran his fingers over the discolored bump as he spoke. "Privates, I'm going to let you in on a secret." He let his hand drop. "In every conflict, there are always more than two sides."

Dong Min frowned. "But aren't we supposed to be the good guys?"

The lieutenant took off his glasses to clean them. He held them up to the light before putting them back on. "That's the lie politicians feed soldiers to do their dirty work."

Lieutenant Lee sat down on a footstool, reached into the file cabinet, and pulled out a small bottle. He motioned the two boys over.

Gun Joo and Dong Min looked at each other, confused. They approached timidly, wondering what the officer was going to do.

The lieutenant unscrewed the lid as he talked. "You should fortify yourselves for what I'm about to say. It probably won't make any sense to you now, but you might understand later . . . if you live long enough."

He took several swigs, grimacing at the sting, before holding out the bottle. "Here, take a swallow. It'll help." He wiped his mouth with his shirt sleeve. "Truth is, boys, there are no good guys in war."

Thirty-Six

2001

Dr. Moon's and Dong Min's voices, which began fraying at the start of their tale, broke apart into mumbles at its terrible end. The monk handed them a plastic bottle filled with water from a spring hidden at the peak. Long shadows from the late afternoon sun striped the green flanks of the mountain.

The monk, whose face was shining with tears, surprised the two friends by taking a turn with the storytelling.

"It was springtime, and my brothers and I were staying at a temple by the sea. Long-term guests, because the mountain was forbidden, and we had nowhere else to go. "

"One morning, very early, women from the village pounded on the temple doors, hysterical. I thought that the village was being attacked by soldiers. But the screaming made no sense. The women kept insisting that the mountain was bleeding. They had been washing laundry when the water started running red."

"Those of us from the mountain temple volunteered to investigate because we knew the secret trails to get around the blockades. We followed the bloody stream to its source. The site is not too far from here, in the foothills, near the main road. Hundreds of people drive by it every day. The stream is in a ravine, with boulders and many beech trees. One side of the ravine is high and rocky, pocked with small caves. The other side, closer to the road, is wide and flat. In the summer, grasses and ferns grow there, but in the winter the ground freezes solid. During the spring thaw, when the stream overruns its banks, water floods that flat section. It gathers behind stones until it can break free, rushing in a torrent toward the ocean."

The monk shut his eyes. His hands trembled around the walking stick. "That's where we found the bodies, lying in a pool of melting blood." He swallowed, wiping away fresh tears. "My brothers and I, We pulled those people to higher ground and buried them as best we could. There wasn't enough soil, so we had finish by covering them with rocks. That's all we could do besides pray for them."

The monk pointed back to the clearing in the foothills below. "The village I told you about earlier? That's where they came from, those pitiful people. In the springtime, the mountain revealed their murder, when the ice melted, and their blood ran down to the sea. I buried their bodies with my hands; you witnessed their murder with your eyes. The Mountain God wanted us to meet."

Dr. Moon turned the monk's water bottle in his hands. He stared down at the clearing, as if he could see the flames. A muscle twitched in his jaw before he spoke again. "After we told the lieutenant about the massacre, he gave us the order to run away. Not immediately, but during the first snowfall, so that we'd leave obvious tracks. We needed to be easy to follow."

Dong Min added, "But we were not supposed to get caught."

"The snow fell two days later." Dr. Moon looked up at the sky. "My wife's grandmother died that night. As if she knew."

Thirty-Seven

1948

Every shade of white fell that night, the night of the first winter snow. In the beginning, the flakes fell singly and in pairs, each tiny crystal distinct. As the darkness deepened, the snow fell in clumps so large that clouds seemed to be falling piecemeal from the heavens. Whiteness clung to every surface, veiling the knobby mounds of dirt in the cabbage fields and capping the stone walls. At dawn, the snow paused, as if to take a breath, before redoubling as a scourge of ice.

Grandmother opened her eyes as soon as the first white flake touched the ground. She sensed the cold blanketing the house and took a shuddering breath. Beside her, Junja lay deeply asleep.

The old woman pushed herself off the floor, muffling a groan. While she was bedridden, she had been visited by feverish visions that struck hard and then receded. Her husband, giving her a bouquet of yellow canola blooms. The boys, splashing each other under the cascades of Cheonjiyeon Falls. Her daughter toddling on the bright sand. Mother, threading a needle with a strand of red silk. Father writing with a wooden brush. In between those hallucinations, when her senses returned, she had been aware of Junja's growing despair but was unable to rouse herself to comfort the girl.

The wind knifed through the room. Grandmother shivered and then went rigid, willing the cold away. There was barely enough heat left inside her to do this work.

She moved in the darkness, without any light, her house as familiar as her body. She broke the film of ice on the water with one crack of the ladle and filled the small cooking pot with water. The kindling burst into flame without any effort, so she thanked the spirit of the hearth for that grace.

She hesitated, then threw all the remaining grain into the pot as she muttered a blessing. The effort came at a price. She doubled over as an invisible blade seemed to strike her in the gut. She closed her eyes, whispered a prayer, and continued moving as moisture beaded her forehead.

She stirred the porridge, trembling, using every bit of strength she could muster. She gathered all her memories together, even the ones she had tried to forget. As she remembered everyone who had been lost, her tears salted the pot.

For a moment, she shook with panic as doubt tried to break into her heart. Oaths had been sworn and promises made, but the hearts of men were weak compared to the whims of the gods.

The knife in her gut seemed to twist. She gasped, doubling over. When she closed her eyes, she saw her fears for what they were and forced herself to stand straight. She pushed the darkness away with a shiver as she whispered another prayer. She thanked all the gods by their names before placing the lid on the pot.

As she walked to the room where Junja lay sleeping, the wind struck the old woman again. This time, she sank to her knees. She crawled to her granddaughter's side and managed to kneel before the sensation ebbed out of her limbs.

Grandmother stroked Junja's hair as she held her hand. She could feel the girl's pulse, a steady beat under her fingers. Blood of my blood, she thought. She remembered her first touch of the child, warm and slippery from her daughter's womb. The infant Junja had smiled up at her before squalling loudly of hunger.

She rested her palm on Junja's warm forehead. The girl's chest rose and fell in a steady rhythm as the old woman's breathing began to grow shallow.

When Junja opened her eyes, the brightness was blinding. She had to blink several times before she could see her grandmother kneeling beside her, haloed by light.

"Junja, try to remember, what did you see in your sea dream?"

The girl smiled. "I'm so glad you're feeling better, Halmung."

As she held her grandmother's hand, Junja remembered her dream.

☽

When Gun Joo and Dong Min arrived at Junja's house, a candle was flickering. They looked at each other, confused. Lieutenant Lee had warned them that the girl would not be expecting them and might be difficult to convince.

Gun Joo whispered. "Hello? Is someone awake in there?"

Snow whirled inside as Junja opened the door. She was fully dressed, wrapped against the cold. She ushered the two boys in while making sure no one was watching.

Gun Joo and Dong Min stumbled into the warmth of the kitchen. Two bowls were set out, and steam rose from a pot.

"Eat all of it," Junja instructed.

Gun Joo was stunned. "Did Lieutenant Lee t-t-tell you what we're going to do?"

The girl shook her head. "My grandmother did." She was wrapping a length of cloth around her leather boots to secure them to her feet.

"She woke up?" Dong Min was already spooning the porridge into his mouth as quickly as he could.

"Briefly, just before she died." The girl appeared calm as she searched through a wooden box for any small valuables she might have missed.

Dong Min looked stricken. "Are we still going to follow the lieutenant's plan? Without, uh . . . you know . . ." His hand waved through the air.

Junja's voice was choked. "There's no time for me to bury her. None of that matters anyways, because she's already had her funeral rites."

The two boys looked at each other, confused. The girl was making no sense. Rites without a burial? Dong Min shrugged as Gun Joo reached out to comfort the girl, who turned away to hide her tears.

She sniffed before speaking again. "Do you have room in those packs for food?" The boys took the two bundles she held out.

"Are you warm enough?" Junja frowned at their thin wool overcoats.

Gun Joo stamped his feet. "We'll warm up once we start walking."

The three of them left the house with quilts wrapped around themselves. The boys carried dried sweet potato, barley, dried seaweed, and bean paste in their packs. Junja's bundle held a small iron pot, dried fish, a candle, and a bag of salt. Around her neck hung a small pouch with a pearl, a hairpin, and a lighter.

The three of them crept along the winding path around the village, which the soldiers trod during guard duty. Enough moonlight shone for them to find their way without losing their footing, but the soft snow did not dampen the sound of their shoes crunching over the frozen leaves. The noise filled the boys with terror, yet Junja felt calm, as if she were experiencing events in a dream. She knew it was bitterly cold, but the sensation did not penetrate her body.

She glanced at Gun Joo. He was anxiously surveying their surroundings, hand ready on his holster. When he noticed her looking at him, he smiled, a brief flash that blinked out as quickly as it appeared.

They reached the main road as the sky began to brighten. Junja turned to Gun Joo, her voice a murmur.

"It's snowing hard. All our tracks will be covered. What should we do?"

Gun Joo glanced behind them, worry plain on his face.

Dong Min scooped up snow and ate some as he groaned. "I'm so hungry, I'd kill for a bo—"

A blackbird shot up into the sky.

Without thinking, Junja pulled both boys behind a large boulder with a scrubby tree growing next to it.

"Did you hear that? Someone said he was hungry. The sound came from over there!" A man's voice, startling in its proximity.

A sudden gust of wind pulled the end of Junja's head wrapping loose and held it aloft above the boulder. Just like a flag signaling their location.

Horrified, she yanked the cloth back down, heart thudding.

"Did you see that? Above that tall rock?" A second man spoke.

"I saw it too! Something rose up and then vanished." A third man, who sounded scared.

"It's a Communist—let's do our job and start cleaning this place up."

"Are you stupid? Why would a Communist be floating above a rock?"

"Didn't you hear what it said? It's a hungry ghost! And it wants to kill someone!"

"I don't believe in such ignorant superstitions."

"Then go investigate by yourself."

"You're the one with the gun."

"Which means I'm in charge. And I'm not wasting bullets on a ghost."

"That was no ghost. It sounded just like a person."

"Don't you know anything? Hungry ghosts sound just like you and me."

"They'll eat our souls if we don't give them food!"

"If we don't bother it, it can't hurt us."

Two gunshots ripped through the night, interrupting the argument.

"Did you hear that?"

"Sounds like they've started without us."

"Let's go back to the village before we miss all the action."

☽

Junja, Gun Joo, and Dong Min stayed crouched behind the boulder until their legs turned numb. When they finally emerged, the snow had ceased falling, and the sky was bright. The footprints left by the three soldiers could easily be seen. Anyone tracking the missing boys would now be led astray.

Dong Min studied the road. "We should leave before they come back."

Gun Joo looked at Junja. His voice was gentle. "Lieutenant Lee told us you would know where to go."

A blackbird cried out, pitiless. *"Gaw, gaw, gaw."*

The forest closed around them, drawing them deep inside its shadows. Junja's feet moved quickly, though her heart lagged far

behind. Her sorrow felt like a stone in her chest, and she wondered if she lived only to ache. Since the loss of her mother, the
blows had kept falling, one right after the next. She would leave
this place, she promised herself, while she ran as fast as she
could.

The two boys chased after the girl, who was following a large
stream toward its source. The trees tried to push them away as
branches clawed at their clothes. Just when they feared they
would lose her, Junja stopped still in her tracks. She wiped her
nose as she sniffed the air. She had found the unlikeliest of scents,
so far away from shore.

The fat boy noticed it too, though he didn't know what it was.
He rubbed his belly and sighed, remembering a bowl of red seaweed soup.

Junja motioned for the boys to follow as she climbed over a
sharp ridge of rocks. There, at the top, were three boulders, each
one shaped like a man. The trio of stones were slouched in a huddle, as if they were sharing a secret.

The girl prayed for permission before reaching into that con-
spiracy of stones. She pulled out the limbs of large branches and
dug out a sodden pile of leaves. The rock guardians seemed to
move apart as a gash opened up in the earth. Junja lay on her
stomach and slipped through, disappearing as if she were swallowed. The two boys followed in her wake, tumbling headlong
into the earth.

The space was too small to stand in, so the three of them knelt
in a crouch. Junja lit a candle, surprising the boys with a lighter.
The cave was part of a tunnel made entirely of stone. Junja left a
dried fish for the trio of stones, in thanks for allowing them passage. As she covered the mouth of the cave back up, the two boys
sniffed, curious. The air underground seemed to move in a

current and smelled salty, like the sea. Junja blew out the candle and apologized. They would be crawling in darkness for a while.

When the boys asked where they were going, Junja's answer baffled them. They didn't ask her to explain, because her voice sounded so bleak.

They were heading back toward the village, to the sea caves

Thirty-Eight

They crawled on their bellies, pushing their packs, grit crusting their mouths and noses. The darkness of the tunnel was so deep that Gun Joo began doubting his senses. Were they moving forward, or were they trapped in place, wriggling in the earth like worms? As his friend whimpered and cursed behind him, Gun Joo kept his silence. He thought of his father stroking his head when he used to wake crying from a nightmare.

Junja clung to the faint scent of brine as she retraced a trail from the past. Mother had taught her how to navigate this twisting route at the end of Junja's apprenticeship. Only full haenyeos were shown the secrets of the tunnel, which wound its way to the sea. *"Imagine you're diving and extend your senses beyond yourself."* Junja followed the memory of her mother as she crept through the dangerous maze.

She was about to despair when she saw the glow, a shimmer in the dark. Candles had been placed near the end of the tunnel by those who understood its terrors.

The girl and the boys stumbled out, blinking at the brightness around them. The sea cavern was filled with people, holding candles against the gloom. Their shadows loomed high on the rocky walls, stretching up to the dome of the ceiling. As everyone rejoiced in their reunion, the villagers thanked them for the risk they had taken.

The plan had been clever, and its execution precise. Young children, elders, and anyone who might cry or stumble in the dark had gone to the caves during the day while the men patrolled the mountain. The last ones to leave were the cooks and the serving girls who prepared the food for the soldiers.

Upon the lieutenant's orders, they had sacrificed the cow. After a bellowing bath in the sea, her body was butchered for a feast. Her ruby flesh was sliced and seasoned, and her bones boiled into broth. Villagers sipped the milky soup, while soldiers grilled the meat. As fat dripped down upon the flames, the fire blazed and roared. That night, the soldiers slept the heavy sleep of men who had gorged on blood. Smoke charred their dreams as the first snow fell, cloaking the world in white.

The first morning watch was still burping when they discovered the missing boys. After following the footprints to the road, the watchmen roused the rest of the camp for the search. The women waited for the signal. Two gunshots, and they would flee, disappearing like foam on the waves.

☽

For seven days and seven nights, the people in the caves ate as much as they could, filling their bellies with food they had hidden from the soldiers: millet porridge with shredded radish and dried anchovies; salads from mung beans sprouted in the dark; kelp soup and stews of fermented cabbage and soybean paste. They cooked at night, near the mouth of the cave, so the winds could blow the smoke out to sea.

As they ate, they shared stories of the past, before Jeju had been overrun by strangers, scaring away all the fairies and sprites. They remembered the old days when the goddess of Hallasan was a young girl who roamed the mountain astride a white deer. They told tales from the time when tigers could talk and dragons slept in the cavern, coiled like gargantuan cats. In the beginning, when the sea king had been in his wild prime, the waves had frothed with his vigor, seeding every oyster with a pearl.

When Junja's turn came, she gave thanks to her grandmother, who had conspired to protect them all. The women of the village beat their breasts and wailed, mourning the old woman's lonely deathbed. Junja, eyes spilling, shared her grandmother's last story: she had already had a funeral once. Long ago, to trick a god.

The ruse had bought her an ordinary life. Yet a dark weed had taken root in the space reserved for the ancestral spirit that she had rejected at her parent's request. After losing their sons to the Japanese, they refused to let their daughter serve gods who had failed in their duties.

The Goh Auntie who harbored the spirit gave precise instructions, to stop the legacy from passing on at her death. The potion she gave her niece made the girl fall into a swoon so deep that her body resembled a corpse.

As the family went into mourning, the auntie closed the door to her house. She had taken with her a chicken, a duck, and enough incense to burn for three days and three nights. The doors and windows of her hut were hammered shut with iron nails, and the seams covered with yellow paper. She wrote incantations on the walls, using her hair as a brush. Nothing could enter or leave that house, not the living nor even the dead.

The auntie prayed for three days, accompanied by the clucking of the chicken and the quacking of the duck. On the dawn of the fourth day, she started pounding on the walls, screaming to be let out. She threatened to curse everyone in the family and singled out her niece, who had awakened from her temporary death.

"There's a space inside you waiting for the spirit, and if you do not fill it, that place will gather darkness instead!"

As the sun set, the auntie's cries grew hoarse, dwindling into croaks that collapsed into whispers. The rising moon finally silenced the auntie, and the family fell into an uneasy sleep.

Around midnight the chicken began squawking so loudly that the noise shattered everyone's slumber. The duck answered that sound with an unearthly barrage of its own. The screaming fowls tore apart the night with their argument. The hideous sounds they made resembled human words by avian tongues inadequate to the task.

When sunlight struck the roof at dawn, the feathered screams were silenced. The two men the auntie had chosen for the task put on their protective amulets and pried open the front door. The auntie's body lay on a mat. Her eyes had turned milky, and her lips bore the faintest of smiles. On one side of her lay the chicken, dead. On the other side lay the duck, panting and unable to move. With gloved hands, the men carried all the bodies to the woodpile.

The flames caught immediately, roaring into a blaze so hot it scalded everyone's cheeks. The air smelled of roasting meat, making mouths water and stomachs churn. When the fire died down, only ashes and knobby white rocks remained, and these were buried with reverence in the forest.

☽

On their eighth night of hiding, the people in the sea cave began their preparations to leave. One last story was shared by candlelight as they finished their final meal. After clearing away every trace of their stay, they filled baskets and bundles with food, as much as they could carry. Children put on every piece of clothing they owned, while mothers argued with fathers over what to leave behind.

Junja led the group, with Gun Joo and Dong Min behind her. They crawled away from the sea this time, back toward the rock guardians in the forest. Grandmother had made a pact with the lieutenant. He would meet everyone and lead them to safety. Shadows pressed upon the girl from all sides, darker than the winding tunnel. What if Lieutenant Lee wasn't there? How long were they supposed to wait?

Junja stopped crawling, her concentration shattered. The tunnel had divided, and she couldn't remember which way to go. Mother had warned her about not giving words to worry; Grandmother always said that fear was more dangerous than the tunnels themselves. The long line of people snaking behind the girl waited, wondering what was happening.

Junja's chest constricted in the scant air. Her blood drummed in her ears. Her fingernails scraped against stone, scrambling for something to hold.

Gun Joo tapped her ankle gently. "Are you all right?"

Junja could hardly breathe.

Behind her, the women of the village understood her silence. The girl had lost her mother and her grandmother. Of course she would lose her bearings here, in this place that tested even the strongest. The tunnel was too narrow for someone else to take the lead, and no one knew which turn had given the girl pause.

A quavering note formed in the dark, so low it sank into the shadows. The note was raised again by another voice, which lifted the tone higher. The tunnel began to swell with a choir of voices, twisting and plaiting together. They sang of drifting tides and fishing boats, of lovers lost and treasures found, of stormy winds and wild waters. The song of the haenyeo wrapped the girl in a promise: she was not alone here in the depths of the earth.

Junja took a shuddering breath. She planted one palm in front of her and swallowed another sip of air. She began to crawl as the singing voices followed her, pushing her forward, helping her remember the way.

☽

As the end of the tunnel drew closer, the air turned sharp with cold. Junja turned to whisper into Gun Joo's ear. She would go out first to look for the lieutenant. He and Dong Min needed to stay hidden, guns ready, until she signaled that it was safe to emerge.

Gun Joo touched her hand in acknowledgment, a light brush with his fingers. "We watch and wait for you."

Junja clawed through a frozen clot of branches and leaves, reaching a layer of crusty snow. She was breaking through that icy barrier when a hand reached inside and grabbed her, yanking her out with force.

Gun Joo immediately turned and tapped Dong Min's head. The other boy repeated the gesture, passing the sign for danger down the trembling line of bodies in the tunnel.

The man who pulled Junja outside was not Lieutenant Lee. The stranger was dressed in animal skins, like a hunter. A bow was slung across his back, and a blade was strapped to his thigh. His fists were wrapped in rags, and his face bundled against the cold. Junja did not know the man by the clothes he was wearing, but when she looked up, she recognized his eyes. They belonged to a boy she had met in the spring, before her mother died.

Thirty-Nine

Suwol did not know Junja at first, though the girl began quivering at the sight of him. Grandmother had warned her that all first loves burnt hot, to quicken the heart, but this one would be branded upon her.

Junja had to swallow, before she could speak. "Where is Lieutenant Lee?"

As soon as Suwol heard Junja's voice, he dropped her arm. His words sounded scorched. "He's recovering from injuries, so I've come in his place." His tone was formal, as if they were meeting for the very first time. "How many villagers are with you?"

Junja kept a polite distance as well. "Several dozen. They're waiting in the tunnels."

The half moon disappeared behind a cloud, casting the scene into darkness. The silence between the boy and the girl expanded. It filled with the memories of promises made, words that the world had broken.

The click of a trigger broke the hush. Gun Joo had crept outside, unnoticed, as Junja and Suwol talked. The moon was shining on his gun. He stuttered, but his hands held steady. "You're n-not Lieutenant Lee. W-who are you?"

Suwol's hand flew toward his blade. His eyes glared, and his voice curdled. He ignored Gun Joo to hiss at Junja instead. "Why did you come with a Nationalist cur? Is this some kind of dirty trick?"

As Suwol's eyes turned feral, Junja took a step toward him, placing herself between the gun and the knife. "His name is Gun Joo, and he's helping us. There's one more soldier in the tunnel. The villagers will vouch for what I'm saying."

"The lieutenant didn't say anything about two soldiers." Suwol's eyes stayed fixed on the gun. His bandaged hands jerked toward Gun Joo. "Tell him to drop his weapon."

Junja watched Suwol's hand clench the hilt of the blade. Her voice shook slightly. "Gun Joo, please put the gun down on the ground." She took a breath before speaking again. "Suwol, let go of the knife. I have no reason to lie; you know that better than anyone here. Please believe me when I tell you this soldier is helping us."

Neither boy moved. Suwol and Gun Joo turned their attention away from the girl who stood trembling between them. They stared at each other, one red with rage, the other white with shock. Neither boy blinked. A gust of wind made Gun Joo shiver as he removed his finger from the trigger. He bent over to lay the gun on the ground, while Suwol drew out the knife.

Junja, who saw the metal glint, shifted her stance, a small half-step. Suwol noticed her move away and understood: she would shield the soldier with her body. His hand dropped, empty, to his side. The manic gleam in his eye faded. His voice was flat when he finally spoke.

"We have to move quickly. Tell everyone to come outside."

))

The people from the sea caves staggered their departures, fanning out across multiple routes. Some groups headed west, toward Mosulpo, while the rest traveled south to seek refuge in the smaller islands.

Suwol distributed the papers that the lieutenant had forged, along with instructions for each group. After guiding the last family to the road, Suwol returned for Junja, Gun Joo, and Dong Min. The three of them would be taking the long route to Jeju City, along the eastern perimeter of the island.

Suwol studied the packs that Gun Joo and Dong Min were wearing, which bulged with supplies from the cave. He asked about the food they were carrying and proposed an alternate route. By cutting across the lower slope of the mountain, they could shorten their journey by half. If he could guide them past the military blockades, would they give him half of their provisions?

Gun Joo understood what Suwol was unable to admit. The need was clear in the pinch of his cheeks and the sharpened line of his jaw. Though desperate enough to ask, he was too proud not to pay.

Gun Joo glanced at Junja, seeking her permission. The anguish on her face was his answer, revealing more than he wanted to know. He reminded himself of how she had stood her ground to defend him. His stutter disappeared as he answered, confident he spoke for them both.

"Get us across the mountain safely, and you can have all the food we're carrying."

Dong Min, who had said nothing since emerging from the tunnels, started in shock at his friend's rash generosity. "Did you just give all our food away?"

Gun Joo's voice held firm. "We'll move faster if we aren't carrying so much."

☽

The four of them crept in silence across the eastern foothills, through naked forests and barren fields of rock. Trees tried to ensnare them, and the shadows of stones made them stumble. The darkness sharpened every noise, giving rise to irrational fears. The snap of a twig rang like a shot, while the leaves seemed to crackle like thunder.

The sounds of the night disappeared as they passed through a dark field of stones. The ground was hard and flat in that place, as if a giant had stomped in a rage. Nothing grew out of the blackened earth, which had been claimed by piles of rocks. The eerie stillness was so absolute that even their footsteps lost their sound. Suwol covered his mouth with his hands, warning them not to speak. He quickened his pace and kept his eyes fixed on the path, gesturing to the others to follow. Though the far end of the field was always in sight, they couldn't seem to reach it. They seemed to be walking in circles, as though they were stuck in a maze.

When they finally crossed to the other side, the forest reached out with its branches. The sounds of the night redoubled in force, pushing away that unnatural silence. Frozen leaves crunched under the ice, which shattered loudly under their steps. The sound of their breathing returned with a whoosh, as did the anxious thump of their hearts.

When Suwol signaled that it was safe to speak, everyone sighed in relief. His voice was a monotone as he explained. "That field is the largest break in the blockade. It's a dangerous place for an ambush. So many soldiers have died there that it's rarely patrolled."

Junja looked puzzled. "I don't understand why it took so long for us to walk through it. The end of the field was always in sight."

"The place was cursed, a long time ago. Some people get lost there and never come out." Suwol looked away as he spoke, his hands balled into fists.

Gun Joo gave Suwol an odd look while Dong Min swore under his breath. "I hope we didn't attract any ghosts," the fat boy said as he touched his mother's amulet.

But the dead were not following them, and neither were the living. They met no other souls as they walked through to the end of that night.

☽

Junja woke up to the sound of water dripping off stones. Dong Min was snoring beside her. His back was pressed up against Gun Joo, whose breathing was slow and steady. The four of them had found refuge in a small cave as the sun began to rise. They would rest and regain their strength before parting ways for good.

Suwol was no longer inside, so Junja crawled out to find him. He would leave at dusk to return to the mountain, going back the way they had come.

He was squatting on the ground, sharpening the end of a stick. White shavings of wood were scattered around him. At his side lay a pile of small stakes. His knife continued to move as Suwol sensed Junja's approach.

"When the other two wake up, I'll show you the path to the nutmeg forest. You'll reach it by nightfall, I think."

Junja knelt beside him and reached for the pouch around her neck. Grandmother had begged her to choose wisely, before the girl understood what she meant. She studied the marks on Suwol's face. Was the scab on his brow from a burn or a blow? Had a knife inscribed that line on his lip? How had she not noticed the hollow of his cheeks, which betrayed his weeks of hunger?

She let go of the pouch as she spoke. Her hands were clenched. "Come with us. To the mainland."

The knife stopped moving. Suwol kept his eyes fixed down on his hands. His breathing formed a cloud of mist. He didn't look at Junja when he finally spoke.

"Duty keeps me here."

The words that rose to Junja's throat tasted like bile. The gods had failed his family, and his country had made him an orphan. The only duty left was to survive. She dared not mention what she had witnessed on the mountain and remind him of what he had lost. She held the bitterness in her mouth.

The knife began moving again, in deliberate strokes. Junja watched the end of the stick turn into a deadly point. Suwol tested the tip with his thumb and set it down before speaking again.

"My cousin, Mr. Lee, has joined our cause."

Junja nodded, feeling numb. "Is he still a lieutenant?"

"Until he's discovered. Or dies." Suwol took out a stone and began sharpening his knife. Sunlight glinted off the blade as his hands moved back and forth. Underneath the wrappings, his fingers were stained, the nails blackened and cracked.

Junja remembered holding his hand on the day they left Jeju City. She had asked for his confession as they walked toward the mountain pass.

No more secrets, the boy had vowed as he told Junja the truth. He was not alone in believing that Korea needed to stand free. Those meddling Americans and their war machines would only bring ruin and grief. If fighting for the sovereignty of his country made him a Communist rebel, he would bear the shame of that label with pride.

He had told Junja about the company he kept, souls far worthier than himself. He described an elderly fisherman whose sons had died in Japan. Because he was illiterate, the Nationalists had hired him as a messenger, not knowing that he could memorize anything he saw in one glance. The former policeman who opened a jail cell to free a village now served as their sniper because he owned the most reliable rifle. A group of haenyeo moonlighting as women of the night would ply the soldiers with drink, kissing their secrets out of them.

These people who bled for their country would never be known by name. They believed that Korea should govern herself, free of ignorant foreigners who understood nothing about them. Patriots in all but name, they fought for this right with their bodies, armed only by flesh and bone. With knives, hoes, and sticks, they defied an intruder of metal and fire.

They were desperately short of funds and supplies, so he had emptied his family's coffers of cash, with his father's permission. The gold rings belonged to his mother, who wept as she took them off. His grandfather gave him the knife he had once used as a member of the royal guard.

Suwol had held her hand gently as he confessed. His hands still felt like a scholar's then, soft and white like paper.

Someone had been tortured, and someone had been betrayed. When they got the warning, they did what made sense in a house of ill repute: they stripped off their clothes and embraced. The shock of two men in such an unnatural pose proved a useful distraction. While the soldiers were beating them in disgust, the bulk of the funds were spirited away by the women who worked the house.

He was bound, by oath and by blood, to these people and this cause. He had pledged his life to protect his country, as the men in his family had done for generations. When she listened to Suwol's confession that day, Junja had been moved by the truth of his words. Once they were husband and wife, she had promised herself, she would seek to join their fight.

But when the bombs fell from the plane, she saw the demon's full strength. The enormity of it felled her grandmother, who begged her granddaughter to flee. When the gods went to war, the old woman warned, men always followed in kind. Nothing would stop the tide of blood that was rising.

Stay and drown, or flee and survive. Her life had diminished to this choice. There was no one left for Junja to mourn, not even the gods. Where could she go from here?

Sunlight glinted through the bony trees as shadows began to lengthen. The chill in the air grew sharper, threatening another night of ice. The girl shivered as she wrapped her arms around herself.

Suwol picked up another stick. His knife began moving again. He laughed, a hollow bark more pained than amused. "I wanted to clear my family's debt to you and your grandmother, but I owe you more now, not less."

Junja wanted to cry, but she had no more tears to spare. She was wrung out by loss, exhausted by grieving.

"There is no debt to pay."

"I promise to honor my obligation. If not in this life, then the next." Suwol was muttering to himself.

Junja watched her breath turn white in the air. She closed her eyes to feel the last rays of the sun. She would keep running as fast as she could until she could run no more. She remembered what she was holding and gently laid the lighter on the ground, where Suwol could see it.

☽

Junja, Gun Joo, and Dong Min reached the nutmeg forest in the darkest part of night. Dazed with hunger and exhaustion, they wandered through the giant trees. They tried to stay awake, fearful of the venomous snakes that guarded the forest, but collapsed into a sleep so deep that neither the stinging frost nor the bright stare of the moon could wake them. Only the sun, at its height, was able to release them from their feverish dreams.

When the three of them stepped out of the forest's shade, they stumbled upon a paved road. A huddle of people stood waiting there, craning their necks and looking expectant.

Dong Min approached a soldier. His voice cracked from thirst. "Excuse me, sir, but what's everyone doing here?"

The soldier didn't bother to turn his head. "We're waiting for the bus to Jeju City."

The fat boy rooted through his pockets and found his mother's money. "We're taking that bus. If I don't eat a bowl of seaweed soup today, I swear I'm going to die. You don't want my hungry bachelor ghost haunting you for the rest of your life."

Gun Joo glanced at Junja. The girl took one last look at the mountain before she nodded.

The bus was jammed with people clutching chickens and sacks of sweet potatoes. The group from the roadside pushed themselves inside, grateful for the warmth. Junja clung to a metal bar as the vehicle rumbled down the road. Whenever the swaying mass of bodies around her shifted, she thought she could see the flash of the ocean, far away on the receding horizon.

Forty

2001

Three shamans will preside over the kut for Dr. Moon Gun Joo: a dancer, a singer, a drummer. The beautiful shaman, who will dance, smoothed a paper banner with her hands. She folded the paper thrice into thirds and picked up a pair of scissors. She cut out the patterns like she was taught, as her grandmother's last apprentice.

Once, there was a time, when the kingdom stood strong, when these ceremonies were fit for gods. Ethereal voices would swell the human choir while the very earth amplified the drums. Rainbow-clad dancers would swirl in unison as silk banners fluttered by the thousands. A banquet of offerings would pass by on parade, held high on lacquered palanquins: roast pig and duck, crackling in brown armor; honey wine in silver goblets; rice cakes, glistening like jewels. Smoke from the incense and candles would rise, billowing like clouds in the heavens.

The beautiful shaman could still hear her grandmother's voice, describing those courtly spectacles. *"Someday, may you preside over ceremonies just as grand. First, you must learn how to dress the altar. Then you must learn to bless the food. When you've mastered all of these, in time, you will learn the drum, the song, and the dance."*

There had been lessons in astrology as well, to track the heavenly bodies. Hours of calligraphy practice, because some words could not be spoken aloud. Herb-gathering trips to the mountain, where strange smells were held under her nose. She had learned to grind powders, mix elixirs, mold incense, brew liquor. All in service to the gods.

They could be fickle and forgetful, Grandmother had warned, with a fondness for flattery and drink. Though immortal, they grew weak at the end of their cycles, to be reborn with every new age. Some gods grew selfish and greedy as they aged, clinging to the dregs of their power. Others slipped away quietly, still full of grace.

The last imperial shamans had been cast out of court for predicting the kingdom's demise. With the dynasty fallen and the country in chaos, Grandmother had escaped with their secrets. *"Ours is an ancient lineage, of high-standing seers and soothsayers. We served the kings and queens of Korea for more than a thousand years. Before that we ruled directly, when only shamans could be kings. Our family is as ancient as this land, our bloodline more noble than royalty."*

The beautiful shaman looked up from her handiwork. The vinyl floor and bare walls made her sigh. No splendor or wonders here, just a bit of threadbare sincerity. She stretched her fingers to release an ache and hoped that her efforts would suffice. She was not expecting the gods, after all, but calling out to simple folk. For them, one more taste of this world was usually temptation enough.

☽

Dr. Moon lit the incense sticks and bowed before the altar. The beautiful shaman poured water, and he drank from the silver goblet. The offering table was an artful abundance, arranged on shiny brass: fruits from field and forest, treasures from the deep, the flesh of beast and fowl. On a table for the gods alone lay the head of a roast suckling pig, lit cigarettes stuck in its snout. The tips of the cigarettes and incense glowed red as smoke curled through the room.

A shaman began to wail, and the drum began to beat. The drummer was wearing blue, and the singer was draped in pink. The beautiful shaman stepped out from the shroud of a long white robe. Her red tulip skirt was embroidered with peonies, and vines climbed up the length of her purple vest. In her right hand she held a handle, tied to a yellow length of silk. The banners above the altar began to flutter, as if swept by a passing breeze.

Dong Min whispered to Dr. Moon as he sat on the floor beside his friend. "Those banners are the doorways to all the other worlds. The spirits will come through them to visit with us in this world. It's like we're throwing them a party." He gestured to the altars. "Those are the decorations and food. Next, the shamans are going to call out to the guests of honor to invite them."

The two men nodded to the monk from the mountain, who was kneeling on the other side of the room. After sharing their stories, Dr. Moon had invited the man to join his kut. The beautiful shaman's eyes had opened wide when the monk arrived, and he had recognized her as well. They both did the work of remembrance in the places where blood had been spilled. They mourned the savagery of those lonely deaths while they prayed for the lost and forgotten. As the three shamans took their places, the monk took out his wooden beads and closed his eyes to pray.

The drumbeat thudded, the cymbal crashed, and the wailing turned into song. The beautiful shaman began to spin, red skirts blooming open. She whipped the silk overhead, the yellow rippling like a snake. As her body trembled in time with the drum, she looped the silk into knots. She freed the knots with a flick of her wrist and began spinning around the room.

The shaman was a whirl of silk, turning and turning in a widening spiral. The air in the room grew thick with smoke, and the floor seemed to tilt. Dr. Moon pressed his palms against the floor, as if to brace himself.

Dong Min nudged him. "Kind of makes you seasick, doesn't it?"

The shaman dropped her outstretched arms. She walked around the room, streamer trailing behind her. She stopped in front of Dr. Moon and squinted. She pulled out an invisible handkerchief and began polishing an invisible pair of glasses. When she leaned forward to speak, Dr. Moon could smell orange blossom under the smoke.

The air promised snow when he pulled the two boys aside to ask for their help. They had to leave tracks and be followed, but they couldn't get caught. Once they reached the mainland, they would stay under cover, leading normal lives. Their mission was to hide in plain sight, until he contacted them again.

While everyone searched for the missing boys, he stayed behind to guard the radio. He drank from his flask as he waited, allowing his mind to wander. If he survived, he would travel to Greece, to drink wine and taste a tomato. How his mother would despair! If he died in this place, her heart would surely break. If he lived, he would only disappoint her.

He tossed the empty flask over his shoulder and went outside. He took a deep breath before he started to run, chasing phantoms only he could see. He circled his tent for emphasis and ran back and forth from the main road. When the tracks suggested the number of bodies he needed, he went back inside and dried off his boots.

He leapt upon the file box, pulling out handfuls of paper. He scattered some pages over the snow and fed the rest to the fire. He attended to the radio next, lifting it with a grimace. As it smashed on the ground, he smiled.

Ready for his final act, he pushed his glasses back up his nose. His eyelids fluttered before he convulsed, snarling as he attacked. He punched his face with his fists and raked his skin with his nails. He punished himself for his weakness, hating the way he was born. He had to force himself to stop, to clean his fingernails of gore. He threw the soiled handkerchief into the fire and watched the silk melt into the flames.

He peered at the sun and winced. Time to call back the hounds. He lifted his handgun and aimed at the dark spot on the wall of the tent. He changed his mind and moved the gun to his head. He stood like that, waiting for courage, until his hands began to shake.

A bullet tore through the top of the tent. He looked up at the hole that glared down at him. When he saw how high the sun was, he fired another round. The soldiers would be returning soon, goaded by those gunshots. With all that meat in their bellies, they would destroy the village in their bloodlust.

He would play no role in that mess.

He poked through the pile of wood, searching for the log he had hidden. It was smooth, so it wouldn't leave splinters, with two bumps that he could grip. He swung the cudgel as hard as he could, feeling his glasses break. The sound of the impact—hollow, blunt—surprised him. He sank to his knees, amused but full of regrets.

As the scent of oranges faded, Dong Min leapt up to speak. "When the war ended, where did you go? Do you have family?" The fat man had always believed that the lieutenant was a hero who had saved their lives.

The shaman cocked her head. Lieutenant Lee had died in cave. He was still waiting to be given a proper burial, but this truth was not theirs to know. She turned abruptly and whirled away, pulling the streamer behind her.

Dr. Moon poked his friend. "Hey, did you tell her about the lieutenant?"

Dong Min shook his head mournfully. "I guess he didn't feel like talking. I should've thanked him instead."

The cymbals crashed, startling the men, who jumped when the wailing grew louder. The thudding drumbeat pulsed through the floor as the dancer stamped her feet, waving the streamer around her.

When she stopped in front of Dr. Moon again, the shaman reached out with both hands. She tousled his hair and pinched his nose, like his father used to do.

"You waited for such a long time." The shaman's voice was husky. "Your father is so sorry that he never came home."

He was returning from Seoul when he was stopped at the border, accused of being a spy. Though they smashed all the melons in his cart and found nothing, the soldiers refused to believe him. He didn't cry when they tortured him, but he wept when they dumped the flour on the ground.

Maybe they didn't like his face. Maybe it was just bad luck. He was the only one detained while the others were allowed to go home. He pressed his neighbor's hand and begged him to deliver a message. "Please tell my wife to take our son and go south, to her sister. I'll join them there when I can."

Gun Joo's mother started screaming when she saw the empty sack. The sound began as a high-pitched shriek and deflated into a guttural moan. When her breath ran out, she fainted.

Gun Joo's father was bound and gagged when the soldiers led him to the forest. As they raised their guns to shoot, the order was abruptly reversed. A tunnel had collapsed in the northern mountains, and more hands were needed for digging.

He dug for days, which blurred into years. He dug until his back hunched over and his hair turned white. He stared down the length of a shovel for so long, he could only see as far as its blade. During the day, he dug underground in the dark, and at night he dreamed of light.

The dream was always the same: the tunnel he was digging led home, back to his wife and son. He would drop the shovel, climb out of the dirt, and walk to the front of his farm. There, at the gate, his son would be waiting, just like he always did. His precious son, his brilliant boy, who could count before he turned two.

He would find his wife in the garden, gathering wild onion shoots. He would give her the flour, with a kiss. For you, my beloved, he would say.

One night, ten years after his arrest, he sleepwalked out of his cot. He was about to open the door to his house when everything turned dark.

He had been shot in the back by a guard, who thought he was trying to escape.

The beautiful shaman released Dr. Moon, who had wept in her arms like a child. "Your father found your mother, and they are together again."

Dr. Moon wiped his nose. "My mother—could I speak to her too?"

The shaman suddenly became shy. She cast her eyes down at the floor, unable to look at Dr. Moon. She rubbed her hands, worrying her fingers, before she finally nodded.

When she saw the empty flour sack, her chest seemed to rip apart. From that moment, her heart was a husk, and she hardly a person.

Everyone begged her to come to her senses for the sake of her pitiful son. But she couldn't bear to look at the boy, whose face looked just like his father's.

The child never complained about his mother, whose presence betrayed her absence. Buckets brimmed over while she milked, and pots scorched as the soup boiled away. Because she no longer felt hunger, she often forgot to cook.

To survive, her son had to borrow beggar's tricks. He drank rainwater to fool an empty stomach and chewed bark to pretend he was eating. He discovered which shopkeepers tossed tasty scraps to dogs and orphans alike. At night, he shut his eyes and pretended to sleep so that his mother would be free to cry.

She endured her grief for as long as she could, until the bombing reached a lull. While the world pretended that the war had stopped, the fighting never ended for her.

When her son finally reached an acceptable age, she allowed herself to give up. She dropped the firewood she was carrying as her legs buckled beneath her. She lay on the ground, not moving, until someone knelt beside her. She opened her eyes to see who it was, and her breath stopped in her throat.

There he was, her beloved, holding out his hand to take her home.

"Your mother is deeply ashamed. She begs you to please forgive her." The beautiful shaman looked sad.

An old tightness released in Dr. Moon's throat, allowing him to respond. "She did her best in terrible times. I promise to honor them both with a proper ceremony every year."

The shaman smiled. "Your father requests peaches. Your mother, noodles."

All the tears he never shed as a boy, the tears that stuck in his throat and made it difficult to speak, burst out of Dr. Moon like a torrent. Alongside him, Dong Min sobbed with abandon, remembering how piteous his friend's youth had been.

The shaman resumed her dervish dance, stomping her feet with the thudding drum and shaking her arms to the cymbal. She tied the streamer into knots and shook out the mortal skein.

A breeze blew open the door, fluttering the flags over the altar. The tips of the cigarettes and incense glowed red as smoke curled through the room. The voices of all her grandmothers whispered in the shaman's ear like an eerie choir of sighs. Invisible hands lent their assistance as the shaman unraveled the tangle of souls that clung to Dr. Moon like burrs.

The space between worlds is as thin as a shadow and as brief as a breath, difficult to cross without dying. Only mediums and seers can bridge this gap, yet even the most impervious of souls can sense it: shivers down spines and gut instincts; good dreams and nightmares; premonition, déjà vu, coincidence.

Being possessed is like being loved: someone must want to hold you, and someone must return that embrace. Some spirits enter with kind intent, bringing the best of themselves. Others break in like thieves, with force, so greedy they drain their host. Lost souls wander through by chance, confused like babes in the woods. As one who moves between the realms, a shaman must host them all.

But there are boundaries to respect and protocols to follow. For what happens in the world of spirits finds a mirror in the world of men.

The two old men stared at the shaman, who was kneeling in the center of the room, head bowed and palms raised. She wasn't moving, yet she seemed to be panting with effort.

Dr. Moon whispered to his friend. "Is it over?"

Dong Min watched the shaman, uncertain. "I'm not sure. Just wait."

The two men were about to stand when the shaman rose and brushed off her skirts. She walked briskly toward Dr. Moon, her mouth curving in a half smile. She placed her hands on her hips, her voice pitched down to a familiar alto.

"Remember the nutmeg forest, yobo?"

Dr. Moon's jaw quivered. "Junja? Is that really you?"

Dong Min swore under his breath. "She's good, this one, spooky good. Even better than my mother."

Forty-One

As she lay dying, Junja remembered how she had floated to the surface, pearl in her palm, her sea dream a trail of bubbles behind her. The years had unspooled like the sea king foretold, a ribbon of bright and dark. How her life ended she never knew, until the moment it happened. A bit of kindness from a god who had learned that a mortal who knew too much would always be haunted by death.

She made the choice to survive and spent the war surrounded by soldiers. She sewed uniforms for the living while Gun Joo studied the cadavers of the dead. They huddled in the dark as air sirens wailed, waiting for the sounds of war. Would it be the sharp crack of bullets this time, or the flat bass thud of a bomb? They swore to each other that their children would never have to know the difference.

In Philadelphia they lived in a Tudor, shaded by oak and dogwood. They drove cars, spoke English, played golf. Every fall, she and her church friends made kimchi in the shade of a Presbyterian steeple while the husbands practiced their putting. As the women brined cabbages with red paste, their eyes would prick with tears. Was it the bite of chili peppers that made them sniff? Or the sting of remembering all the women before them who had taught them how to taste with their hands?

In the spring she planted seeds she had smuggled against her body—green onion, mung bean, chili, perilla, cucumber—that she fed to her family in the summer. She grew accustomed to the shock of eating meat every week, but her mouth always longed for the sea: the slip of kelp, the bristle of anchovy, the chewiness of squid.

The work of surviving the present had spared no time for mourning the past. But as the thunder of war grew distant, she began to remember what she thought she had forgotten. Sometimes she heard voices in the dry whispers of falling leaves. The sight of a blackbird made her look twice. Whenever the first flake fell from the sky, her heart seemed to crack wide open.

The gods of her mother and grandmother had failed her, yet she still found a way to persist. She brought to that new world an inherited conviction, a Korean will to believe. Her faith was more than a cultural habit; it was practical too. Why place all your bets on a mortal coil when divinity might offer a hedge? Between a life too brief and an endless death, it seemed only sensible to improve the odds.

☽

Junja watched the beautiful shaman turn, arms open wide in welcome. Her spirit felt moved by that earthly embrace, its promise that her life had mattered. While the shaman stretched up to the sky, Junja reached down to the ground below. Together, the two women formed an ecstatic duet, a bridge between heaven and earth. As a swelling of voices rose in song from the depths, the skies thundered their timpani. Whirling and spinning until she grew giddy, Junja began to laugh, remembering that as many times as a life could end, it would start back up, all over again.

Junja, Gun Joo, and Dong Min reached the nutmeg forest during the poisonous part of the evening, when the snakes guarding the trees roused themselves to go hunting. Junja sang out to the snake god to create a safe path for their feet. The three of them tiptoed past the warning signs into the hulking trees.

They found a dry patch of ground in a ring of slender saplings. The three of them were so hungry that they gnawed on nuts scratched out from the snow. The strange medicinal taste made them dizzy, confusing the ache in their bellies.

The girl listened to the branches as they fiddled in the wind. The boys danced a silly dance, giggling until they collapsed. As the forest played a wild lullaby, the three of them curled against the trees and closed their eyes.

Junja woke up to find Gun Joo sleeping against her. While the trees whispered overhead, she touched his face to make sure he wasn't a dream. He sighed as a tear slipped down his cheek. She caught the warm drop with her fingertip and touched it to her tongue.

Love tasted necessary, like salt.

As the threesome slept in the forest, moonlight crept over the rocky crevices, awakening the snakes in their burrows. The creatures slithered around the slumbering bodies, forked tongues flickering. The snakes didn't taste any prey in the wintry air, so they slid back to their holes, curled up, and resumed their dreaming.

The drum beat stopped. The dancer left the dance. The kut ended as it began, with the doorways to all the worlds fluttering shut. The incense, candles, and cigarettes turned into ash as the haze drifted out of the room. The food from the altar was shared by the living, who ate in memory of the dead.

☽

The shamans and the monk bowed in farewell as the two friends drove away. Their small gray car looked like a beetle as it crept toward the silver sea. There it paused, by the water's edge, to let the two men leave. Together, they walked on the beach, pants

rolled, feet bare against the sand. The surf crashed over their murmuring voices, as mist stung their eyes. Seagulls floated overhead,
crying as they circled. The water rushed toward the land, waves
rolling over in the wind, white on black and black on white. The
men held up their hands as they watched, waiting for a god to
touch them.

The three shamans and the monk drove up the mountain pass,
which was once an old road before the Japanese paved it. Though
the passage had changed with the years, the surrounding forest
looked the same as it always had, the branches reaching out like
arms. The vehicle turned onto a gravel road that faded into a rut-
ted dirt trail.

The drumming shaman turned off the engine and looked at
the singing shaman, who nodded. The beautiful shaman and the
monk gazed past the trees, up at the sky beyond.

The first two shamans carried the drum and cymbals. The
beautiful shaman and the monk bore the incense and offerings.
The foursome stepped over sticks and small stones, venturing
deep inside the forest, where the air was cool and still. As they
entered the clearing, the ground began to slope, forming a deep
depression. They picked their way through a sunken antechamber
at the hidden opening of a cave. They set down the ceremonial
objects to clear away fallen branches and leaves.

The loneliness of that place made the monk fall to his knees.
Weeping, he began to dig at the crumbling earth, which smelled
sweet and stained his hands. More lost souls were waiting to be
found, deep in the mountain's heart.

With the first beat of the drum, a horde of black exploded
from the green, spiraling up high toward the blue.

"*Waw, waw, waw . . .*"

"Do you have any matches left?" The darkness seemed to be reaching into Suwol's body, for his bones. He held his hands against his chest, trying to staunch the blood. He couldn't stop shaking. It was so cold here underground.

Lieutenant Lee didn't answer. He was saving the last match for the bundle of homemade explosives. The bomb was likely a dud and would smoke them out, into the arms of their pursuers. If it made enough noise, however, some of these people might be able to escape. Unless the tunnel collapsed and buried them all alive.

Outside, dogs were barking and soldiers shouting.

"The fugitives are near! Get your guns ready!"

The child whimpered. One of the women whispered to Lieutenant Lee. "Thank you, sir, for trying to save us."

The grandmother muttered a prayer under her breath.

A man crawled to Lieutenant Lee. "Leave us, sir. Tell them we were holding you hostage. Escape while you still can, so you can help others."

Lieutenant Lee thought of his mother, who had sent him to Jeju to keep him safe. War, she had warned, was a demon, one that would try to steal his soul. Live as a man or die as a man, but don't be tempted to survive as anything less.

If he walked out and sacrificed these people, he would never be able to face her.

Lieutenant Lee lit the match. He could see Suwol's face, drained white. He saw the men, resigned. The mother's anguish. The praying grandmother. The child, silent. And himself.

The match died in his hand as he wept.

Another light flared in the darkness. Suwol was holding a small lighter. The lieutenant wrapped his hands around the boy's trembling grip.

The flame touched the wick, as tender as a kiss.

The mountain cradled the boy, drawing him deep into her heart as his body relaxed against her. She murmured a lullaby to soothe the boy, water bubbling over stones. When the boy's spirit began to wander, the mountain mourned, summoning the winds and the rain.

The roots of trees grazed upon the boy's flesh, while insects crawled upon the bridges of his bones. His thoughts turned to vapor, collecting as dew on the grass above.

When the mountain began vibrating with drum beat and song, the boy's ears flew back, to listen. Deliciousness scented the air, so his nose rolled back to sniff. His mouth watered as his questing tongue followed his yearning stomach, eager to end their long fast.

The boy stretched. Every bone, sinew, and muscle exulted in their reunion.

His reluctant eyes, the first to leave, were the last to make their return. He blinked at the yellow dog, which wriggled under his hands. Mother and Father were kneeling beside him, dressed in festival finery.

His little sister pulled him up from the ground, laughing. She had found his hiding place at last.

His mother and father embraced him, wiping the dirt away from his hair and his clothes. The little girl scrambled onto his back.

As they approached the shimmering feast, the boy could see his uncles, aunts, and cousins, all tasting from platters piled high with food. Grandfather was peeling tangerines for the children, who surrounded him like baby birds.

Sweetness upon sour—a contradiction only the living could taste. With every morsel, he remembered more of what he had forgotten. Anger burned. Regret was bitter. Love could be salty and sweet all at once.

When the boy had eaten to fullness, he decided to search for the rest of his human longings, scattered over the mountain like leaves. He returned to the forest, where he found his secret trail.

The path had been walked by someone before him.

☽

The woman lay curled on the ocean floor. The waves kept time, a mighty pulse swelling and subsiding with the moon and stars. Currents rippled around her, caresses from the god of the sea.

The sun shot beams through the watery dark, rousing the woman from her dream. She swam up, following the shafts of light. Sparkling motes glimmered in her wake, the dust of stars.

She stepped onto the shore, wearing a veil of water. She lifted her face to the heavens and bowed.

She began to walk. The ground rose to meet her feet with every step. Pebbles rolled in place as the earth massed to form a path that sloped, winding up toward the mountain.

As the woman walked, her hair grew longer. Tendrils covered her shoulders, hunched from threading a needle, and crept past her breasts, spent from nursing children. The woman's hair snaked past the sag of her belly and hid her wrinkled knees.

When thirst parched the woman's throat, a stream burbled up. When hunger hollowed her gut, branches dangled fruit.

As she drank, she remembered who she was. As she ate, she remembered the lives she had lived before and the lives that were yet to come, all of them blossoming out from an ever-present moment that was here and now, forever. She remembered all the times she had traveled this path between goddess and god.

When her passage ended, the woman knelt. She clasped her hands and closed her eyes.

As the woman prayed, her hair twisted and turned as it continued growing. The strands burrowed into the soil, turning into roots that searched for succor and found it, buried deep. Gleaming sap traveled up the shaft of the woman's hair, turning white into black. Luster returned to her skin, fullness to her flesh, strength to her bones.

The mountain had more gifts to share, sending vines to twine up the woman's body. Leaves unfurled to clothe her, and trees spread out their branches to create shade. Whorls of green looped and curled around the kneeling woman, waiting for her prayer to end.

As the boy entered the clearing, the girl looked up. Her hands stopped in midair. Next to her was a basket, spilling over with ferns.

Here is a secret: The dead, they dream too. Just like the living.

☽

One Last Story

Ten thousand years ago, the gods created the heavens and the earth and everything in between. Giants walked the land and swam in the oceans while dragons flew through the air, breathing fire and water.

One night, the king of the seas rose up from the depths to admire the new stars. Amongst the twinkling lights, a young dragon played, so beautiful that the king of the seas wished to possess her. He sent forth a wall of water that rose to the heavens and ensnared the divine beast, bringing her down to the depths of the ocean, where her flames were extinguished.

The dragon floated in the ocean, angry with the sea king, who dared rob her of flight. She stood on her new legs and rose to a massive height. She stretched out her arms and reached into the water to scoop the sand from the bottom of the sea. With seven mighty handfuls, she created the island of Jeju. When she finished her work, she lay down. She stretched to her full length as she gazed up at the sky, remembering her place among the stars.

When she died, her five hundred sons swore never to allow anyone to disturb their mother's rest. They kept watch over her body, mourning for a thousand years, their tears blackening into stone. Whenever the winds blow, you can still hear weeping.

Author's Note

This story was born in a Seattle hospital in April 2013. My father had just been admitted after collapsing from what would later be diagnosed as pancreatic cancer. While he dozed, attached to an IV, I settled into a chair beside his bed. Suddenly, in my mind's eye, I saw a woman cough, followed by the sound of crashing waves and the cries of sea gulls, as clear as if I were standing by the sea. After a moment of shock, I began writing as quickly as I could.

During the following year, I raised my three children while accompanying my father to doctor's appointments and chemotherapy treatments. I would wake at dawn to work, possessed by these strange images. The more I wrote, the more I began to believe that the tale was a true one, rooted in a reality I knew nothing about.

As I tried to connect the story to history, it became clear that the events took place in Korea around the time of the Korea War. However, the details were baffling. The only female free divers I had heard about were the pearl divers of Japan. And why were American planes bombing targets in South Korea? Much of the narrative made no sense to someone who had no knowledge of, much less any interest in, the Forgotten War.

Once the basic bones of the tale were excavated—another year as I grieved for my father—I had to flesh out the details. In October 2015, a year and three months after my father died, I traveled to Korea for further research. The trip would be my first to Korea as an adult since I left Seoul as a one-year-old infant. There had only been one other previous visit, when I was 10 and bedridden by chicken pox.

I had already connected the story to Jeju Island, home of Korea's deep-sea diving women, the haenyeo. The tragic events were linked to a bloody period of political unrest, referred to as the April 3 Incident in history books. I thought that I was mostly finished with the writing and that I was only traveling for a bit of local color, to add more authenticity to the tale. When I got to the island, however, that assumption was turned on its head. What I would learn on Jeju over the next three years would change everything—about the story and about my entire life.

An easy one-hour flight from Seoul, Jeju Island is located off the southernmost coast of the Korean Peninsula and is the largest of Korea's three thousand-some islands. A UNESCO Natural Heritage site, Jeju is a tourist magnet, popular with Korean honeymooners and Chinese tourists for its mild climate and natural beauty. Gorgeous and massive Mt. Halla, much of which is conservation land, dominates the landscape in every direction. Many Koreans, Jeju residents in particular, regard Mt. Halla as a sacred peak with spiritual significance, much like Peru's Macchu Picchu, Japan's Mt. Fuji or Nepal's Mt. Everest—all tourist attractions as well.

Jeju's current sunny reputation, however, belies a darker past. Due to distance, size, and geography, Jeju—called Quelparte by the Dutch—developed a unique history, culture, and even language of its own, distinct from the mainland peninsula. During the Three Kingdoms period (50 B.C.-900), Jeju was known as Tamna, enjoying various degrees of autonomy until it was officially annexed and renamed Jeju in the early 1200s. The puppet-kings of the Goryeo Dynasty (900-1300) would cede to the Mongolian Yuan Dynasty of China later in the century, and Korea would become a vassal-state. The Mongols established a cavalry outpost on Jeju with the hope of using it as a staging ground for an invasion of Japan. Sturdy indigenous ponies, which had existed on the island since the Stone Age, were crossbred with Mongolian imports until the 1400s. To this day, horse meat is still served at speciality restaurants in Jejudo, and a record is kept of all pedigreed heritage stock.

During the disintegration of the Mongol empire and the establishment of the Joseon Dynasty (1392-1897), Jeju transitioned into an island of undesirables, a dust-bin where political prisoners, religious exiles, and former slaves languished alongside crossbred horses. Jeju islanders were considered second-class citizens, easily recognized by their distinctive dialect and often barred from traveling to the mainland.

With the Japanese annexation of Korea in 1910, life on Jeju, which had always been difficult, grew even more so, as local men were conscripted onto Japanese ships and taken away to Japan as indentured labourers. Because of the chronic shortage of men, the women of Jeju, who had long been diving for sustenance, assumed the role of primary wage earners. When the close of World War II in 1945 removed the Japanese invaders from the Korean Peninsula, sixty thousand Jeju citizens were able to return to their native land, the vast majority of them men. They thought they were returning to the safe serenity of their island home, but they were wrong.

On my first trip to Korea I landed in Jeju City in the evening, reeling from jet lag. My guide picked me up and took me to a hotel on the beach, where I immediately fell asleep. In the middle of the night, I was awakened by a nightmare and the feeling of being icy cold. All the windows of my hotel room had somehow blown open. I closed them and fell back asleep again.

I was awakened again, this time by voices shouting in panic. I opened the door to see if the noise came from outside, but the hallway was completely silent. I went back to my bed and listened more carefully. The voices were somehow within my room but not—there is no other way to describe it. Shouts of "Gothis way!" and "Runaway!" were interrupted by random panicked screams. Finally, I heard a man screaming a very specific word: "Doguljengi! Doguljengi!" Because of my limited Korean, I had no idea what the word meant. I wrote it down phonetically in English to ask my guide to translate it the next morning. I lay awake until dawn, listening until the voices faded away.

When my guide finally arrived, I asked him what "doguljengi" meant. Startled, he asked me where I had heard it. I explained what happened the night before. He cringed and backed away, studying me fearfully with his arms over his face. When he was satisfied that I was not possessed, he explained that the expression—"murderous thieves"—had been shouted by victims fleeing their killers during the April 3 Incident. He refused even to say the word. The location of the hotel I was staying in was known to be one of the more notorious massacre sites: so many people had been murdered on the beach that the sharks grew fat from the corpses.

My guide begged me to consult a shaman. Apparently, I was seeing and hearing ghosts.

Acknowledgments

The first draft of this novel was completed in 2018, the seventieth anniversary year of the April 3 Jeju Incident, the tragic massacre alluded to in this story. The year 1948 was rocked by turmoil, similar to another rat year, 2020, when this book was published.

It takes a very long time to weave such a tale. Foremost thanks to the teachers, who taught my hands how: Dr. Lucy Chu, Prof. Sylvia Zaremba, and Mary Alice Fite of Columbus, Ohio; Prof. Philip Fisher of Harvard; Lucie Brock-Broido; and Prof. Frederick Crews of University of California, Berkeley.

For all matters Korean, I bow to the original Kim Dong Min of Jeju; shaman Lee Young Sook of Jeju; paksa Hyung Il Pai of University of California, Santa Barbara; lawyer Jennifer Sohn of Bellevue; and the original Gongja, my gomo Marie Lee of Los Angeles.

On Jeju Island, I am indebted to the Seong Up Folk Village Senior Center (especially members Kim Chang Ok, who was a policeman in Mosulpo during the tragic events, and Cho In Hung, who sang songs from his childhood); the April 3 Memorial Peace Park (especially Son Myoung Ki); the Seong Up Jeju Folk Village; the Jeju Folklore and Natural History Museum; the Jeju National Museum; and the Jeju Haenyeo Museum.

The haenyeo of tiny Gappado Island gave me blunt answers while sharing their catch. On the mainland, the War Memorial in Seoul was a trove of wartime paraphernalia and propaganda. For the medical facts: Dr. Ralph Rossi of Seattle and Dr. Ha Jong Won of Seoul.

The credit belongs to everyone else; the blame is mine.

Friends and family I must thank, in order of their appearance in my life: Boomee, Jennie, and Arlene; Nellie Kim; Nina Lee; Dwight Huffman; Kathleen Bulger Webb; Ari Jaffe and Lena Verkhovsky; Tyrone Hayes and Katherine Kim; Jane Po; Brad Berens; Margaret Stude Michael; Holly Kim; Emily Baillargeon Russin; Edwin Curry, Tara Young, Brobson Lutz, and Gerri Jumonville; David and Marita Almquist; Brooks Whitney Almquist; Chewie; Martha Brockenbrough; Wendy Minick Heipt; Divya Krishnan; Linda Berger Bean; Mary Ingraham; Ruth Dickey; Anne Kalik; Daniel Moceri; Dong Mei and Robert Peng.

The two men who gave my words a chance to be heard: Seattle's David Brewster and New Orleans's Jim Amoss.

The two women who believed that this story would take flight, even as a misshapen hatchling: Jenny Chen of Alcove Press, truly a beautiful shaman, and Priya Doraswamy of Lotus Lane Literary, with her clairvoyant eye.

Thank you all for keeping me company.

May this book serve as a jesa, of sorts, for my parents: Hahn Seong Hack (1937–2014) and Kim Yung Hee (1940–2012). Their graves may be far away in America, but I know where their spirits have gone.

Glossary of Korean Terms

ahjumma—an older woman, with a dowdy connotation

aigoo—an expression of frustration or dismay similar to "oh no" or "aargh"

baksa—scholar. Today, a PhD would make someone a baksa.

banchan—Korean side dishes that accompany rice

bangsatap—a pile of stones, like a cairn

bing-tteok—a buckwheat crepe filled with julienned radishes and other vegetables

boshintang—dog meat soup, believed to have curative power

bulteok—fire circle used by haenyeo to warm themselves

dolchu—stone anchor used by haenyeo to hold their nets and floating gourds in one place

doldam—the stone walls of Jeju, made from black volcanic rock

dol hareubang—the stone grandfather statues that once guarded the entrances to traditional villages, they are now a ubiquitous Jeju icon for tourists

dotchebbi—the Jeju term for goblin. In mainland Korea, the term is dokkebi.

dwenjang—along with soy sauce (ganjang) and chili pepper paste (gochujang), one of the primary flavorings used in Korean cuisine. Made of fermented soybean, the paste is pungent and salty and resembles Japanese miso.

eum yang—the Korean version of yin yang. Eum is generally associated with the female while yang is associated with the male.

gashin—a minor family deity

gosari—fiddleheads from bracken fern

gumiho—a nine-tailed fox that would transform itself into a beautiful woman to entrap men

gwishin—ghosts or spirits

haenyeo—the woman free divers of Jeju Island who forage for seaweed and shellfish in the waters around Jeju Island. Once the economic backbone of the island, their numbers are in steep decline.

halmung—Jeju for grandmother. Mainland Koreans use halmoni.

Hallasan—Mount Halla

han—a rather complex term to express a quintessentially Korean sense of angst

hangul—the Korean phonetic alphabet, created in the fifteenth century by King Sejong the Great.

hanbok—traditional Korean dress, with a high-waisted tulip skirt and cropped jacket

hindoongi—a derogatory term for white people

jeong—A uniquely Korean sense of empathetic connectedness and social obligation between people

jesa—ceremonial rites for the deceased

gehsekki—literally a dog's whelp; figuratively a bastard

jook—rice porridge

kimbop—rice roll wrapped in seaweed containing meat and/or vegetables; Korean sushi

kkaennip—perilla leaf. This broad, serrated herb is mildly astringent, with a slightly peppery taste.

kut—ceremonial rites conducted by shamans for spiritual purposes of varying kinds, often to communicate with dead relatives

makgoli—milky white fermented rice wine made with cultures

manggeon—headband worn by boys and men around their foreheads

noonah—a younger boy's term for an older sister

ohmanah—an exclamation of surprise like "oh my!' or "whoa!"

ohrabang—Jeju term for big brother, as said by a younger sister

olle—the old trails and walkways that once crisscrossed Jeju. Some coastline olle have been renovated and are now maintained as walking trails for tourists.

omija—a type of magnolia vine whose medicinal berries are described as tasting of all five flavors at once: salty, sweet, sour, earthy, bitter

Sim Cheong—In Korea's famous Cinderella tale of filial piety, an impoverished girl is sacrificed to the sea king, which results in her becoming queen and restoring her blind father's eyesight.

soju—a clear vodka-like spirit so popular with Koreans that it is, by volume, the most highly consumed liquor in the world

sollani—Jeju word for okdom, a delicious type of tilefish

soondae—Korean pork sausage

sunnim—monk

sumbisori—the whistling exhalation made by haenyeo as they come up for air

ummung—Jeju term for mom or mommy

yangban—Korean noble class

yobo—term of endearment used by married couples

Readers Club Guide Questions

1. Junja cannot help feeling guilty about her mother's death. Do you think that she would have inevitably felt some form of survivor's guilt regardless of the circumstances? How does the death of a parent change a person? At what age do you think that kind of loss is felt most keenly?

2. Many kinds of love are featured in this story. Who would you consider to be Junja's first love? Are all first loves doomed to end? What kind of love appeals to you more: the lightening strike of first attraction or a love that endures over a lifetime? Can a person have both kinds with one person? How does our ability to love change over time and as we mature?

3. Junja eventually leaves the water, despite it being a major part of her. Have you ever had to leave something that was integral to your identity behind in order to survive or evolve? How difficult was that transition?

4. Readers tend to split into two camps: Those who prefer the first part of the book (Junja's story) and wish that the story had continued in that time frame and those who found the change in perspective to Dr. Moon a pleasant surprise. How does your group divide?

5. Junja's grandmother is a master storyteller who meets her match in Lieutenant Lee, a master manipulator of appearances. Do you think that the unique abilities of these two scheming plotters gives them additional insight into the perils

of their historical moment? Does reading historical fiction like this story offer insight into the present political situation?

6. A crisis can make or break a person (even an entire society). Junja experiences a crisis of faith that causes her to change her religious beliefs. What causes her crisis, and how is it resolved? Can you think of a crisis in your life or in society that had a transformative effect? Was this effect negative or positive?

7. It's a commonly held belief that the telling the truth is always the best path forward. And yet the white-haired shaman believes that "not all truths were meant to be told." Similarly, the beautiful shaman holds back information because "this truth was not theirs to know." Can telling the truth sometimes cause more harm than good? Might this harm be justified in the end? Is knowing the truth indeed a "right" that should be granted universally?

8. The term synesthesia describes how the stimulation of one sense can trigger sensations in another area of perception. The word "nice," for example, is often associated with light blue, pink, or yellow. Junja ultimately concludes that "love tasted necessary, like salt." What does love taste like for your group? What is its color? Does it have a sound? A tactile feel?

9. Ghosts appear everywhere in this novel, both literally and metaphorically. Do you have any personal experience with ghosts?

10. This is a war novel, and there are five death scenes in it, with the protagonist dying in the first two pages of the story. But is this a violent story? How does depicted violence in language and in visual images affect you as a person and how you receive the story?